BENEATH

an

ITALIAN SKY

BENEATH

an

ITALIAN SKY

STACY
HENRIE

Mirror Press

Print edition

Interior Design by Cora Johnson
Edited by Kelsey Down and Lisa Shepherd
Cover design by Rachael Anderson
Cover Image Credit: Arcangel

Published by Mirror Press, LLC
ISBN-13: 978-1-947152-59-5

Books by Stacy Henrie

The American Heiress Series

Night at the Opera
Beneath an Italian Sky
Among Sand and Sunrise

Love Inspired Historical

Lady Outlaw
The Express Rider's Lady
The Outlaw's Secret
The Renegade's Redemption
The Rancher's Temporary Engagement
A Cowboy of Convenience
Their Wyoming Courtship Agreement

Of Love and War

Hope at Dawn
Hope Rising
A Hope Remembered
A Christmas Hope

Other Titles

Love for All Seasons
The Keeper of Her Heart

Prologue

Somerset, England, Summer 1890

Free at last! Emmett burst from the carriage the instant the door was opened by a footman. He raced up the stone steps of Hadwell House. The weeks ahead shone as bright as a new toy to the ten-year-old. No studying, no scowling teachers, no smarting backside from discipline. Nothing but roaming the estate with his greyhound, Bran, and riding his horse and spending time with his grandfather, his favorite person in the world.

His mother's father wintered in Sicily, but every summer he came to stay at Hadwell House for several months. For Emmett, it was the best time of the year. Grandfather was never too busy to listen or offer an encouraging word to a boy who often felt adrift in a house full of sisters. There was always a unique gift from Italy for him too.

Entering the house, Emmett paused just long enough in the foyer to wave hello to his parents before he hurried to the library to find his grandfather. He peeked inside, but the room stood empty. Perhaps his grandfather was upstairs reading.

"Grandfather? I'm home!" he called out as he took the stairs two at a time.

Emmett heard his parents calling after him, but he was too eager to see his grandfather to find out what they wanted. What trinket or piece of fruit awaited him this time? He'd once overheard his mother say that he and Grandfather got on so well because they were alike—both kindhearted and jovial in personality. Emmett could think of no greater compliment.

He ground to a stop outside his grandfather's door and knocked. But there was no answer. Was Grandfather resting? Emmett quietly pushed the door open. However, the bed stood vacant, and so did the chairs in front of the fireplace.

A stab of disappointment cut through him. Had his grandfather gone somewhere, forgetting Emmett would be returning home from boarding school today?

No, Emmett reassured himself. *Grandfather wouldn't forget something so important.*

Besides, his grandfather had written him two weeks ago and shared how much he was looking forward to his and Emmett's summer adventures. Perhaps Grandfather had just gone for a walk. Emmett backed out of the room, intent on returning downstairs and asking his parents where his grandfather might be. But to his surprise, his parents were already waiting for him in the hallway.

His father, the Marquess of Hadwell, was scowling. "You needn't run through the house like some wild savage," he said in a brusque tone.

"Where did Grandfather go?" Emmett asked.

A flicker of unease passed over his father's face. Emmett couldn't recall ever seeing his father look anything but confident. "He is . . ."

The marquess visibly swallowed, then glanced at Emmett's mother. Dread began tightening Emmett's throat.

Something was wrong. His father never let his mother do the explaining unless it was something very unpleasant.

"We didn't wish to worry you." His mother fixed her eyes on something farther down the corridor. "At first, we thought it was only a cold. But then he took a turn for the worst the next day." She pressed her hand to her mouth as if to stop a sob.

Emmett frowned, not understanding. "So Grandfather is sick?" Had they put him in another part of the house so no one else would catch what he had?

"Your grandfather passed away four days ago." His father wouldn't look at him either. "It was sudden, yes, but the man was already quite advanced in age."

His grandfather was . . . Emmett shook his head to keep the awful word *dead* from settling inside his mind. His father must be mistaken.

"We didn't think it right to call you away for the funeral before your final exams." His mother placed her hand on Emmett's shoulder. "I'm sorry, Emmett. I know how much he—"

Emmett twisted out of her grasp. "No! Grandfather isn't . . . isn't dead! He wrote me. He said we were going to a fair this year." His voice rose in volume as tears stung his eyes. "He wouldn't go without seeing me. I know it."

"The timing of it is unfortunate," his father said. "However, there is no need to carry on in—"

He'd had enough. Emmett spun on his heel and dashed down the hallway to his bedroom, desperate to get away from them. Raw emotion burned inside him. His dog, Bran, hopped up from the rug and trotted toward him as he entered. Emmett slammed the door shut, pressing his back against it. Any moment now, he'd get a dressing-down for his behavior. And yet no one came.

Had his mother somehow checked his father's rebuke for once? Emmett didn't know. After a minute or so, he slid to the floor. Then, burying his head in his dog's brown-and-white fur, he wept.

He eventually cried himself to sleep and missed dinner. The next day Emmett refused to leave his room. A maid brought up a tray, but he just picked at the food. He sat at the window, remembering funny stories his grandfather had told him. But the memories only made the ache inside him hurt worse. So he'd try to think of something else, like joking with his best friend, Avery Winfield, at school. That made him feel better for a little while. Only then he'd remember how he had wanted to tell Grandfather those same stories, and the hurt and tears would start all over again.

That night, Emmett slept fitfully. He kept dreaming he was in a carriage, one that moved so slowly it finally stopped altogether. He kept pleading with the driver to hurry, that he wouldn't make it in time. At one point, he stirred awake and found his mother sitting by his bedside.

"I'm so very sorry, Emmett," he heard her whisper. "We should have sent for you." He fell back asleep as her cool hand brushed his hair off his forehead.

The following morning, Emmett awakened to the voices of his parents outside his door. Curious, he tiptoed across the room to listen. ". . . Now his title and estate have been lost to some no-name cousin of yours," his father was saying. "We would have faced the same fate had we not had Emmett. Still, there are days I wonder if Alder would have made a more fitting marquess."

Emmett winced at the reference to the older brother he'd

never known. Alder had died as a child, several years before Emmett was born. But his two oldest sisters had told him that Alder had been the apple of their father's eye.

"You dote on Emmett too much," the marquess continued from out in the hall. "If he's going to be the man he must become, a future marquess, then he would do well to follow in my footsteps rather than his grandfather's."

The twisting of the door handle sent Emmett leaping backward. He scrambled to his bed and slid under the covers. It wasn't his mother who entered, as he'd expected—it was his father. Normally Emmett was summoned to the study when the marquess wanted to speak with him.

"Good, you're awake." His father crossed to the bed as Emmett slowly sat up. "It's time for you to dress and join the family downstairs for breakfast. All of these tears and refusals to eat are further upsetting your mother and sisters. And they will not bring your grandfather back." The marquess's rigid stance softened as he added, "His death is a tragedy none of us foresaw, but we cannot wallow in grief. Strength is found in forging ahead."

Guilt filled Emmett. He didn't want to upset anyone, least of all his mother.

"Do you understand what I'm saying?"

Emmett nodded. He needed to stop feeling sad, so he didn't upset his family members who'd already been through enough. First with Alder and now with his grandfather. "I understand, Father." The marquess didn't smile, though he did look pleased.

"Once you've scrubbed the tears from your face, you may come down." He started for the door.

A question Emmett had always longed to ask but never dared rose into his throat for the hundredth time. However, today it wouldn't remain there. "Father?"

The marquess turned. "Yes?"

"Do you . . ." His heart began to pound. "Did you like Alder more than you like me?"

His father looked taken aback. "Of course not."

"Do you think he would've made you prouder?" Emmett risked asking next.

Stepping back toward the bed, the marquess waved him forward. "Come here, Emmett." He climbed out of bed and went to stand before his father.

"Your brother, had he lived, would have made a fine marquess. God didn't leave us without another heir, though." His father settled an awkward pat on Emmett's head, but the rare show of affection still felt like a gift. "That's you now, and if you'll heed my counsel and do as I have done, you may even surpass the hopes and plans I had for Alder."

There was still time to make his father proud? Emmett felt a rush of relief. He would be every bit the heir, perhaps even more, that his older brother would have been. But his determination teetered a bit when he recalled something his grandfather had told him last year.

You have your own unique strengths, Emmett. Different than your father's or mine or anyone else's. God knows what they are. And He will help you and place you in situations to learn them for yourself.

His grandfather's advice was to find his own strengths, yet his father wanted him to follow a set example. Who was right? Emmett wanted to make them both proud, and yet his grandfather was gone.

Looking up at the marquess, Emmett made his decision. He could still win his father's love and approval as Alder had done. His father had told him how.

And that was what Emmett would do.

Chapter 1

Somerset, England, December 1908

At twenty-eight, with a courtesy title and a wife, Emmett Markham was long past boyhood. But he still experienced a familiar twist of nerves at being summoned to the study by his father, the Marquess of Hadwell.

"What do you suppose he means to ask now?" he murmured, setting aside the book he'd been attempting to read for the last half hour. His brown-and-white greyhound, Bran the Second, lifted his head from off the rug as Emmett stood. "Come, Bran."

Whatever the reason for the meeting, Emmett would face it with Bran at his side. The dog had been his loyal companion for years. Bran preferred country life, though, so he remained at Hadwell House year-round. But the dog still greeted his master with fondness whenever Emmett returned home from London—and more recently, from overseeing the renovations on his own estate house.

Emmett exited the library, Bran at his heels. As they crossed the foyer, the dog stopped and sat, his large brown eyes watching the ornate front door. The ritual elicited an ache inside Emmett—as it had every day since he'd come home nearly two weeks earlier.

"She isn't coming today, boy."

In truth Emmett wasn't certain when his wife, Clare, would return to England. Not until after the holidays. Possibly not before spring.

Clare struggled with the cold, which was something Emmett's maternal grandfather would have understood. The man had wintered for years at his Sicilian villa, which Emmett had inherited from him. Grandfather had returned to England each summer—up until the year Emmett turned ten and his grandfather had caught the illness that had ended his life. The pain of that loss was something Emmett still carried with him.

He suspected there was more, though, to Clare's sudden trip to Italy than trading England's blustery winter weather for a more temperate, sunny climate. Did it have anything to do with the rumors he'd heard about her last week?

Forcing his thoughts from lingering on such an unpleasant topic, he rubbed his dog's head. "I don't believe she's forgotten about you," he reassured Bran. Emmett, perhaps, but never Bran.

It was one of the things Emmett had been most pleased about after he and Clare had come to stay at the family seat in Somerset, following their honeymoon to the villa. She and Bran had instantly got on with each other, in spite of Clare never owning a dog before. And while the creature was still loyal to Emmett, it stung a bit to know he no longer claimed Bran's undivided devotion.

Emmett called for the dog to follow him again, anxious not to keep his father waiting. Entering the study, he found the marquess seated at the large desk. The man's gray hair and impeccably trimmed beard gave him a distinguished air, rather than an aging one. And though Lord Hadwell was not overly tall—Emmett, on the other hand, had inherited his grandfather's height—his bearing made him seem imposing.

"There you are, Emmett." No one except his family and Clare called him by his first name. To everyone else, Emmett was known as the Earl of Linwood, the courtesy title he'd inherited from his father. "I was beginning to wonder if you meant for me to *repeat* my invitation."

Repetition wasn't something the marquess countenanced. *Listen and obey the first time* had long been his motto. "I apologize for delaying you, Father." Emmett sat in one of the chairs facing the desk. Bran lay at his feet.

The marquess nodded with obvious approval at the contrite words. "I have something important to share with you."

It was not the first time—nor was it likely to be the last—that Emmett had heard such a phrase. Last year, before the start of the social season, the important thing to share had been that it was time for Emmett to marry. All of his sisters were married with children of their own, and it was now Emmett's turn to enter into the institution of marriage. He was told to find a suitable bride—which meant a wealthy young lady with plenty of cash to update Hadwell House and secure its future for generations to come.

Included in that request had been a reminder of his duty to produce an heir who would carry on the title and oversee the estate. It was up to Emmett to guarantee a distant cousin did not become Marquess of Hadwell.

Unfortunately, while Emmett had fulfilled his father's former directive by marrying a lovely red-haired heiress from America, he had failed in the latter. He and Clare had not yet been able to have a child, though she'd been pregnant twice. Both times had ended in miscarriage. Emmett had experienced his own grief with each loss, but he hadn't wanted to upset Clare further by sharing his sorrow with her. Instead he'd kept his sadness to himself, along with his feelings of failure. Still, those darker thoughts threatened to resurface in this moment, until his father spoke again.

"I have decided you are to become an MP." The marquess smiled at what he clearly felt was his own brilliance.

Emmett blinked and sat back. "You want me to try for a seat in the House of Commons?"

"Precisely." Lord Hadwell stood, his waistcoat bowed from the slight girth at his middle, and began to pace from the desk to the window and back. "As I see it, you have plenty of time to establish yourself as an MP, perhaps even become Leader of the House one day, all before you assume the family's seat in the House of Lords after my death." He turned to look at Emmett, but his gaze appeared to be seeing something other than his son. "You will be able to do and achieve what I myself was denied when I became marquess."

Lord Hadwell had inherited the title from his father at the age of eighteen, which ended any plans he had of sitting in the House of Commons. Emmett had heard his father relay the loss of his dream, and now it appeared he would need to fulfill that dream if he wished to continue following his father's path.

"I'm not sure I am as knowledgeable or passionate about politics as you, Father."

Emmett enjoyed political debates now and then with his friends. But in those situations, it was the socializing and being with other people that he liked best—not the actual content of the discussions. Lately, he'd had little time for even that the past few months, with overseeing the renovations and developments to Barksley Hall, an estate he and Clare had bought on the opposite side of the county, near the sea.

The marquess stopped moving and frowned. "It's high

time you changed, then. We need everyone qualified and like-minded doing their bit in the House of Commons."

He didn't say he needed Emmett specifically. Or that he'd be proud if his son became an MP. Or that in doing so, Emmett would finally gain the love and approval the marquess had always held just out of reach—seemingly in wait for the day when Emmett would finally live up to his older brother Alder's lost potential.

He glanced at the boy's photograph that hung on the study wall. The stoic brother staring back at him was a stranger, and yet his picture—captured only months before his death at age seven—had taunted Emmett for years from its prominent place inside their father's study.

Lord Hadwell had adored Alder, for whom he'd had such high hopes, and the boy's death had supposedly been very difficult for him, not the least because he had no other sons at the time. With his wife delivering four daughters in a row, the likelihood of the title passing to someone else had been a reality until Emmett was at last born. But despite Emmett's best efforts to heed his father's counsel and do all that was asked of him, he still questioned whether he'd ever measure up to what Alder would have been as a future marquess.

Would becoming an MP change that? Would this be the thing that made Lord Hadwell truly proud of Emmett at last? He may not have won his wife's unwavering approval, but this could secure his father's. The possibility was too great to dismiss, whether he was enthused about politics or not. He had welcomed and embraced the challenge of improving things on his own estate. As an MP, he'd be at the forefront of improving things for the whole country. There was quite a lot to be said for that.

Likely sensing his tension, Bran sat up and put his head on Emmett's knee. "Since the election isn't for another two years," Emmett said, scratching the dog behind his ears, "I could wait to start campaigning until my estate was up and running—"

"No, no." Waving away Emmett's words with his hand, Lord Hadwell resumed his pacing. "That isn't soon enough. You must start now, especially since you'll need to improve the public's opinion of you before you ever begin campaigning."

He needed to improve the public's opinion? Had the marquess heard the same rumors Emmett had? A chill crept through him that had little to do with the cool air inside the study. "I'm not sure what you mean, Father."

"How does it look to the county"—the marquess's voice increased in volume with each word—"for a future MP to spend the holidays away from his own wife?"

Emmett's jaw went slack at the accusation, then tightened with barely swallowed anger. It wasn't his wish for Clare to go to the villa. He hadn't sent her away, at least not intentionally, though he'd begun to wonder if there might be wisdom in some time apart.

The moments of strain between them, which hadn't started until after Clare's first miscarriage, had grown more pronounced for some time now. It hadn't helped to hear someone remark at a party last week that his wife had only agreed to marry him to obtain a title—and that, in the absence of an heir, Clare was preparing to begin a separate life away from him.

Emmett hadn't wanted to believe such rumors. Especially not after the blissful two weeks he and Clare had spent together at Barksley Hall at the end of October and into November. He would have asked her to extend her stay longer, except Emmett hadn't felt right about her sleeping in the servants' quarters as he planned to do while the main rooms and bedrooms were being renovated. However, in his wife's absence, he had begun to wonder if things were as resolved as he'd hoped or if the closeness they had shared those two weeks had been much like their honeymoon—more a dream than reality.

After she'd returned to Hadwell House, work on the estate had thankfully kept his focus elsewhere, at least until Clare's letter had arrived. In it, she'd told Emmett that she wished to spend the holidays somewhere warmer. Her plan was to depart for Sicily in three days. The announcement had greatly hurt and surprised him. Worst of all, it had given new strength to his misgivings about their relationship. It wasn't until he'd overheard the gossip last week, though, that Clare's decision to leave England finally made sense.

"What are you saying?" Emmett hoped he sounded more curious than frustrated. His father did not condone outward bursts of emotion.

Lord Hadwell sat at his desk once more. His light-blue eyes, the same color as Emmett's, gleamed with satisfaction. "You will leave immediately for Sicily."

"I won't arrive before Christmas. That's four days away, and it takes five to get to Taormina."

The marquess's smug look only increased. "It makes no difference if you are actually in Sicily for Christmas or not. The idea is that you are *going*. That will be the first step to building a more positive political image. An image that includes a happily married couple."

The dread inside him iced over into a solid mass. "A happily married couple?"

"Yes, Emmett," Lord Hadwell snapped. "How else do you think you'll obtain the votes you need? It certainly won't be on your merits and parentage alone. You need that beautiful, rich American wife of yours and her charming smile to win votes.

That's why you are going to Sicily: to convince Clare to return to England forthwith."

Emmett kneaded his forehead with his fingers in an attempt to think clearly. His father was asking too much this time. It was one thing to agree to go into politics, something Emmett believed he could actually come to enjoy. However, it was another matter entirely for him to go to Clare, convince her to come back with him, and then parade around England with her as if they were the contented couple they clearly weren't. But he knew better than to voice such an argument. His father didn't need more evidence that his only remaining son always fell short of the mark.

"If she won't listen . . ." The words were barely spoken aloud, but the marquess evidently heard him.

"Nonsense. Be as charming as you were when you were courting her, and she'll agree."

That hadn't been about artifice back then. "Is it really necessary that she return now?" Perhaps he could wait and see what Clare said in her first letter from Italy before he started on what might become a fool's errand—for both himself and her.

"I have failed you if you cannot grasp the importance of this." Lord Hadwell shook his head as if disappointed with himself. Emmett knew better. His father was really saying Emmett wasn't up to snuff—not sufficiently intelligent or insightful to understand why his wife needed to come back to England as soon as possible.

Uncertainty warred with determination inside him. His task held as much potential for failure as it did success, and yet he had to try. If Emmett could convince Clare to return with him, his father would surely be proud of him. Although, at what cost? The distance between him and Clare might grow worse, at least in private. He missed her, even after everything that had happened, but how did she feel about him? His father had been clear about what he wanted from Emmett. But with Clare, Emmett didn't know anymore what she wanted.

"Very well." He managed a strained smile as he stood. "I shall leave for Sicily tomorrow." If nothing else, he would get to see Clare sooner than he might have otherwise.

Lord Hadwell gave the desk a victorious slap, then rose to his feet as well. "That's my boy."

The happiness Emmett felt at the small bit of praise lasted only until he and Bran reached the door. "One more thing, Emmett." The marquess circled his desk. "I've arranged for a reporter to accompany you and your valet to Italy. He's the son of an old friend and will be writing stories about you and Clare as a couple for the London *Times*."

His father had already arranged things with a reporter? That meant the marquess had been quite confident what Emmett's answer would be, regarding both pursuing a political career and going after Clare. He wasn't sure whether to feel pleased or dismayed by that fact. But one thing Emmett did know—he wouldn't show up to the villa with a reporter in tow. That wouldn't be fair to his wife.

"No reporter," he said, facing his father directly.

His heart thumped faster at the marquess's look of surprise. He hadn't challenged his father in such a way in more than eighteen years. Doing so now poked painfully at Emmett's fear of his father's disapproval, but he wouldn't back down. If he did, he would be denying Clare the time to prepare for a more public life as the wife of an MP before any sharp-eyed reporter began hounding her with questions. Emmett might not know how she felt about him, but he still cared enough about her to do this.

Lord Hadwell scowled. "You need this sort of press right away."

"I'll go and convince Clare to come back to England with me, but I won't have a reporter tagging along with us."

The marquess didn't stop glaring, but he did concede after a long moment's pause. "Fine. I will tell the reporter his services are not yet required." He shook a finger at Emmett. "But you had better be on your way the instant breakfast concludes tomorrow, or I will change my mind."

"Thank you, Father. I will."

Emmett headed upstairs, Bran beside him. Should he have his valet, Rushford, pack a suitcase or a trunk? How much time would he need in Italy? He wasn't sure. But whether it took a few days or a few weeks, he would do everything in his power to be successful.

Taormina, Sicily, December 1908

From her painting spot among the ruins of the ancient amphitheater, Clare Herschel Markham, the Countess of Linwood, could view the city's beauty spread out below. Sunlight illuminated the blueness of the ocean, and where there weren't stone buildings, the hills still boasted greenery. In the distance, the snow-topped volcano, Mount Etna, inspired as much fearsome respect as it did awe.

When finished, this painting would be Clare's fourth, and she'd only been here for two weeks. Apparently the spark of creativity she'd feared had been erased over the last year had just been lying dormant. Her second morning back in sunny Sicily, Clare had woken with the almost-forgotten need to put brush to canvas. And so she had.

She dabbed a lighter shade of blue across the stretch of sky. The walls of the amphitheater framed one side of the scene. The other featured the city, the hills, and the ocean.

Her completed paintings, those back home in New York and the few she'd created since her wedding to Emmett, were all landscapes—save one. She'd attempted a portrait of her husband during their honeymoon in Taormina. Clare had placed him on the bench that circled the fountain in the villa's walled garden. And while she didn't think it an exact likeness of the handsome Earl of Linwood, with his dark-blond hair and broad shoulders, she prided herself on having captured Emmett's light-blue eyes perfectly. At least the way they had once looked, full of delight and adoration.

His mother, Lady Hadwell, had taken an instant liking to the portrait and wanted it displayed at Hadwell House instead of in the Linwoods' house in London or at their recently purchased estate, Barksley Hall. Clare had complied, up until she'd made her decision to leave England. The night before her departure, she'd slipped downstairs after the family was asleep, removed the painting from the frame, and replaced it with one she'd done of Hadwell House. Only Bran, Emmett's dog, had witnessed the change.

Clare hated to add to the family's list of disappointments when it came to their daughter- and sister-in-law. But for reasons she hadn't been ready to name, she'd wanted the painting of Emmett to come with her to Italy. If nothing else, it reminded her that they'd once shared happiness instead of only loss, regret, and failure.

"I suppose we ought to get back," she said, turning to look at her lady's maid, Miriam, who sat reading nearby. "If we're late for lunch, Signora Russo is sure to give us both a thorough scolding."

The eighteen-year-old girl, two years Clare's junior, shut her book and hopped up. "She does sound a mite more cross when she speaks Italian."

Clare smiled in agreement as she stood to gather up her

painting supplies. In truth, the villa's cook and housekeeper had a warm heart and maternal way about her that reminded Clare of her own mother. But there was nothing like a good meal left waiting until the food turned cold to incite Signora Russo's strongest disapproval. That, and eating very little of the woman's generous cooking.

"Allow me, my lady." Miriam hurried to take the easel from Clare's grasp.

She gave in but didn't relinquish her paints or canvas. "I may be with child, Miriam, but I can still carry things."

"I know, my lady. It's just that . . ." The girl let her voice trail off as she glanced away in obvious embarrassment.

It was just that the other two times Clare had been pregnant this year, she'd miscarried. Miriam had largely been the one to hold Clare's hand and let her cry. The caring letters from her parents had helped, but it wasn't the same as having them nearby, eager to embrace her while she wept.

She'd longed to share her feelings with Emmett, but he hadn't empathized with her grief, especially after the second miscarriage. He hadn't seemed to notice her pain or feel any of his own. And that was why Clare hadn't yet told Emmett about this pregnancy. If she miscarried a third time, there wouldn't be a need for a discussion anyway. She would simply weather the sorrow and pain alone, here in Italy, without fear of Emmett not understanding. No need for him or any of his family to know she'd failed—yet again—to fulfill her duty to produce an heir.

Still, Clare was hopeful and prayerful that this pregnancy would be different. She had good reason to feel more confident this time around. The doctor she'd consulted back in England had suggested that wintering in a more temperate climate may well increase the likelihood of Clare remaining with child. So she had made the impromptu decision to return to Sicily at once.

Their driver, Alessandro Russo, was waiting with the wagon as Clare and Miriam left the amphitheater. The man helped them stow the paint supplies in the back, then turned to Clare. "Ready, Signora Linwood?"

She nodded. "*Sì. Grazie.*" He helped her onto the seat. Clare carefully balanced her canvas on her lap while Miriam climbed into the back of the wagon.

Soon they were rolling along the cobbled streets toward the villa. A wave of queasiness had Clare gripping the side of the wagon, but she welcomed the feeling too. She hoped it was an indicator that she was still pregnant, at least for the moment. Signora Russo's delicious fare and special tea typically eased the worst of her sickness throughout the day.

A group of dark-haired, olive-skinned children raced past the wagon, their giggles rising above the clatter of the wheels. Clare watched them before they darted around a corner up ahead. The familiar yearning to be a mother, to watch her own children running about, filled her with a physical ache.

As an only child, she'd often dreamt of having a home with lots of children. A home filled with the same laughter and warmth she'd known growing up—one far different from what she'd found at Hadwell House. When she'd faced the difficulty of bringing a child to term, her dreams became more modest. If she could only have one child, as her parents had, then she would choose to be as grateful and content as they had been.

Any child would be a cherished blessing. A boy would, of course, be a particular cause of celebration for her husband's family, who needed an heir. However, if this baby was a girl, Clare wasn't sure she wished to raise her daughter in England.

Maybe they could remain in Sicily instead, far away from the place where she'd struggled and failed to fit in, far away from the stigma that a daughter wasn't as valued among the gentry as a son.

The villa came into view, with its balconied windows and grand stone staircase running in parallel curves on either side of the front door. An unfamiliar wagon, with a horse and donkey as its team, sat out front.

Clare let Signor Russo help her to the ground and rounded the vehicle to collect her paint box. "Miriam, do you recognize that wagon?"

The maid shook her head as she picked up the easel. "Are you expecting company, my lady?"

"No."

Clare's friend Helena had also come to Sicily for the holidays. But Helena was hosting a birthday party for her husband, the Viscount Vickley, tomorrow night at their villa in Messina. It wasn't likely the young woman would make the two-hour train ride to see Clare in Taormina, when Clare was expected at the viscount's home this evening to help with the preparations. Maybe the visitors were relatives of the Russos. Though Signor Russo made no comment about the mystery guests as he drove the wagon toward the stable.

Clare led the way up one of the staircases and through the front door. It had taken her a little time to adjust to not having a butler as they'd had in London and at Hadwell House. But after hiring and overseeing a staff of fifteen at her and Emmett's London residence, Clare had come to appreciate the villa's small contingent of servants.

Voices drew her toward the open doorway of the drawing room. Signora Russo wouldn't have allowed her relations to settle there. The older woman insisted on entertaining them in her domain, the kitchen.

"Should I take your things upstairs, my lady?"

Clare handed Miriam her canvas at the same time someone inside the drawing room moved into her line of sight. Someone with light-blue eyes and a face she knew well.

In her shock, Clare accidentally dropped her box of paints. It hit the floor with a *thwack*, with two immediate results—Emmett looked directly her way . . . and the box upended its colorful contents onto the marbled tiles. Heat scoured Clare's face as she and Miriam crouched to right the mess. Signora Russo entered the foyer and told Clare not to worry about the clutter, but Clare ignored her. She needed something for her trembling hands to do.

"May I help?" she heard Emmett ask, though Clare didn't lift her gaze above his shoes.

She couldn't speak or nod or shake her head. He wasn't supposed to be here. What if he learned she was pregnant? Nausea grasped at her again, and she knew she was going to be sick.

"I'm sorry," she murmured. Rushing to her feet, she clapped a hand to her mouth and rushed up the stairs, away from her husband.

London, April 1907: Twenty months earlier

Her cheeks flushed from dancing, debutante Clare Herschel navigated the crowded ballroom to where her mother sat in a chair along the periphery. The dance wouldn't be over for some time yet, but her mother already looked weary. Clare couldn't blame her. The past three weeks had been a constant whirlwind of social engagements and late nights that rivaled Clare's debut into New York society.

Frances Herschel didn't thrive on societal events, but she and Clare's father still wanted the best for their daughter. That was the reason her father, a poor apple farmer, had sought to make a better life for his family. Eventually Gifford Herschel became a self-made millionaire as a hair-pomade manufacturer. Unfortunately, the eligible bachelors back home had still turned up their noses at Clare's new money, prompting her mother to take action. Frances decided that she and Clare would go to London for the season, as many other American matrons and their daughters had been doing for decades. The Herschels already had American friends living in England's capital city anyway, and a few letters were all it took to set things in motion—securing a place to stay and ensuring that all the proper introductions and invitations would follow.

Clare had been both eager and anxious at leaving her

home behind, but she'd found comfort in knowing her parents would never let her marry anyone they didn't consider kind, faith-filled, and respectable. Of course her large inheritance would likely attract the interest of an Englishman with a title. And yet more than anything, her parents wanted what Clare did—to make a match founded first and foremost on love.

"Are you ready to leave, Mama?"

Frances glanced around the room. "I don't want you to miss the rest of the dancing."

"I appreciate that," Clare said with a smile, "but there will be other opportunities."

"No." Her mother stood, her expression changing from hesitation to resolve. "We left the last dance early on my account, and I want you to experience this one fully. I think a cup of tea is all I need to revive me."

"Are you sure?"

Frances looped her arm through her daughter's and patted Clare's hand. "Stop fussing, Clare. It reminds me of your father, and I'm liable to get weepy if I get homesick for him again."

"I miss him too."

Clare fingered the silver rose brooch pinned to her dress. It had been a gift from her father on her eighteenth birthday. He'd told her the beautifully crafted yet unpretentious piece of jewelry reminded him of her. Her father had then counseled her to remember that in his eyes, and more importantly in God's, she would always be of worth, whether she was an heiress or still the child of a once-humble farmer.

Lowering her hand, she gave her mother's arm a gentle squeeze. "Letters just aren't the same, are they?"

"No, they aren't," Frances said softly, her tone full of love and longing.

They entered the refreshment room together. It wasn't as crowded as the ballroom, but it still held a fair number of patrons.

"I'll get the tea, Mama, if you want to find a seat for us."

When her mother agreed, Clare approached the refreshment table. Two gentlemen stood conversing at her left. They were both tall and lean with broad shoulders, though their coloring was different. The gentleman she could see most clearly had nice-looking brown hair and eyes, while the gentleman whose back was largely to her had dark-blond hair.

"Come now, Winfield," the blond one was saying. "The night is young, and there are plenty of lovely girls to dance with."

Winfield scowled at his companion. "Yes, lovely girls who at the behest of their mothers wish to sink their matrimonial claws into me."

"I believe you're right, old chap." His friend folded his arms and leaned forward. "I've heard they gather at night in one of their drawing rooms to plot your nuptial demise."

He lowered his voice and affected a woman's falsetto. "Tonight's the night, my dear ladies. The heir to the Duke of Moorleigh will succumb at last. We shall see him trussed up and hauled to the nearest church, or we shall perish in the effort. *Vive le mariage*!"

A laugh tumbled from Clare's lips. The sound drew the immediate attention of the blond gentleman, and he turned to face her. She blushed at being caught listening, but he didn't look annoyed. If anything, his pale-blue eyes were full of teasing warmth.

"Does my friend's misfortune inspire laughter?" His features were every bit as handsome as his friend's, though Clare preferred his light hair and eyes.

She feigned a serious expression as she accepted the tea

cup handed to her. "Oh no. Calculating mothers with claw-wielding daughters are no joking matter."

"Ah. Then you feel his pain?" She could tell he was trying hard not to smile.

"Indeed."

He nodded slowly as if thoroughly pondering her answer. "Perhaps it was my faulty performance that made you chuckle then?"

"Not at all." Clare shook her head. "It was the accuracy of it that prompted my response." Stepping past him, she directed her final comment to his friend. "I wish you the best of luck in fighting them off, sir."

The blond gentleman's deep laughter filled her ears as she walked away. Clare wanted to stay and banter with him longer, but they hadn't been properly introduced. Still, she couldn't help glancing at him over her shoulder. To her pleasure, she saw he was watching her too, a warm, attractive smile lifting his mouth. She pressed her lips over her own smile and carried the tea to her mother.

Since coming to England, Clare had met plenty of gentlemen. Many of them were nice-looking and adept in both conversation and compliments, but none seemed to possess a great sense of humor. Until now. As her mother sipped her tea, Clare studied the blond gentleman, at least as much as she could see of him from her chair.

A regal-looking, dark-haired beauty soon approached the two men and placed her gloved hand on the blond man's arm. Disappointment cut sharply through Clare at the familiarity between the pair. They didn't look enough alike to be related. Was this his wife? Or maybe his fiancée? As she watched, the three of them left the refreshment room.

Clare and her mother followed several minutes later. Frances guided Clare to an empty chair beside their London hostess—an American named Mrs. Poole. Her daughter Helena was a friend of Clare's and had married a viscount the year before.

As their mothers began talking, Helena turned to Clare. "Are you enjoying the dance?"

Clare gave a distracted nod. She was searching for the blond gentleman among the faces of those dancing. Sure enough, he and the dark-haired young woman waltzed past. "Helena?" She linked her arm through her friend's. "Who is that gentleman dancing there? The one with the blond hair? I believe he has a friend named Winfield."

Her friend followed her gaze. "Ah, that's the Earl of Linwood. His father is the Marquess of Hadwell."

"And the woman dancing with him?"

"Lady Melinda. Her husband died last year, making her a young widow with four children."

Clare watched them dance. They made a striking couple with his light hair and her dark. "Is there an . . . understanding . . . between them?"

"Their families have been friends for years," Helena answered in a half-whispered voice. "Apparently Lady Melinda hoped to marry Lord Linwood when they were younger, but her dowry was too small for the marquess's liking. I get the impression that she still hopes Lord Hadwell will change his mind, especially now that she's able to marry again. As for Lord Linwood, I've never detected anything but friendship between him and her."

Helena's words restored Clare's anticipation. "Will you introduce me to him when the waltz ends?"

"Of course." Her friend arched her eyebrows in a teasing manner. "But you've never asked me for an introduction before. Why the sudden interest in Lord Linwood?"

Clare gazed again at those dancing as she replied, "He

managed to do what no other English gentleman has done so far."

"What's that?"

She let her smile show through at last. "He made me laugh."

Chapter 2

"I'm fine, Miriam. I promise." Clare set her half-drained cup of tea onto the vanity table. Nothing about the reflection staring back at her from the mirror hinted at the torrent of shock and emotion still swirling inside her. Her copper-red hair, styled on top of her head, had remained in place despite her being sick. Her cheeks were no longer pale either, nor did her green eyes look as panicked.

Her maid didn't seem convinced, though. "Are you sure, my lady? Should I have a tray brought up?"

"No, that isn't necessary. I'll eat downstairs." *With my husband.*

Miriam nodded and left the room to inform Signora Russo that Clare would be eating lunch in the dining room after all. Swallowing her apprehension at Emmett's sudden appearance and what they would talk about, Clare finished her tea and rose to her feet. She could endure one meal, one conversation, in order to find out why Emmett was here. After that, she would decide how best to proceed.

Thankfully she had an excuse for leaving the house right after lunch. Going to Helena's and attending the party tomorrow would allow her to keep her pregnancy a secret, at least for the next few days. But what about after that?

I don't know what to do, Lord, she prayed as she descended the stairs. If Emmett intended to remain for some time in Sicily, her plans would be complicated. And if she miscarried while he was still here . . . Clare shuddered at the thought. Hopefully her prayers for this baby would be answered, even if those she'd voiced regarding her marriage hadn't been so far.

Signora Russo was setting a tempting plate of food on the table for her when Clare entered the dining room. Upon seeing her, Emmett stood. He appeared to have eaten half of his lunch in the time Clare had been upstairs, mastering her queasiness and her courage.

"I wasn't certain you would join me, or I would have waited."

She acknowledged his remark with a nod. "You were fine to go ahead."

He helped her with her chair, since there were no footmen at the villa, then returned to his seat. "Is everything all right?"

Clare didn't answer right away. Instead she took a moment to arrange her napkin across her lap and pick up her fork. Emmett was probably wondering why she'd bolted at the sight of him. "I'm sorry about earlier. I didn't expect you."

"I would have sent a telegram, but . . ." His gaze briefly met hers before dropping to his food. "I wasn't sure I'd be welcome."

Guilt pricked at Clare as she took a bite. Honestly, she *didn't* welcome his presence here, but not because she didn't want to see him again. Just not now, when she needed more time to see what would happen with this pregnancy.

"This is your home too, Emmett."

A flicker of something she couldn't interpret entered his eyes, then disappeared. "How was your Christmas?"

"It was rather unconventional by society's standards." She couldn't help the smile that tugged at her mouth. "I didn't want to eat alone on Christmas Eve, so I joined Miriam and the Russos and their married children in the kitchen. The meal was loud and boisterous and simply wonderful." It had reminded her of holiday celebrations back home.

Emmett chuckled. "Unconventional was the order of the day then. Rushford and I spent a rather quiet Christmas aboard the steamer. Several of us did share a holiday toast with the captain."

The reminder he'd come to Taormina, unannounced, and had been traveling instead of spending Christmas in England eroded some of her mirth. "I imagine your family wasn't too pleased to have you leave right before the holiday." Every one of Emmett's sisters and their families came to Hadwell House to celebrate Christmas.

"Actually it was my father's idea that I come."

Clare's surprise at his answer quickly gave way to wariness—and a thread of hurt. Her husband wasn't here because *he* wanted to see her but because his father wanted him here.

The marquess was a shrewd man with uncompromising expectations, ones Emmett had clearly been trying to meet for years. Why would Lord Hadwell want Emmett to come to Sicily now? Especially when Clare had already defied the family's expectations by coming to stay at the villa alone?

"What business does your father have for you here?"

Emmett began twisting his goblet in a slow circle. He seemed unusually nervous, which only increased her suspicions. "My father would like me to become an MP," he said at last.

"To run for Parliament? Why?"

He glanced at her as he answered. "Because he sees the

need for more like-minded men in the House of Commons." Emmett pushed his plate forward as if he was done, though there was still food there. "As for myself, I like the idea of influencing changes for the betterment of the nation and its people. Overseeing the work at Barksley Hall has taught me that."

The mention of the country estate they'd purchased called to Clare's mind a mixture of pleasant and unpleasant memories. At first, she'd naïvely believed this project would be something they would oversee together. After all, though she'd been an heiress when she'd married Emmett, she wasn't a stranger to hard work or business organization.

She still recalled her early childhood, when her family had struggled to make ends meet on their apple farm in Vermont. And she had witnessed—and joined in—the labors along the way as her father had worked to perfect the right recipe, which eventually led to the creation of his famous hair pomade. Building the business, gaining customers, overseeing production, growing distribution . . . her father had discussed all the details openly with his wife and child, giving Clare a business education that she doubted a grand university could surpass. She hadn't yet told Emmett about that part of her life, afraid of what he might think of her humble origins, but she'd been excited at the prospect of showing him the skills she'd learned from her father.

However, like many situations since her wedding, the estate project hadn't turned out as she'd hoped or imagined. She and Emmett had spent two full weeks at Barksley Hall, discussing ideas and plans for the inside of the house. But when it came time for the actual interior work to begin, he'd insisted she would be more comfortable living back at Hadwell House. Four weeks later, she'd learned she was pregnant for the third time and that leaving England might help her remain that way. Clare hadn't been brave enough to tell Emmett her travel plans in person, so she'd shared them in a letter. A part of her had hoped he would come see her before her departure, but he hadn't.

"If being an MP is what you want to do," she said, willing her thoughts to stay in the present and not the past, "I think you should. But I still don't understand how that relates to you being in Sicily."

Emmett took a sip of his drink. "It does when my wife is here."

"What are you saying?" The roiling in her stomach had nothing to do with her usual nausea this time. Clare instinctively knew they were finally getting to the real reason her husband had shown up with no warning.

He rubbed a hand across his jaw, drawing her attention to its strong outline. She'd thought him handsome from the moment she'd first seen him, and that hadn't changed.

"There's no easy way to say this, Clare." As she waited for him to continue, she set down her fork and grasped her hands in her lap. "If I'm to become an MP, my father believes it's vital for me to present a . . . a more positive image to the public."

"Which means?"

Emmett blew out his breath. "He feels it's best for my campaign if you and I are seen together and looking as a happy couple should."

His expression conveyed his own discomfort at repeating his father's edict, but that didn't stop a seed of anger from germinating inside Clare. She'd already experienced enough decrees and opinions from the marquess within the past year to last her two lifetimes. Worst of all, even when Emmett seemed to disagree, he never failed to comply with his father's edicts.

"I see." She kept her voice calm. "Then you'll be staying in Italy as long as I am?"

Sweet relief flooded her when he shook his head. But his next words renewed her frustration—and her fear. "I've come to ask you to return to England with me, Clare, as soon as we can make the arrangements. Once there, we'll begin laying the groundwork for my campaign."

His unexpected appearance made perfect sense now. He was here to collect her as one did a piece of luggage that had gone missing. She herself wasn't even needed in this political scheme of his and Lord Hadwell's—not in any way that truly mattered. She was only necessary as the other half of a smiling couple and, of course, as the one supplying the money to fund the campaign.

A dreadful memory, one Clare had attempted to squash time and time again, returned to her mind now. Lady Melinda had once commented on how Clare's marriage seemed happy, even though it was based solely on money. She hadn't believed the widow's audacious assumption at first, instead chalking it up to Lady Melinda's resentment over Emmett not marrying her. And yet Clare had been left with a niggling doubt when the woman went on to claim she'd heard the marquess congratulating his son for following his instructions to find a wealthy wife.

The pain Clare had felt that day gripped her anew and merged with her anger. Dropping her napkin on the table, she pushed her chair back and stood. "I can't go back to England with you, Emmett. Not right now. I'm sorry."

"Can't or won't?" His own irritation revealed itself in his tight tone and creased brow.

"I can't. Now, if you'll excuse me, I have to prepare to catch the train to Messina."

He climbed to his feet as well, his frown deepening. "What's in Messina?"

"Helena is hosting a party for Lord Vickley tomorrow,

and I agreed to help." She walked to the doorway, more than ready to be done with their conversation. "I'll be staying at their home tonight and tomorrow, so you'll have the villa all to yourself for the next few days."

Emmett swallowed a frustrated growl as Clare exited the dining room. His first attempt at convincing her to return to England hadn't exactly gone well.

Was her reason for not agreeing to come back with him as he feared? Had she truly left because she no longer cared about him and was eager to start a new life separate from his? He pushed the fear aside with the consolation that she hadn't treated him unkindly. So perhaps he wouldn't count their conversation as a total failure. However, being at the villa while Clare was in Messina wasn't going to help matters either.

Thinking fast about what to do next, he followed after Clare. She'd nearly reached the staircase landing, her steps nothing to her rapid ones earlier. The way the color had drained from her face right before she'd hurried upstairs had been unnerving. Had it only been shock at seeing him, or was something else wrong?

"Clare?" he called from where he stood at the bottom of the stairs. "May I come to Messina with you?"

She turned to face him, her hand on the banister, her eyebrows lifted. "You just came from there. Why would you want to go back?"

He didn't want to, but repeating the two-hour train ride would afford him more time—both to spend with Clare and to come up with a plan for how he was going to convince her to leave Sicily sooner than she apparently wanted. Besides, he preferred the idea of attending a party than staying here alone.

Talking with Clare just now had served as a powerful reminder of how much Emmett had missed their conversations. Until today, he hadn't seen or spoken to his wife in weeks, and he wasn't keen on their brief time together ending so soon. And while he couldn't forget that he had a job to do, he was also hoping that if he and Clare could reconnect, even tentatively, the transition to public life might go more smoothly once they were back in England.

"Vickley and I are friends," he said, choosing to only give voice to the more logical reasons for accompanying Clare to Messina. "And I'd like to attend the party, if that is amenable to the viscount and to you. The train ride there would also give us time to talk."

Her lips turned down at the corners. "If you want to talk more about returning to England, then no, I don't want you to come." She flinched as she spoke, as if she didn't enjoy saying such a refusal out loud.

It was a small thing, but it gave Emmett hope—and another idea. He would get nowhere in convincing her if she felt backed into a corner. They did need to talk about his campaigning at some point, but he could be patient. Especially if it meant talking about the future without one or both of them getting frustrated. In the meantime, they could converse about other things.

"I promise, if I come with you, I will not speak of politics, campaigning, or returning to England."

Clare eyed him silently for a moment. "All right." The line of her shoulders relaxed slightly. "You may come, and I'll speak with Helena tonight about you attending the party." He opened his mouth to express his gratitude, but she wasn't finished. "You and Rushford will have to stay in one of the hotels in Messina. It wouldn't be polite to arrive after giving no notice and insist you stay at the viscount's villa with me."

Emmett nodded. "Agreed. Rushford and I will be quite comfortable in a hotel for two nights." He offered her a grateful smile, which she didn't reciprocate. But she didn't look as upset or horrified as she had upon his arrival.

"I'll be ready shortly," Clare said, "then we can head to the train station."

As she continued upstairs, he went in search of his valet to let Rushford know the change in plans. Emmett found him eating his own lunch in the kitchen. With typical patience, Rushford took the news of a return trip to Messina in stride and promised to gather the luggage from Emmett's room, where it had been stowed earlier.

Signor Russo drove the four of them to the station. Emmett selected a seat beside the window in one of the train cars, and Rushford sat next to him. He half expected Clare to sit in a different car, but she surprised him. She and Miriam joined them in their car, settling themselves on the bench across from the two men. Clare even chose the spot nearest the window, which put her directly opposite Emmett. He hoped that meant she might be willing to converse some more with him.

As the train rolled away from the station, quiet settled over their car. Rushford leaned his head against the back of the seat and was soon dozing. Having removed a book from her satchel, Miriam began to read. Other society women likely wouldn't condone their maid reading while in their presence, but Clare didn't mind. In fact, Emmett had overheard her encouraging the girl to read whenever she could. It was another way his wife differed from the type of women he'd known all his life.

Clare had told him that her parents had always treated their servants more like members of the family than hired help. That way of interacting with the staff had been difficult for her to change when she'd needed to hire servants for their London townhouse. She'd adjusted somewhat to meet his family's expectations of what was right and proper, but she still treated everyone, servant or gentry, with the same grace, poise, and kindness. It was a quality Emmett had come to secretly admire about his wife; it had even influenced his own interactions this last year with the servants at Hadwell House and the tenants at Barksley Hall.

"How is Bran?" Clare asked, once the train was steadily moving.

"Doing well. I would have brought him, but he would have hated the steamer." Emmett cast a glance at her. "He misses you."

A shadow of a smile appeared at her mouth. "I miss him too."

And me? he nearly asked. *Do you miss me, Clare?*

He swallowed the words before they could spill out and turned to look at the Sicilian countryside rolling past. What if she hadn't missed him? He wasn't sure he could bear hearing her say it aloud.

"How is your family?" she inquired next.

He welcomed the change in topic and the fact that she was even talking to him at all. "They're well. The house was full to the eaves with nieces and nephews the night before I left. Mother was enjoying every minute of it."

Turning to face the window, Clare appeared to focus on the scenery outside the car. But Emmett hadn't missed the mixture of sorrow, wistfulness, and what looked like resolve shining in her green eyes before she turned away. He felt a twist of guilt; he shouldn't have mentioned his sisters' children. Not when they hadn't yet been able to have children of their own.

Hoping to redeem himself, he asked, "Have you done

some painting while you've been here? I noticed your box of paints when you came in." The same box that had tumbled from her hands when they'd first seen each other through the drawing-room doorway at the villa.

"I've finished three, actually, and I'm almost done with a fourth."

Emmett raised his eyebrows in amazement. "That's impressive, Clare."

"Thank you. Apparently my muse just needed sun like I did."

Or time away from her husband, a pessimistic thought argued.

Emmett cringed inwardly, then countered the accusation with the reminder that Clare had painted a portrait of him when they'd last been here, on their honeymoon. Before leaving for Sicily, he'd gone to view the painting one more time. But a different picture had been in its place. Neither his mother nor any of the servants knew where the portrait had gone. He'd felt a physical sense of loss at the thought of never again seeing Clare's painting of him. It was almost as if the memory of that happy time was fading and would eventually disappear too.

Clare glanced at him again. "How goes the work at Barksley Hall?"

This was a subject he could happily talk about for hours. Not so long ago, he and Clare had done just that. "It's going well," he answered with a smile. "At least it was when I left for Hadwell House before Christmas. The bedrooms and kitchen are finished, and the bathrooms have likely been completed by now."

Having a bathroom adjoining each of their bedrooms, complete with indoor plumbing and flush toilets similar to those in her home in New York, had been Clare's idea. She'd also suggested putting in electricity and radiators, which Emmett had agreed would be nice. He'd liked the idea of modernizing the four-hundred-year-old house while preserving its history too.

"Will you be able to oversee the changes if you are campaigning for Parliament?"

Emmett nearly replied with his potential schedule of plans, then thought better of it. After all, he'd made a promise not to speak of politics or his campaign. In truth, he wasn't sure how much time he would be able to devote to Barksley Hall. Hopefully all of the updates and renovations would be finished sooner than later.

"Very clever, my dear," he said, wagging his finger at her. "However, I won't be so easily tricked into breaking my promise."

"Breaking your promise . . ." Clare echoed, her tone full of confusion.

He was happy to hear she hadn't purposely been baiting him with the way she'd phrased her question. And with her sharp mind, he knew she'd quickly realize what he was referring to. Sure enough, a moment later, she smiled. It wasn't a full smile, but it was still aimed his way.

"Evading tricky questions is surely the first test of a true politician, my lord."

Her witty reply made him laugh out loud. Rushford stirred in his sleep, and Miriam glanced up from her book to smile at them. Right then, Emmett could almost believe things hadn't changed so much between him and his wife. Only in the next moment, Clare faced the window, and the connection between them faded.

Desperate to bring it back, Emmett searched for something else to say. "Are you feeling queasy at all?"

"What?" The horrified expression on Clare's face when

she turned to look at him made no sense. "Why would you ask that?"

Emmett frowned. "Because you sometimes feel queasy when you ride on trains or steamers."

"Oh yes, of course." She laughed, but the sound held little merriment. If Emmett didn't know better, he would say she was nervous. "I have some peppermints with me if I feel sick."

He nodded, still puzzled at her odd reaction but willing to let the matter drop since it seemed to upset her. "Have you enjoyed being here in Sicily again?"

"I have." Her gaze returned to the countryside beyond the train. "I think I understand why your grandfather loved it so much. It's beautiful and peaceful and still so green, even in winter."

"He did love it here," Emmett murmured.

Thoughts of his grandfather still invoked the painful memory of the man's death. But the wonderful memories were there too. Like the long walks they'd taken around the estate, talking about everything from school, to the family, to Emmett's current collection of rocks or bugs or glass bottles. With Grandfather, Emmett had been allowed to simply be a child—not just the future Marquess of Hadwell.

There had been plenty of conversations about God as well—about the world He'd created for them, about how He watched over and loved each person, old and young, and about how He heard every prayer. In this way, Grandfather had shared his deep, quiet faith, and in doing so, had awakened and solidified a similar faith in Emmett.

He'd once asked his grandfather if God loved the marquess. "He certainly does," Grandfather had said without a moment's hesitation. "Your father is as much God's child as you or I, Emmett."

"I don't know that Father cares much for God in return."

His grandfather had chuckled, then grown serious again. "Be that as it may, God still loves him. And because God can and does love your father, He's asked us to do the same."

Emmett looked at Clare. Her eyes were now closed, her hat slightly crushed as she rested her head against the section of wall next to the window. She looked tired. Was his presence the reason for her exhaustion? He hoped not, though things weren't likely to be any less wearying for a long time to come, not with a political career potentially ahead of them.

What would his grandfather think of Emmett wanting to become an MP? He wasn't sure, though he suspected Grandfather would have been supportive if this was what Emmett wanted to do. And he did, didn't he? If he could be a force for good, for change, in England, then surely he would be the sort of man a father could be proud of.

But first he needed the help of another Father, One whom Emmett had forgotten to petition before coming to Sicily. It was time to change that. In the silence of the train car, he shut his eyes, but he didn't sleep. Instead he silently asked God to give him the strength to do what he needed to here, to soften his wife's heart, if possible, and to make more of Emmett's future than he could on his own.

There was a carriage waiting in Messina to convey Clare and Miriam to the viscount's villa. It was large enough to accommodate Emmett and his valet too, but since the recommended hotel where they'd be staying wasn't far, they opted to walk.

"I'll ask Helena about a party invitation for you," she told Emmett, "and send word to the hotel in the morning."

He nodded. "I hope to see you tomorrow then."

Did she hope to see him as well? A large part of her did. After all, talking with him on the train hadn't proved to be as unpleasant as she'd feared. And it was nice to see his face again and hear his voice.

She was still frustrated with him over his sudden arrival in Sicily and his plan to return her to England, but some of her ire had cooled in the past two hours. Especially since Emmett had kept his word to her. He hadn't brought up his newest plan to run for Parliament, nor had he pressed her for why she wouldn't go back to England with him straightaway. He'd even refrained from answering her innocent question about Barksley Hall because it would have meant talking, indirectly, about politics.

"Until tomorrow." Clare stepped toward the carriage, but before the driver could help her, Emmett held out his hand.

"May I?"

She stared down at his hand, her pulse flitting faster. As her hesitation stretched longer, her cheeks began to heat. She must look silly debating something so simple as accepting her husband's offer of help. Finally, she placed her gloved hand against his palm. A zing of feeling swept her head to toe. She shot a glance at Emmett's face and found him watching her. Had he felt the same charge of sensation that she had? Or was the spark between them only on her side?

The warmth she'd felt at his touch wasn't manufactured, though. And the growing look of surprise in his eyes told her she wasn't the only one to experience a rush of emotion at their joined hands.

Confused, she lowered her gaze as Emmett assisted her into the open carriage. He helped Miriam in next, then shut the door. The vehicle rolled forward. Clare couldn't help peering at her husband, who watched her as well until the carriage turned a corner. With a heavy sigh, she sat back against the seat.

"Are you well, my lady?"

Was she? Despite sleeping a little on the train, she felt fatigued—and hungry. But it was more than just physical tiredness. Right now she felt weary in heart too.

"I'll be all right, thank you, especially once I have some dinner."

Eating might help assuage her pregnancy sickness, but it wouldn't cure everything. Clare still didn't know what to do about Emmett's request to return to England. She'd found little happiness living there, and she couldn't go with him anyway, not if she wanted to prevent another miscarriage. Yet the longer he stayed in Sicily, attempting to convince her, the harder it would be to keep her pregnancy a secret.

She'd been terrified on the train when he'd asked if she was queasy, certain he'd somehow guessed her condition. Her relief that he hadn't had been profound, but it also made Clare aware of how careful she had to be. Over the next few days, she would need to keep eating regularly to stay her nausea. Tomorrow night, she'd also be sure to drink some tea before the party, since Emmett would likely be in attendance.

The viscount's villa rose before her a few minutes later. The driver helped her and Miriam alight from the carriage, and Clare led the way to the front door. Squaring her shoulders against her worries and exhaustion, she put on a smile and knocked firmly on the door. "I believe we have a party to help with."

Miriam smiled back. "We do indeed, my lady."

As they were ushered inside and Clare was greeted with an enthusiastic embrace from Helena, she held tightly to her resolve. She'd weathered difficult things before, especially in the last fourteen months since she'd been married. One party and a few days in Messina with Emmett would surely prove to be an easy thing to manage.

London, May 1907: Nineteen months earlier

Up until a few weeks ago, Emmett hadn't realized how his interactions with other young ladies were lacking. He had been tasked by his father to find and marry a suitable—meaning rich—woman before the year was out, and he'd decided the best way to do so was to meet as many of the young women in London as he could. Hopefully one of them would fit his father's requirements but also his own. Emmett wanted a marriage with more laughter, affection, and closeness than he'd observed over the years in his parents' relationship.

Lord Hadwell had let it be known around town that his son was looking for a bride, and Emmett had experienced no shortage of interested young ladies. But he'd begun to despair of finding one who saw him as more than his title. None of them seemed sincerely interested in coming to know him—and there wasn't one who inspired a true interest in Emmett to know her.

Then he'd met Miss Clare Herschel. Her lovely laugh and clever banter had captivated him from the moment Emmett had turned and found her watching him with those bemused green eyes and an attractive blush on her cheeks.

Emmett nearly told his father later that night about the

meeting but thought better of it. The immediate connection he'd felt with Miss Herschel still seemed too private to share with anyone. Besides, he wasn't entirely certain what the marquess would think of his interest in an heiress from America. She had a fortune, to be sure, but she'd still been raised in a world of customs and obligations that differed from his.

Rather than risk his father asking him to find someone else, Emmett kept his growing admiration for Miss Herschel to himself. But he sought her out at every event of which they were both in attendance. He especially enjoyed dancing with her—that, and inspiring her laughter.

Tonight he'd had the good fortune of securing two waltzes with her. However, since this was their second dance of the evening, he would now have to be content with partners who were far less witty, genuine, and interesting.

"Thank you for the dance, Lord Linwood." Miss Herschel's smile never held any pretense, only gentleness and honesty.

Emmett smiled in return. "The pleasure is mine, Miss Herschel." He led her toward the edge of the dance floor, happy for an excuse to keep her elbow in his gloved hand a little longer. "You waltz beautifully."

"I think that's a compliment meant as much for you as for me, my lord. Since you are, in fact, the one leading the waltz."

He feigned a thoughtful expression. "I concede your point. May I say then how beautifully you waltz with *me*?"

"Only with you?" It was clear she was trying not to laugh.

"Miss Herschel," he began again, "how beautifully you waltz with every gentleman lucky enough to partner with you. How's that?"

Her lips twitched with hidden delight. "I'll allow it. However . . ." A small laugh escaped her mouth before she pretended to be serious once more. "To be truly sincere in the compliment, you would have to observe me waltzing with others before making such an observation."

"And who is to say I haven't?" he countered, no longer teasing.

She blushed, but there was also a look of pleasure in her eyes. Could she be as fascinated with him as he was with her? As if in answer to his unspoken question, she asked, "Will you be attending the theater tomorrow night, my lord?"

The hopeful note in her voice nearly had him leading her back onto the floor for another dance, the possible ruin of both their reputations notwithstanding. "I was considering it. Will you be in attendance?"

"Yes."

Then he would attend too.

Miss Herschel had entered his life less than a month ago, but there were times when Emmett felt as if he'd known her for years. He'd been to visit her and her mother twice at the townhouse where they were staying and had covertly learned which social events they would be attending. He had even begun to entertain the hope of courting Miss Herschel.

Emmett released her arm as propriety dictated, but he didn't step away. Instead he studied her open, graceful countenance. She didn't break his earnest gaze either. In that moment, the music, the crowds, the overly warm room ceased to exist, leaving only them. A desire to kiss her tugged him forward a step.

"Miss Herschel." The marquess's voice sounded as loud as symbols in Emmett's ears. He fell back a step as his father placed a firm hand on his shoulder.

She nodded politely. "Lord Hadwell."

"If you'll excuse us, I need to speak with my son."

"Of course."

Emmett offered her an apologetic smile. "Thank you again for the waltz."

"You're welcome, my lord."

He lost sight of her as his father steered him toward the opposite side of the ballroom. Would Lord Hadwell demand that Emmett stop interacting with her? His heart thudded with consternation at the thought. He didn't wish to choose between his growing feelings for Miss Herschel and his father's displeasure, but he couldn't imagine never seeing her again either.

"Is she the one whom you've set your sights on?" his father asked after he stopped them beside a pillar.

Should he speak the truth of what he felt? Emmett glanced around to buy himself another moment before answering. Nearby Lady Melinda, a longtime family friend, was conversing with another young lady. They didn't seem to be paying Emmett and his father any attention though.

Summoning his courage, Emmett pushed out a deep breath. "I admire her very much," he said, steeling himself against his father's reaction.

"Excellent. I believe she'll do quite nicely for you and—"

Emmett reared back. "Wait. You're saying . . . you approve of my choice?"

"Why shouldn't I?" His father actually looked offended.

"Well, for one she's American."

The marquess waved his hand dismissively. "A very wealthy American. Have you heard the size of her inheritance?"

"I have," Emmett answered, somewhat warily. Despite his efforts to conceal his attentions toward Miss Herschel, had his father noticed anyway and gone digging for information about her?

Lord Hadwell smiled as he gazed at the gathered crowd.

"You know how much Hadwell House needs someone like her. Her cash will ensure the estate is kept solvent and in good repair for several more generations."

His father talked as if an understanding was already in place. Not that Emmett would mind. He wanted to proceed naturally, though, rather than feel rushed by the marquess's expectations.

"I haven't even started courting her."

Turning to face him, the marquess frowned. "Why ever not? You need to hurry, or some duke's son is liable to come along and snatch her millions right out from under you. That's what these American heiresses want, after all—a title."

Miss Herschel had never given any indication that she cared whether Emmett had a title or not. "I'm not interested . . ." He lowered his voice to avoid being heard. "That is to say, I don't wish to court her for her millions, Father."

"There's no shame in it," his father remarked in a patronizing tone. "However, if it eases that conscience of yours to believe you admire her for her charm and beauty, then go ahead."

Emmett's jaw tightened with irritation. "Miss Herschel has far more qualities to recommend her than simply being a beautiful heiress."

"Yes, yes, of course." The marquess studied something in the distance, then clapped a hand to Emmett's shoulder again. "No need to be glum, my boy. Congratulations are certainly in order. You've done as I asked in finding a wealthy wife. You should feel proud of yourself."

The compliment felt hollow. "I'm grateful I met her."

"As am I. Now, I need to go speak with Lord Huffing."

As his father walked away, Emmett took a moment to calm his frustration. He ought to be elated that his choice had met with the marquess's approval. The victory had been robbed of some of its sweetness, though, now that he knew his father believed Emmett's interest was based on monetary reasons. Still, he was relieved that he no longer had to hide his interest in Miss Herschel. And with that newfound freedom, Emmett knew the first thing he wished to do.

He headed back toward the spot where he'd left Miss Herschel. Only she wasn't there. He studied the faces of those dancing but didn't see her. Growing desperate in his search, he asked Winfield if he'd seen Miss Herschel. Emmett's best friend had always been adept at observation, though lately, Winfield's gift seemed even more honed. As expected, the man reported having seen Miss Herschel and her mother leaving the ballroom.

Emmett found them as they were collecting their coats. "Miss Herschel? Might I have a word?"

"Of course, Lord Linwood." She exchanged a curious glance with her mother, though she didn't look displeased that he'd detained them.

That knowledge had him standing straighter. "I'd be honored if you would allow me to accompany you and your mother to the theater tomorrow night. We would have the use of my box." He looked at Mrs. Herschel as he added, "If, of course, that is agreeable to the both of you."

Mrs. Herschel offered him a kind smile. "Thank you for the invitation, Lord Linwood. Clare and I would be happy to accept."

"Wonderful," he said, glancing at Miss Herschel again. Would she recognize his intention to have this invitation be the start of courting her? "I shall send a note tomorrow morning with the details."

Her answering smile struck him straight through the chest. "I look forward to the evening, my lord."

"As do I," he murmured.

He bid them goodnight and returned to the ballroom. But he was hardly aware of anyone or anything after that. In his mind's eye, Emmett was already at the theater, seated beside Miss Herschel, for the first of what he hoped would prove to be many more outings in her unequaled company.

Chapter 3

Emmett had been dreaming of the night he'd first invited Clare to the theater when a violent shift of the bed woke him. He had only a second or two to recall he was in a hotel in Messina before he was flung to the floor, striking it with a hard *smack* that reverberated through his entire body. He sat up, dazed and confused, but the vibrations in the floor didn't stop.

Across the room, large cracks began to spread like spiderwebs across the plaster. A rush of rain-drenched air jerked his attention to the long, rectangular window and its now-gaping hole. Emmett shivered as much from growing horror as from the cold.

He managed to get his feet beneath him, when a terrible sound rose up from somewhere within the hotel, peppered by piercing screams. Never had he heard such an awful racket. It seemed to come from the very depths of some fiery inferno. The entire room swayed around him, and Emmett threw his arms out for balance to keep himself from crashing to the floor again.

This had to be an earthquake. They weren't uncommon in this region, but Emmett had only ever experienced two or three mild ones. Was Clare safe? Would they feel the quaking at the viscount's villa? Or were the hotel patrons suffering the worst of the vibrations?

The reality of his situation hit Emmett full force, and he knew he had to escape this madness. Then he had to find Clare.

Grabbing his clothes from off the nearby chair, Emmett traded his pajamas for shirt and trousers as quickly as he could before he pushed his feet into his shoes and rushed toward the door. But no matter how hard he tugged on the handle or shoved the wood with his shoulder, the door wouldn't budge.

"Oh please, God, help me," he murmured as he frantically searched the room for another means of escape. The window provided the only other way out, but he and Rushford were on the second floor. Rushford! Was his valet all right?

Emmett stepped to the door again and shouted, "Rushford?" He didn't know if the man could hear him or not, but he had to try. "I'm going out the window."

White dust from the eroding plaster began filling the room. Emmett coughed as some of it entered his mouth. He hurried toward the open window, his shoes crunching against the broken glass. There was little to see beyond the rain. No light shone along the street below or in the buildings across the way.

A bolt of an idea sent him darting back to the bed. Tugging the mattress free, Emmett dragged it to the window. He maneuvered the mattress over the balcony rail and let it fall. The building rocked again, causing the balcony to tip to one side, as if angered at Emmett's attempts to flee. He could just make out the white of the mattress below. Keeping his gaze fixed on the object, he climbed over the balcony and jumped.

His stomach seemed to leap into his throat as he fell through the air, but miraculously he landed on the mattress.

For one long moment, he didn't move. Emmett simply lay there, sucking in great gulps of rain. He was alive, for now.

A yell drew his attention upward. On another balcony stood two people. "Help!" one of them screamed. "We can't get out."

"You'll have to jump." Emmett scrambled to his feet and positioned the mattress beneath the other window. "I have something for you to land on."

No sooner did he have the mattress in place than one of the pair hurdled themselves over the balcony. The person struck the mattress near the side. Emmett saw it was an older woman, dressed in a long, white nightgown. He helped her up before the second person jumped.

"Oh, thank you," the woman sobbed, throwing her arms around Emmett. "The stairs are gone, so we couldn't get out that way."

Her husband stumbled toward them. "We should find shelter. It's not safe to linger in the streets."

As if on cue, one of the buildings across the street tumbled to the ground with a loud crash. Emmett covered his head with his arms and crouched low. A shower of debris fell around him and the older couple, who were hunkered down beside him.

"Look at that!" the man called out, when the falling stones appeared to have stopped. "Half the hotel is already gone."

Emmett jerked his chin up. Sure enough, the hotel looked as if someone had sliced the building in two with a giant knife. The half he'd been staying in still stood but at a tipped angle. The other half was nothing but a heaping pile of rubble. Which half had Rushford's room been in? Emmett couldn't remember.

Terror rendered him immovable as he took in the

devastation around him. The crash of masonry mingled with the screams and cries for help that rent the air in every direction. Fires now lit the sky, while people in nightclothes and bare feet scurried down the littered street and up and over the mounds of rubble. The ground continued to quake beneath him. As Emmett gaped in shock at the nightmarish scene, a stone parapet tumbled to the ground, crushing several pedestrians beneath it right before his eyes.

He couldn't stay here. He needed to move, to act—or he was as good as dead himself.

Emmett ground his teeth together as he pushed against the paralyzing fear and forced his legs to rise. He had to find Rushford. That was all he would think about for now. After that, he would find Clare. One task at a time.

He bolted to the nearest mass of rubble from the hotel. Shouting Rushford's name, Emmett began pulling away the debris with his hands. Immediately moans rose up from the wreckage. Someone was buried there. Emmett worked faster. Even if the person wasn't his valet, he couldn't stop helping now that he knew a fellow human being lay hurting somewhere below.

"Hold on," he called down to the victim. "I'm going to get you out."

God willing, he silently added.

He had no way of knowing how long he dug before he saw a face staring up at him through the hole he'd made. It wasn't Rushford's face, but the cry of relief from the stranger made all the effort worth it. Emmett reached down and grasped the other man's hand. Then carefully, so as not to bury him again, he pulled the chap from the mound of rubble that had almost been his tomb.

The stranger looked to be younger than Emmett, though the blood covering a good portion of the man's face made it difficult to know for certain. "God bless you," he murmured over and over again in Italian.

Emmett decided to use part of his shirt as a bandage for the stranger's injury. The garment was so frayed by now that the fabric broke away easily when he ripped it. He wrapped the makeshift bandage around the young man's head. "I'm sorry I don't have anything else." He hated leaving the stranger here, alone and injured, but there was nothing more he could do for him. He had no water, food, or medical supplies to offer.

"Lord . . . Linwood." The words were spoken in a hoarse voice, but Emmett recognized it at once. He whirled around and saw his valet moving slowly toward him. Rushford cradled his left arm to his chest, but otherwise, the man appeared to be unharmed.

"Rushford!" Emmett closed the distance between them and grasped his valet's uninjured shoulder in a rush of relief and joy. "Are you all right? I thought you might have been caught in the rubble. What happened?"

His valet bent forward, his breaths coming hard and fast. "I was sleeping . . . and suddenly the ceiling crashed in, and the floor sank." Rushford sucked in another long breath. "I fell into a rubble pile and nearly gave myself up for dead. After a bit, I found a hole in the wreckage and worked my way out. Afraid I broke my arm, though."

"We can make a temporary sling until we can find a doctor to set it for you."

Emmett searched among the debris for something to use and found a black shawl. Shutting his mind to what might have befallen the garment's owner, he placed the material around Rushford's back and chest and tied it at the man's shoulder.

"Thank you, my lord."

The valet visibly winced as he placed his injured arm into the sling. But it would have to do for now.

"We need to see how Clare and the others have fared."

As the two of them started down the street, Emmett glanced back to where he'd left the wounded young man. The stranger had already disappeared. He sent a quick prayer heavenward for the young man, along with a plea for protection for Clare and Miriam, for himself and Rushford, and for those at the viscount's home.

Emmett hoped to reach them soon, but his and Rushford's progress was constantly slowed by the chaos around them. In nearly every street and square, mounds of rubble blocked their path. Emmett lost count of how many piles they scaled. Or how many times he stumbled and fell from the vibrating earth and broken cobblestones. The rain hadn't let up either, and both he and his valet shivered from the cold. They weren't the only ones fleeing the toppling buildings either. The streets were as clogged with fleeing people as they were wreckage.

Far worse, though, than the damp or the constant threat of being crushed to death by falling objects were the terrified wails of those trapped beneath the rubble. Should he stop and try to help them? Emmett asked himself that question again and again. It tore at his heart to walk away from anyone in such desperate need, but he couldn't assist everyone, and he needed to get to Clare. The urgency he felt to find his wife screamed at him to move faster, but he hated not being able to rescue others.

A sort of numbness began to seep into his mind and threatened to overwhelm him. Emmett fought it back by picking a point ahead of him. He could make it that far. When he reached that point, he would select another, then another.

Hours seemed to pass as he and Rushford trudged

forward. Eventually Emmett could tell daylight was creeping over the world, lighting the horrors around them in ever-increasing detail. In the growing light, he thought he recognized the square ahead of them. If he was right, they were nearly to the viscount's villa.

They picked their way across the square, veering far to the right at one point to skirt the rubble of another fallen building. The one beside it hadn't collapsed yet, but like the hotel, it leaned at a precarious angle. Any minute now it would join the fate of those around it.

Emmett was nearly past the teetering building when a boy cried out to him in Italian. The pleading voice stopped him in his tracks, and he turned back. On a balcony above him stood two children, holding fast to each other's hands, their faces pale with fear. The boy looked about twelve years old, while the little girl couldn't be more than seven or eight. Their dark hair, large black eyes, and matching chins identified them as siblings.

When the boy repeated his call for help, Emmett looked at Rushford. Staying would delay them from reaching Clare and would likely put their lives in even greater risk. And yet the same determination and newfound energy he felt surging inside him filled his valet's eyes. They couldn't leave without trying to help.

Praying God would keep his wife safe a little longer, Emmett picked his way toward the building. Rushford was right behind him.

"We'll need some way to reach them, my lord."

The two of them rummaged carefully through the debris around the building. It wasn't likely that they'd find a ladder, but Emmett couldn't help hoping anyway. There seemed to be nothing in the way of tools, and they were running out of time to save the children before the building collapsed.

Rushford suddenly cried out in triumph and lifted a length of rope into the air. After tying one end to a stone, Emmett directed the children in Italian to stand back. He swung the rope and tossed the stone toward the balcony. It landed with a thud. He instructed the boy to untie the rope from the stone and secure it to the balcony rail. Once that was complete, Emmett climbed the wreckage and gave the rope a gentle tug. He was relieved when it held. But would it support a grown man's weight?

Since his valet had a broken arm, Emmett would have to be the one to ascend the rope. "I'll climb up for one of them," he explained to Rushford. "Then hand the child off to you before I go back for the other."

His valet gave a solemn nod. "I'll keep an eye on the building."

Emmett silently voiced another prayer for help and protection before he slipped off his shoes and approached the rope. He gripped it as high as he could reach, then pulled himself upward. For a second, he hung there, bracing himself for the snap of the rope or the sudden crash of the building as it fell. But nothing happened. Taking in a deep breath, he climbed, hand over hand. The muscles in his arms were on fire, and his palms smarting by the time he was halfway to the balcony. Yet he couldn't stop. He instinctively knew if he did he would likely not be able to start climbing again.

The pitiful cries of the little girl spurred him on until he could at last reach up and grasp the balcony rail. The boy insisted his sister go first. Her expression turned to sheer panic as her brother lifted her over the balcony toward Emmett. She screamed and held fast to the railing. The boy tried soothing her, but she shook her head.

"What's her name?" Emmett asked.

"Antonina."

He attempted a smile, though it was getting harder and harder to hold himself up. "Antonina," Emmett soothed in her native tongue. "I want to help you and your brother. But I need you to come with me now. Is that all right?"

She studied him through large, dark eyes before she finally nodded. "*Sì*," she whispered.

Her brother told her to climb onto Emmett's back. This time she obeyed without any protest other than a whimper. Her little arms wound around Emmett's neck and held fast. He released the balcony and grasped the rope with both hands again. A loud creak sounded nearby. The building leaned farther, causing the rope to sway. Emmett heard the girl's frightened yelp in his ear, but she didn't scream.

"The building's listing even more, my lord," Rushford hollered up to him.

Emmett would need to hurry. The extra weight on his back made it almost as difficult going down as it had been to climb up. Finally his feet touched ground instead of air. Emmett let his arms sag as he bent forward to catch his breath. Rushford hurried forward to take the girl from him, but she wouldn't release Emmett.

"It's all right, Antonina," he said, trying to reassure her. "You're safe."

No sooner had the words left his mouth then Rushford shouted, "Watch out, Linwood!"

A dreadful rumble roared in Emmett's ears. He snapped up and stumbled away from the building with the child still clinging to him. Pulling Antonina off his back, he cradled her against his chest and crouched to the ground, doing his best to protect her small body. Dust rained down on them, and something struck Emmett in the back. He winced and choked on a cry of pain, but he didn't think any real damage had been done.

After a minute or two, Antonina squirmed in his grasp. "Angelo? Angelo?" she yelled in a tear-filled voice as she looked over Emmett's shoulder.

He slowly straightened his aching muscles and turned. The building had crumbled into ruins. There was no more balcony, and no more Angelo waiting to be rescued. Nothing but stone and plaster and beams.

Rushford came to stand beside him and placed his hand on Emmett's shoulder. Instead of comforting, his valet's grip felt heavy and final. "There's nothing more you could have done for him, my lord."

"We can't be certain he perished—the boy could still be alive." After all, that other young man had survived being buried in the rubble. Emmett attempted to set Antonina down again, but she clung all the tighter to him. Too tired to protest, he shifted her to his side and began to move away what he could of the wreckage with one hand. "Angelo?" he called loudly. "Angelo? Can you hear us?"

Rushford joined the effort. But there was no answering cry from the boy. Emmett finally set Antonina on her feet, though he kept hold of her thin shoulders. "We need to go," he explained. "But I will come back . . ." Emotion made his voice hitch, and he had to cough to clear it. The girl didn't need to hear his own shock and regret at the loss of her brother. "I will come later today and look for Angelo again."

Tears had made streaks in the white dust that covered her face. He'd never seen such a mournful expression, especially on one so young.

"How old are you, Antonina?"

"Eight."

"And where are your parents?"

She wordlessly pointed at the mound of ruins. Had her parents been killed first, leaving her and her brother to escape alone?

"Would you like to come with me and Mr. Rushford?" He nodded to his valet, who watched them with a sorrowful look of his own. "I must find my wife now and see if she is safe. She is very kind, and I think you'll like her. Will you come with us?"

Emmett held his breath. He didn't want to leave the child behind, and yet he wouldn't force her to come with them either. Perhaps there were other family members or friends who lived close by who would be anxiously looking for her. But a glance at the toppled buildings around the square proved the futility of such a thought. Even if the girl's friends or neighbors had survived, they'd have no shelter to offer her.

"I's come with you," she said in broken English.

She tugged one of his hands from off her shoulder and placed her small one inside his large palm. A lump filled his throat, momentarily robbing Emmett of the ability to speak. He responded instead by giving her hand a gentle squeeze.

Somewhere beyond the square another roar sounded. It still wasn't safe to remain long in one place. Echoing his thoughts, Rushford said, "We need to keeping moving, my lord."

"You're right." Emmett shoved his feet inside his dust-filled shoes and scooped Antonina into his arms. "We need to go." He would do all in his power to keep his little charge safe, along with anyone else that came under his care.

At first, Clare believed she was simply more tired than she'd thought when she swayed on her feet on her way up the grand staircase of her friend's villa. She'd woken before four thirty in the morning and couldn't get back to sleep, her mind racing with thoughts of Emmett and his abrupt arrival in

Sicily. Unfortunately, her wakefulness had also renewed her nausea, so she'd gone down to the kitchen to make herself some tea. The warm liquid had soothed her queasiness and eased the early morning chill. It was still dark outside, but Clare had heard the rain drumming against the kitchen window.

The tea hadn't helped with her apparent dizziness at rising so early though. She could hardly put one foot on the stair above her without listing to one side or the other.

She'd nearly reached the landing when she was thrown into the wall. Clare cried out more in surprise than from actual pain. A painting near her ear tumbled off the wall and crashed to the floor. In the dim light, she could see that the entire foyer was shifting around her. The banister swayed, and vibrations shook the stairs beneath her bare feet.

"Helena!" The viscount's sudden shout from above made Clare jump. "Grab the baby! It's an earthquake." The man yelled for the rest of the household to assemble in the upstairs hall.

Clare stumbled up the stairs, fear pushing her faster. A pale-faced Miriam met her in the hallway where the others were gathering. "Oh, my lady, are you all right?"

"I-I think so. I need to grab something though."

Without waiting for the maid's response, Clare moved quickly into the guest room where she was staying. She grabbed her silver brooch from off the dressing table and slipped it into the pocket of her robe before she hurried back into the hall. Tightening the robe's sash around her long nightgown, she awaited the viscount's instructions. Helena stood beside her husband, her ten-month-old son on her hip.

"All of us will go downstairs," the viscount said in a grave tone. "We'll take shelter in the window arch in the dining room. Understood?"

Murmurs of assent rippled through the assembled group before the viscount started down the stairs. The steps were still swaying under her feet as Clare followed the others to the ground floor. A rumbling noise from somewhere in the back of the house filled the air.

"Hurry," Helena's husband directed, waving them into the dining room. "The walls are starting to fall."

Clare moved as if in a dream, numbly following the person in front of her. Nothing felt real. Fear was beginning to resurrect her nausea.

"Mind the glass as you sit." The viscount kicked aside a large piece.

The arched window in the dining room was pockmarked with holes, allowing the rain inside. Cold, damp air hit Clare's face and neck, and she shuddered. A fire-like glow lit the sky outside, in spite of the storm, and pushed back the early-morning darkness.

Beneath the enormous archway, Clare took a seat on the floor beside Helena. Her friend looked every bit as terrified as Clare, though her little boy appeared to still be dozing. Miriam sat near Clare. The whole group had to squeeze together in order for the ten of them to sit beneath the protection of the arch. But huddling together also meant staying warmer.

Creaks, groans, and crashes could be heard from elsewhere in the villa, making Clare flinch. Particles of white dust began floating through the air. No one spoke, except for the occasional whispered prayer. Clare prayed too for those assembled here and for Emmett and Mr. Rushford. Was her husband safe? Had he found a place to take shelter at the hotel?

Soon the awful sounds drew closer and seemed to engulf them, pressing in. Clare wished she could block out the noise. Without warning, the ceiling to the left of the arch suddenly collapsed, showering stone, plaster, and dust into the room. Someone screamed, and the baby, waking abruptly, started to wail. Clare covered her head, but that didn't protect her fully from the dust. It entered her mouth and nose, making her sputter and cough.

"We're trapped!" one of the viscount's maids cried in a panicked voice.

Clare lowered her arms and lifted her head. The girl's statement was correct—wreckage surrounded them on all four sides now, blocking out all but a bit of light near the top of the window. They could no longer feel the rain, but that was paltry compensation.

A clammy feeling filled Clare's chest, making her heart race. She tasted bile on her tongue and feared she might be sick. Clapping a hand to her mouth, she forced herself to breathe evenly. Miriam clutched her other hand and squeezed hard. Somehow the human contact eased a little of Clare's shock. She clutched the girl's hand in return.

"What do we do, Leo?" Helena whispered to her husband. The baby hadn't stopped crying, and any attempt at soothing him was rebuffed.

The viscount cleared his throat. "We will simply wait for rescue. Someone will come."

Would they? Was rescue as imminent as he believed? Or was the viscount only trying to pacify them into remaining calm?

Helena's baby began another round of wails, but his distressed mother made no attempt to shush him this time. The fussing child gave Clare something else to focus on, and she welcomed the distraction. Untying the sash at her waist, she gently took the boy from Helena and set him on her lap. She dangled the sash before the little boy. The diversion did the trick, and he stopped crying. Clare tickled his cheek next.

She could just make out the crooked smile that appeared on his dusty face. The sight of it was so incongruous with their situation that it felt surreal, and yet it also brought Clare the tiniest glimmer of hope.

Somehow, in spite of being trapped inside the villa behind walls of debris, she believed they would be all right. As the viscount had reassured them, someone would come. Clare repeated that refrain over and over as she entertained the baby. Someone would come.

London, June 1907: Eighteen months earlier

Judging by the lack of horse traffic along Rotten Row, the threat of rain had kept most riders at home this morning. But Clare didn't mind the prospect of a drizzle. She was enjoying her ride, especially since it meant spending more time with Lord Linwood.

"You look quite at home on your horse, Miss Herschel," he said from atop his own mount.

Clare turned her head to give him an amused glance. "Is that a compliment or a critique, my lord?"

"It's an observation of delighted surprise." His eyes were full of teasing, and yet there was admiration in them too. "I was not aware when I issued my invitation for a morning's ride that I'd be in the company of such an excellent horse-woman."

His candid tone sent warmth tumbling through her—a phenomenon she experienced more and more in his company, especially now that he was her suitor. A week after taking them to the theater, Lord Linwood had asked for permission to court Clare. She'd waited outside the drawing-room door as he spoke with her mother, but Clare stayed close enough to overhear him describe his intentions. The thought that he wished to court her—and the affectionate, knowing smile he'd sent her way as he left the townhouse—had made it difficult for her to stop smiling for long or to sleep. Or to think of anything else besides this warm, caring, handsome man who wanted to spend more time with her.

"Thank you, my lord. I've loved to ride since I was little."

"Me as well. Though riding in London is nothing compared to riding in the country."

Without thinking, Clare agreed. "There's something about racing across open countryside, isn't there?"

"You speak as if from experience. Does your family own a house in the country?"

She swallowed hard. Did she dare confess that as a girl she'd ridden bareback around her family's farm and to and from the nearby village? It wasn't until after her father's hair pomade had become successful that Clare had taken formal riding lessons and learned to manage a side saddle.

"No, we don't have a house in the country. I lived in Vermont before my family relocated to New York when I was nine years old. There was plenty of countryside to ride through near our first home." She urged her horse into a faster gait, hoping to bring an end to this particular direction of conversation.

Thankfully Lord Linwood didn't inquire what had necessitated her family's move or what life had been like before that time. Maybe he sensed her reluctance to talk about her childhood. Whatever the reason, Clare was grateful when he began to tell her a story about an impromptu horse race with some of his boyhood chums at his family's estate in Somerset. Clare liked his funny stories and the animated way he told them. It made her feel as if she were experiencing the events right along with the boy he'd once been.

For herself, she wasn't ready yet to reveal details about her earliest growing-up years—the ones from life on the farm.

Did they even really matter now? The Herschels' fortunes had eventually changed for the better. And while Clare appreciated and remembered the lessons gleaned during those hard, lean years, those times were in the past. If she'd continued as nothing more than a struggling farmer's daughter, she'd likely have never even seen London, much less been welcomed into high society and courted by a nobleman.

"Do you miss your family's home when you're in London?" she asked when he'd finished his story. She greatly missed her father—the three of them had never been apart for more than a night or two prior to her and her mother coming to England. Clare wished he could have come too, so she could learn his thoughts about the man riding beside her.

Lord Linwood cocked his head as he considered her question. "I miss the countryside and my dog, Bran."

"You have a dog?"

"Yes, a brown-and-white greyhound and the most loyal, intelligent creature of any on the planet. Save perhaps for your dog, Miss Herschel."

Clare laughed. "I've never actually owned a dog."

"You jest," he said, stopping his horse.

She did the same with her mount. "It's true." Farm animals, yes, but she and her parents had never gotten a dog. "If I did have a dog, I don't know that mine would live up to your Bran's illustrious reputation."

"He is rather brilliant." Lord Linwood smiled and urged his horse forward again.

"I hope I get to meet this extraordinary dog of yours." Her face grew hot when she realized how presumptuous that might sound. "That is . . . if I'm ever in Somerset."

The seriousness of Lord Linwood's expression as he looked her way disrupted the regular beating of her pulse. "We would like that as well. Bran and I both." They rode in silence for several moments, though it was a comfortable quiet. "My grandfather was the one who gave me Bran the First."

"You have two dogs named Bran?" she inquired with a chuckle.

He didn't join her, though. "No, the first dog passed away about a year after my grandfather did. I didn't acquire Bran the Second, the dog I have now, until a few years later."

"Was this grandfather the previous Marquess of Hadwell?"

Lord Linwood frowned and gave a quick shake of his head. "I never met that grandfather. This was my mother's father."

The reverential way he spoke of the man suggested they'd been close. "It sounds as though his death was very difficult for you."

"It was, yes."

Clare felt his grief as if it were a tangible thing he'd handed her. She was as honored by his trust in sharing it as she was surprised. Although they could easily talk of anything, she'd noticed Lord Linwood often steered a conversation in a more lighthearted direction if the topic held too much sorrow.

"I'm sorry," she said sincerely. She'd never known any of her grandparents, but the type of relationship he hinted at sounded wonderful. "How old were you when he died?"

His hands visibly tightened on the reins before relaxing. "Ten."

"That kind of loss wouldn't be easy to experience at any age, but especially as a child."

Lord Linwood shrugged. "I grew up rather quickly that summer." He didn't elaborate on what he meant, and Clare didn't feel right about asking. Maybe one day he would feel comfortable enough to share more with her. He glanced at her, his look apologetic. "I'm afraid that sort of talk is as gloomy as the weather."

"I wasn't thinking that at all."

Clare met his gaze directly to show she meant it. She didn't wish to shy away from talking about difficulty or loss. She'd experienced both, though in different ways, as a girl.

Besides, she wanted him to feel at ease discussing anything with her. After all, it wasn't just his ability to make her laugh or the thrill of bantering with him that had her looking forward to when she would see him next. The easy camaraderie between them was something she'd come to appreciate and cherish. She had never felt this relaxed and happy with a gentleman before. With him, she didn't have to think carefully through her responses either. They simply accepted each other as they were, right now.

"I very much enjoy talking with you, my lord, on any and all topics of conversation."

He studied her in a way that made Clare's middle flutter with feeling. "So do I, Miss Herschel."

Before she could think of how to respond, the clouds gave up their rain, spilling a deluge of heavy drops on them. Clare stopped her horse and peered around for somewhere to take shelter from the increasing downpour.

"We can wait out the worst of it beneath that tree," Lord Linwood said, pointing with his crop in that direction.

She guided her horse after his. Lord Linwood climbed down from his mount beside the tree and helped Clare dismount too. He secured the horses so they wouldn't wander off as Clare shivered near the tree's trunk. The branches above were thick with summer foliage, but they didn't completely block the elements.

"Unfortunately, I didn't bring along an umbrella." Lord Linwood joined her under the tree.

Clare could feel her riding hat beginning to slide. Removing the pins that secured it, she took off the hat to reposition it. "It's all right. There's little more the rain can do to us at this point. I'm not sure we can get any wetter."

He chuckled. "That may be true, but what sort of gentleman would I be if I didn't offer you some sort of covering?"

"If you can rummage up a covering," she teased, "then you'd be more than a gentleman—you'd be a magician." She tucked her hat beneath her arm and attempted to fix her falling, wet hair.

"A challenge I can't refuse." Lord Linwood made a show of studying the branches and base of the tree before a grin appeared on his face. Pulling off his hat, he took hers in hand as well and hung them both on nearby branches. "Are you ready for your magic trick, Miss Herschel?"

She laughed with as much amusement as doubt when he pulled off his jacket and positioned it over their heads. Though she was initially doubtful, the pelting of the rain did lessen beneath the cover of the fabric. "Bravo," Clare said, clapping her hands. She grabbed one of the corners to help hold the jacket in place, so Lord Linwood could lower one of his arms. "I'll admit this is much better."

"Yes, it is," he murmured.

Clare didn't think he was talking about the rain. Not when his attention remained fixed on her. She realized in that moment how close they were standing to each other, his shoulder pressed to hers, his warmth adding to her own. She knew she probably ought to step away, but she didn't.

"You have some . . ." He motioned to her cheek with his free hand.

Embarrassed, Clare reached up to touch her face and discovered a strand of wet hair plastered to her skin. Was that why he'd been staring intently at her? She blushed and swiped at the hair. Only half of it obliged her cold, trembling fingers by releasing its hold.

"May I?" Lord Linwood asked quietly.

She nodded in agreement. His blue eyes held no mockery, which eased her humiliation a little. Gently he detached the hair from her cheek and pushed it behind her ear.

The intimacy of the gesture and his close proximity caused her heart to trip faster. He didn't lower his hand either. Instead he stroked the side of her face with his thumb. Clare couldn't look away; she could hardly breathe. Beyond the shelter of his jacket, nothing else existed save the two of them and the intense light that returned to Lord Linwood's gaze as he glanced down at her mouth.

Tipping her chin up slightly with his knuckle, he met her lips with his. She leaned forward, her hand settling against the front of his jacket as she reciprocated his kiss.

Her feelings for him had been growing steadily for some time. But as they kissed, Clare could no longer deny the depth of those feelings. She was falling in love with him.

And the adoration in his smile when he stepped back several moments later filled her with hope that maybe he could love her in return.

She'd left behind everything dear and familiar to come to England in order to make a good match with a respectable gentleman—to have a relationship similar to what her parents had. Could she and Lord Linwood share that sort of loving bond? Clare was beginning to believe so. And if he felt the same way, then she would bravely embrace both a marriage to him and a new life, far from home, with all of her heart.

Chapter 4

Emmett raced up the drive leading to the viscount's villa, mindful of the broken cobblestones and split earth. He still carried Antonina. Rushford was only a few steps behind them. The three of them had managed to survive the death traps awaiting them in every other street and square up to now. Emmett had even driven the guilt he felt at not saving Angelo from his mind with the reminders that his next task was to see to Clare. However uncertain their future or relationship, he had to be sure she was unharmed.

The mass of rubble where the house had once stood halted his frantic pace and caused him to stumble. "No," he whispered, his gaze roaming the ruins for any sign of life.

"They may have escaped." Rushford drew alongside him. "Before it collapsed."

After what they'd witnessed and lived through so far, Emmett recognized it was a rather fragile piece of a hope his valet offered. But it was hope nonetheless, and Emmett held to it as tightly as he cradled the girl in his arms. "Right. We'll call out and see if anyone answers."

His feet moved forward almost unbidden, a likely result of narrowing his thoughts to a single focus throughout all the horrors of the morning. "Clare?" he shouted as loudly as he could. "Vickley? Anyone?"

Silence rumbled in his ears, then a tiny sound breached the mound of rubble. "Emmett! We're here!"

His wife's voice had never sounded sweeter. Emmett dropped to his knees in relief and exhaustion amid the broken stones. They were alive—Clare was alive. God had mercifully answered Emmett's petitions. He blinked hard against the tears forming fast in his eyes.

"We're trapped," the viscount called out. "Near the east side of the villa."

Emmett rose onto one foot, keeping Antonina secure against his chest. "Is anyone hurt?"

"No."

Standing fully, Emmett replied back, "Hold on. We're going to get you out." But first he needed to convince the frightened little girl clinging to him that he wasn't going to abandon her if he let her down.

"Antonina, I need to set you down now." As he'd expected, her dark eyes widened and her arms tightened their grasp around his neck. "I am not going anywhere, and I will not leave you. I'll be right here. But I need both my hands to help the people trapped inside this house. Understand?"

She looked toward the toppled villa and back at him. Emmett held his breath. He didn't want to frighten her further by forcibly putting her down, but he couldn't join in Rushford's efforts to clear a hole in the rubble while still carrying the child. Finally Antonina nodded and loosened her grip. Emmett's breath came out in a whoosh of gratitude.

"You can stay right by me while I work," he reassured her as he set her on her feet. "You can even help, if you want."

With another nod, she let go of him and took a tentative step to the side. Emmett mustered a quick smile for her, then bent forward and grasped a stone. After a few seconds, Antonina picked up a small section of plaster herself and dragged it to the pile Emmett and Rushford were beginning to make. Her willingness to pitch in brought the renewed sting of tears to Emmett's eyes. No child should have to endure what Antonina had so far this morning, and yet she still had the strength and compassion to recognize that others were in need too.

That kind of attitude reminded him of Clare. She too had a great capacity to see others, to put them at ease, to treat them kindly, to encourage them—be they members of high society, children, or servants.

Thoughts of his wife drove him to work faster. He and Rushford cleared away stones, plaster, wooden beams, and furniture, while Antonina helped with the smaller pieces. Bit by bit, the hole in the rubble widened in depth and size. From time to time, Emmett or Rushford would call out to the occupants below to ensure they were still all right. Each time an answer came back, relief and resolve coursed through Emmett, infusing his aching muscles with fresh energy.

The constant bending and hauling intensified the pain in his back where he'd been hit during the collapse of Antonina's home. A quick examination of the back of his shirt revealed no blood though. He'd likely have a rather large bruise, but it was nothing to the injuries he'd seen on the race to the viscount's villa or what poor Rushford must be enduring with his broken arm.

At last the hole in the debris was large enough that Emmett could see several dust-covered heads below. They were through! "I'll help you climb out one at a time," he called down.

He positioned himself alongside the hole and reached down. Rushford crouched slightly behind him so Emmett could hand off the person to the valet. Antonina stayed close to Emmett, her gaze on the hole too. Helena appeared first and placed her hands inside Emmett's. He carefully tugged her forward and up until she was free.

"Thank you, thank you." She was covered head to toe in white dust and sobbing. "It's a miracle you were here!"

Her baby was handed up next and Emmett settled the squalling child into his mother's arms. He heard Clare encourage the other women to go before her. And while Emmett appreciated her kindness, it didn't lessen his anxiety to know she remained imprisoned inside the collapsed villa. After helping Miriam, he assisted three other female servants, all of them looking like ghosts emerging from the grave.

At last he saw Clare. Like the others, she was covered in white dust, but Emmett knew the shape of her face, the red-gold color of her hair, and the green of her eyes. He pulled her out and reluctantly handed her over to Rushford. Emmett wanted to embrace her, if only to be certain she wasn't hurt, but he wasn't sure if Clare would welcome that. Besides, there were more people who still needed rescuing too.

The viscount was next, followed by his valet and a footman. Ten people in all, and all of them alive. Emmett shook his head in grateful astonishment and rose shakily to a standing position. At once, he felt a small hand grip his.

He looked down at Antonina. "*Grazie*," he said to her. The little girl had been a part of the rescue too.

"Emmett!" Clare broke away from the group and hugged him. "Y-you saved us." Her voice hitched with tears. "Thank you."

Without thinking, he wrapped his free arm around her, pulling her securely against his chest. It felt marvelous to hold her like this, to feel her heart beating in time with his. But did Clare feel the same way? He loosened his grasp slightly and braced himself for her to pull away. When she didn't, he guessed it was only because of the awful ordeal she'd lived through. Her embrace was likely as much about needing comfort as it was about the affection she might have given him once.

The realization saddened him, and he released her. She didn't need to feel beholden to him. He'd done what any self-respecting husband would have done.

"You're all right?" she asked, searching his face. "You weren't hurt?"

He shook his head. "I'm fine. Rushford broke his arm, though."

"Who is this?" She looked at Antonina.

Emmett glanced down at the girl too. "This is Antonina. She and her . . ." He swallowed hard against the rise of guilt. "She was in need of rescuing too." He looked at Clare, hoping she would glean from his expression that he didn't wish to elaborate further within the girl's hearing. Clare studied him, then nodded with apparent understanding. "Rushford and I couldn't leave her behind."

"Of course not." Despite the horror of being trapped inside the rubble earlier, Clare offered Antonina a real smile. "*Buongiorno,* Antonina. *Mi chiamo* Clare." She pointed at herself.

"Clare," Antonina repeated.

Now that everyone was rescued, it was time to leave. "We need to get moving," Emmett said, addressing the whole group. "It isn't safe to stay in the city, so I suggest we head for the open countryside." When no one argued, he nodded. "All right then. Be careful, and follow each other as closely as you can."

He hoisted Antonina onto his back and began to navigate his way up the hazardous drive a second time. A glance over his shoulder showed that the group was hurrying after him, Rushford at the rear. After a few minutes, Emmett turned the corner onto an adjacent street, but he hadn't gone far when he realized the footsteps behind him had stopped. He spun around to determine the delay and found everyone, except for Rushford, gaping in shock at the scene before them. They'd had no of way of knowing their ordeal inside the villa had been the fate of nearly every other home and building in the city.

"Come on," he called out. "We can't stop!"

He hiked up a pile of ruins and down the other side. The constant shifting of the earth beneath him was painfully familiar by now. So too was the constant stumbling and the striking of his knees on the debris with regularity. Emmett forged onward though. He had an entire group of people depending on him to get them to safety.

Every few feet, he peered back to ensure they were still following. He did his best to shut out the continuous cries for help and the sight of broken bodies littering the streets. Antonina remained silent. Once when Emmett shot her a look over his shoulder to see how she was holding up, he thought he saw that her eyes were shut tight. He wished he could do the same.

A cry from behind sometime later made Emmett whirl around. Her baby still in tow, Helena was leaning over the viscount. "He's bleeding," she cried out.

Emmett hurried back toward them. Up close he could see that the viscount's head sported a nasty gash. "I . . . don't know . . . what struck me," the man said in a dazed voice.

"Can you stand?" Emmett freed a hand to grip the viscount's elbow. The other man didn't answer, though he managed to rise shakily to his feet.

Emmett looked around for the viscount's valet or footman. The two men were a ways behind, only now turning the corner onto the street. They would have to catch up as best they could. It wouldn't be wise to wait for them, or others might end up hurt and bleeding too.

"Rushford?" Emmett said. "Can you help the viscount walk?" The valet nodded and took Emmett's spot beside the injured man.

Helena was openly weeping now, her eyes wide with shock. Clare must have noticed too, because she took the baby from her friend's arms. "I'll hold Little Leo for a while."

Emmett sent her an approving nod, then returned to his place at the head of the group. "We must keep going."

The crying and crashing on every side didn't cease as they moved from one street to another. Each time he looked back, though, Emmett saw the other members of their group plodding along as quickly as their bare feet would allow. The earthquake had struck before any of them had risen and dressed for the day. If only he had shoes for everyone.

When the ruined buildings and wreckage seemed to grow farther apart, Emmett wondered if it was only his imagination—that he was seeing what he wanted instead of what was real. Then he spotted a country road up ahead. No rubble barred this path, though the ground was still badly broken up in spots.

Emmett didn't stop walking until he reached a field with no trees or houses nearby to come crashing down upon them. Only then did he lower himself to the earth and helped Antonina sit beside him. He was relieved when Clare, still holding the baby, came to a stop a few feet away. Helena, Miriam, and the other three young ladies joined them, while the viscount hobbled forward with Rushford's help. Everyone collapsed to the ground in exhaustion.

"Where are the footman and the other valet?" Emmett asked, peering past them to the road. He'd hoped both men would have caught up by now.

One of the maids burst into tears at the question. After a moment, she managed to speak in between her wails. "H-he was struck down, sir, right behind me. I-I don't think he's still . . . alive."

"The same thing happened to his lordship's valet," another maid added, her face gray. "I don't know how the rest of us survived."

Emmett hung his head as defeat stifled his relief at escaping the city. His efforts hadn't met with total success. A heavy, smothering silence blanketed the group, broken only by the sound of the maid's weeping and the viscount's moans of pain.

After a time, Emmett lifted his chin and studied the remaining members of their group. Like him, most of them sported cuts on their faces. Several of them, including Clare, had bruises and gashes on their feet too. Their nightclothes were dirty, dusty, and torn, and the baby was sucking desperately on the sash of Clare's robe as if he might find sustenance there. Every expression reflected the same fatigue and numbness Emmett felt. They still needed food, water, clean clothes, and a doctor . . . and a way to leave Messina.

Emmett ran a hand over his face as he considered what to do next. The action likely just smeared the grime and dust there rather than wiping it off. Was it best to stay here and watch over all of them? Or should he risk returning to Messina to see if he could find some supplies?

Antonina leaned her head against his arm, her gaze as haunted as everyone else's as she stared straight ahead. Emmett had promised to go back and search for her brother. However, keeping his word would mean leaving her and the others to fend for themselves.

As he struggled with his decision, he remembered what his grandfather had once told him. "When you're torn over what path to take, ask yourself why you wish to do something. If your motive is out of compassion and honesty, you cannot go wrong, regardless of what anyone else says about your outward actions."

Was he thinking more about his grandfather because he was in a place the man had lived and loved? Or was it because Emmett was away from the constant demands and opinions of his father? Whatever the reason, his grandfather's words brought him a measure of comfort and direction.

Looking down at the little girl at his side, Emmett knew why he wanted to return to the city. He'd made a promise, and he would keep it. Hopefully in doing so, he could find aid to bring back to the group too. He turned to Antonina and nudged her to sit up. When she did, he looked her in the eye. "We need some help." He spoke the Italian words quietly, so as not to alarm her or alert the group to his plan just yet. "I also want to go look for Angelo."

"Angelo?" she repeated, a bit of animation creeping into her voice.

Emmett nodded. "I hope to find him—and also some water and food and a doctor." He looked toward the viscount and Rushford. "I also want to find a way to get to our house in Taormina."

"I can come to Taormina too?"

"Yes, but first I have to go back to the city." Her brow puckered with her frown, but Emmett forged on with his explanation. "I need you to stay here with Clare."

At the mention of her name, his wife looked at them. She could understand and speak a little Italian, though not enough to carry on a full conversation as he and Antonina were doing.

"But you'll come back?" the little girl asked him.

He dipped his head in another nod, praying God would help him honor this promise too.

"I will wait then."

A rush of compassion prompted him to kiss the top of her dark head before he stood. "I'm going back," he announced to the rest of them. "To see if I can't find supplies for us."

No one but Clare and Rushford reacted. His wife immediately passed the baby to Miriam and got to her feet. Emmett's valet started to rise too, but Emmett waved him back down. "With the viscount hurt, I need you to stay here."

The valet glanced between Emmett and Clare, then sat back down. "If this is where you need me most, my lord, I'll stay."

"Thank you, Rushford."

Clare stepped in front of Emmett, almost as if she meant to prevent him from leaving. "You can't go back there," she pleaded. "You could be killed."

"I know." He was aware of Antonina's gaze on his back. "I wasn't able to save her brother . . ." Remorse nearly choked him until he swallowed. "I knew I needed to get to you and make sure you were safe, but I gave her my word that I would go back and look for him. Not to mention, we're in desperate need of food and water and medical supplies. Securing a way for us to get to Taormina is necessary too. That is, if it hasn't been destroyed." Emmett hated to think of anything happening to the Russos or his grandfather's villa.

His wife folded her arms tightly against her ragged robe, but her panicked expression had softened. "We could use some blankets and extra clothes too."

"I'll see if there's anything to be salvaged from Helena's villa."

Clare dropped her voice to almost a whisper. "What about Antonina? She can't follow you, Emmett."

"I spoke with her," he said, matching her low volume.

"She understands she needs to stay here. I promise I'll be careful, Clare, and return as soon as I am able."

Her lips trembled. "That doesn't mean you won't be in danger."

The distress she seemed to feel on his behalf made him wonder if perhaps she did still care for him, at least a little. Of their own accord, Emmett's fingers reached out toward the line of her pale face. But instead of touching her, his hand fell away when Clare suddenly spun around and rushed away from the group. A moment later he heard the sound of her retching into the grass.

Brushing her lips clean with the back of her hand, Clare straightened. Her head and heart pounded, and her stomach desperately needed something to assuage her growing sickness. She had no food or tea, though, or even water to wash the taste of bile from her mouth.

Had Emmett seen her heaving into the grass? She mentally shook her head. Of course he'd seen her. She heard footsteps approaching her from behind and knew it was her husband.

"Are you sick, Clare?"

"It's been an awful morning," she answered. It wasn't a direct response, but it was still the truth.

She waited for Emmett's reply, but the quiet at her back stretched wider. In its wake, she thought back to what had happened before she'd raced away to avoid vomiting on Emmett's shoes. Had he really been about to touch her face? She wanted to believe it. Such a caress would surely have felt as wonderful and comforting as being held by him earlier.

Clare allowed herself to hope for a moment, but it was

short-lived. After all, Emmett had been the first to break away from their embrace outside the ruined villa. His reaching out just now was likely about offering simple human kindness, and nothing more.

Something warm and firm rested on her shoulder. Clare turned her head to see it was Emmett's hand. Her heartbeat leapt in response, as it had yesterday when he'd helped her into the carriage. No amount of chiding or rationalizing would calm it.

"Everything I've seen so far feels like something out of a child's worst nightmare," he admitted quietly. "It doesn't seem like any of it could possibly be real."

She twisted to face him, stunned at this rare glimpse of emotional honesty from him. "That is exactly what it's been like."

Emmett lowered his arm to his side, but he didn't retreat. He didn't try to disguise the haggardness of his expression or the conquered look in his light-blue eyes either. The raw pain Clare had seen earlier when he'd told her he couldn't save Antonina's brother was still there too. Someday, would he share with Clare the tragedy behind finding this little girl? She very much hoped so.

He glanced at the group, then back at Clare, his gaze full of concern. "I can stay a little longer if you need me here."

How many times during her miscarriages had she longed to hear him say those exact words? To have him really look at her in this way? But she couldn't ask him to stay now. All of them desperately needed supplies, and if she hoped to keep this baby, Clare couldn't remain long outdoors with no shelter and nothing to eat. Of all of them, he was the best equipped to brave Messina's shattered streets. She might hate the idea of her husband facing the danger all over again, but she could choose to be strong by letting him go.

"No," she said with conviction. "I'll be all right."

He hesitated a moment longer, then determination filled his features. She'd seen this same look many times before, though typically it came in regards to something his father had asked of him. It was refreshing to see Emmett's resolve at doing something he'd decided for himself that he needed to do.

"I'll look for Angelo," Emmett explained as he walked back toward the group. Clare matched his footsteps. "Then I'll see if I can find some food and blankets. Wait for me here."

She gave him a brave nod. "We will. I'll watch over Antonina."

The suggestion of a smile pulled at his mouth. "I know you will."

His praise warmed her, even though she shouldn't let it. Emmett wouldn't be praising her if he knew she was pregnant and didn't plan to tell him for some time still—maybe not at all if she miscarried a third time.

"I'll keep praying for you, Emmett." That was something she could do.

"Thank you."

She wished she understood the lingering look he sent her way. Before she could make sense of it, though, he turned, gave a reassuring wave to Antonina, then hurried across the field toward the road.

A confusing mixture of relief and disappointment wound through Clare as she watched him go. Eventually Emmett disappeared beyond her sight. She fingered the cherished brooch in her pocket, thinking of her father. Such thoughts brought her a measure of much-needed courage. She turned away from the empty road and faced the beleaguered group. It was time for her to think of what she could do to help all of them.

London, October 1907: Fourteen months earlier

"Are you nervous, old chap?" Avery Winfield asked from his spot beside Emmett at the front of the church.

Emmett shook his head, his gaze fixed on the cathedral doors. Any minute now his bride-to-be would enter, and he couldn't wait to see her. Today he and Clare would start their life together.

"The unusual way you're bouncing about," Winfield drawled, "and seem unsure whether to cross your arms or not would suggest otherwise."

Chuckling, Emmett finally turned to look at his best friend. "Fine. I'm a bit nervous. Are you happy now?"

"Indubitably." Winfield's mocking look became a sincere smile as he clapped Emmett on the shoulder. "I'm happy for you and Clare. I believe the two of you will suit each other marvelously."

"Thank you." Emmett gave Winfield a firm handshake to show he meant the words.

He was grateful for his friend's support—especially the way it hadn't waned from the moment Emmett had shared the news that he wished to marry Clare. Winfield was likely the only other person besides Clare who understood the true reasons why Emmett had chosen her. She was so much more to him than an heiress with plenty of money to secure the future of his family's estate. Did his own family understand that yet? He wasn't sure, and not knowing accounted for the small knot of tension in his gut as he waited for his wedding to begin.

Emmett glanced to where his parents, sisters, and brothers-in-law were seated, near Mrs. Herschel at the front of the assembled crowd. His father looked smug, as though the marquess himself had arranged the marriage. And though his sisters weren't frowning like Lady Melinda, they hadn't yet seemed overly interested in coming to know Clare either. To them, his American bride was still something of a curiosity. His mother, at least, had expressed her happiness at seeing him happy.

Perhaps his family simply needed more time to adjust to the idea of him being married. After all, as heir to the Marquess of Hadwell, Emmett's marriage marked an important event for all of them. He hoped some distance, while he and Clare were on their honeymoon in Sicily, would do them all some good. If not, then maybe living with his parents at Hadwell House before the start of the season would help bridge the distance.

The sudden swell of music drew his attention back to the doors. Clare was moving slowly up the aisle, her arm tucked into her father's. Emmett smiled broadly, his worrisome thoughts forgotten. Clare looked exquisite in a cream silk dress and flowing train. A long veil covered her hair and face. But as she came closer, he saw her green eyes shining beneath the thin material. The same love and anticipation stirring inside Emmett and making his heart thump faster shone in Clare's gaze.

For a moment, his vision blurred with tears of happiness. Emmett quickly pressed his thumb into the corner of each eye and straightened as Mr. Herschel and Clare stopped beside him. After lifting his daughter's veil, Mr. Herschel placed a tender kiss on her forehead.

"I love you," the older man whispered, looking near tears himself.

Clare squeezed her father's hand. The tenderness between them prompted a twinge of envy inside Emmett. If only his own father would express the same unconditional love and approval for Emmett that he'd seen Mr. Herschel openly give his daughter again and again since the man's arrival in England.

Finally Clare turned to face him, her lips curved into a radiant smile. It was the same smile Emmett had seen six months ago at their first meeting. Would anything ever be more beautiful to him?

At the instructions from the priest to hold hands, Clare passed her bouquet to the younger sister of her friend Helena. Then she slipped her hands into Emmett's. Immediate calm replaced the last of his nerves. Everything would be all right. He'd made his choice of a wife, and in doing so, he had never felt happier. Looking into her lovely gaze, he saw a bright future stretching before them.

Chapter 5

Clare studied the landscape surrounding the field where their group had sought refuge. Could she find a source of water or something for them to eat among the trees and hills? She clamped her teeth against another wave of nausea and breathed as evenly as she could until the surge lessened in intensity. Even a little bit of food would surely help her and the baby she carried—not to mention the rest of their weary assembly.

Crouching down by Miriam, Clare placed a hand on the girl's arm. The maid lifted her chin, revealing red-rimmed eyes and dusty cheeks. "May I help you, my lady?"

"No, Miriam," she said gently. "I just wanted you to know I'm going to search for some food. I'll take Antonina with me."

The maid seemed to collect herself. "I ought to come too."

"I'll be all right. If you want to help, you can see if there's a way to bandage Lord Vickley's head." Clare glanced at the man, who still looked ghastly pale. "You could help with the baby too when he wakes." The poor boy had fallen into an exhausted slumber, but he kept stirring and whimpering in his sleep.

Clare stood and went to tell Rushford her plan to search for food. Like Miriam, the valet felt it his place to accompany her. But she wouldn't allow it. From the expression on his face, she could tell his broken arm was hurting. Hopefully Emmett would find something to help. To spare the valet's pride, Clare reminded him that the group still needed someone to look after them, especially in Emmett's absence. Rushford finally conceded to staying put.

"Antonina?" Clare approached the little girl, who sat with her arms wrapped around her legs, her chin on her knees. "Will you come with me? To find food?"

The girl looked puzzled by some of the English words. Would Clare's limited Italian be enough to communicate with Antonina while Emmett was gone?

She pantomimed eating. "Food. We need to find some food."

"Ah, *cibo*," the child said, her black eyes lit with understanding.

Clare held out her hand to Antonina. After studying her a moment, the girl rose to her feet and placed her hand inside Clare's. The simple act of trust inspired tears in Clare's eyes.

As she and Antonina started toward the opposite side of the field, Clare heard Helena cry out, "Clare! Where are you going?" Her friend had seemed to be in a sort of shocked stupor ever since witnessing the destruction of her house and her husband's injury. Clare didn't blame her. The horrors they'd passed through would have been all the more frightening with a baby in tow. But now, it seemed, the haze had cleared enough for her to be aware of her surroundings again.

Clare turned back to answer her friend. "We're going to see if we can find some food. Just wait here." She motioned to Helena's husband. "Miriam can help you figure out how to bandage that gash of his."

"I can do that." Helena straightened her shoulders. "Here, Mary. Take the baby." She passed her child to one of the maids and moved to kneel before the viscount. "Let's find a bandage for you, Leo."

Her friend's determination was proof Helena was going to be fine. Relieved, Clare led Antonina through the field. Her feet ached from rushing through the debris-filled streets earlier, but at least here, the ground wasn't covered in wreckage.

She cast a glance at the silent child walking at her side. From the little Emmett had said, she gathered that Antonina had lost her parents today and likely her brother too. A swell of sorrow and compassion nearly overwhelmed Clare. What must this little girl be thinking and feeling after what she'd experienced? Clare wished she knew enough Italian to find out. She did manage to learn Antonina's age. At eight years old, she wasn't much younger than Clare had been when her family's situation had changed. But where Clare's change in circumstances had brought wealth and opportunity, Antonina's changes were full of loss and tragedy.

Clare squeezed the little girl's hand, grateful to have her here and that Emmett had been able to save her. Regardless of the troubles in their relationship, Clare still felt proud of her husband and his heroic actions. Emmett, with help from God, had saved many lives today.

Please continue to preserve his life, she silently pled.

When they reached the field's edge, Clare glanced in each direction. Some trees to her right looked to be orange or lemon trees. "This way," she said to Antonina. They moved toward the grove. Among the grass, Clare spotted an orange. She bent and picked it up. It looked overripe, and yet it was still something to eat.

She and Antonina walked a little farther and found

several more oranges in the grass. The trees themselves were bare of the fruit, which meant these had been left behind after the recent harvest. Removing her robe, Clare placed the oranges in the center of the garment and lifted the sides like a sack.

"Let's see what else we can find." Antonina may not have fully understood her, but the girl kept in step with Clare as she headed in the opposite direction of the fruit trees.

Before long, they came across what appeared to be a wild olive tree. Clare and Antonina picked up what olives looked edible and added them to the oranges. Excited about what they'd discovered so far, Clare kept walking. After a bit, though, she stopped. Apparently they'd found what they could. She started to turn back when Antonina bent down and lifted something off the ground. The little girl held it up for Clare to see. It was a nut.

"That's perfect, Antonina. Are there anymore?"

The girl didn't smile, but her troubled expression eased as she studied the ground. Soon she had a whole handful of nuts that she placed inside the robe.

"We probably ought to get back," Clare announced.

The fare wasn't much, but it was still something to assuage everyone's hunger. She led the way toward the field, but a new idea made her pause. Little Leo could eat the orange pulp, but the olives and nuts would be too difficult for him to chew. They would need a knife or a rock to smash the food. A flat stone caught Clare's eye. She gathered the robe in one hand and bent down to grab the rock. Antonina gazed at the object in obvious confusion.

"We can use it like a plate to mash the food on." Clare set down her load and pretended to pound her fist against the rock.

The girl's eyes widened, and she hurried past Clare.

Reaching down, Antonina scooped up a rock about the size of Clare's hand. "This . . . good?" she asked in an expectant tone.

"*Bene.*" Clare smiled.

The child said something in Italian as she motioned to the rock Clare held. After a moment, she realized Antonina was volunteering to carry both rocks while Clare carried the food. With a nod, she handed the other rock to the girl. Side by side, they returned to the field.

Lord Vickley's head had been bandaged with the sash from Clare's robe, and Helena's baby was awake now. Everyone still looked bedraggled and weary, but they watched with intrigued expressions as Clare unfolded her robe.

"We found some oranges and olives, and Antonina found the nuts."

At the murmurs of approval, and the grateful smiles aimed their way, Clare saw the little girl's mouth lift slightly at the corners. Clare peeled one of the oranges and handed the first slice to Antonina. Rather than popping it into her mouth, though, the child looked over at the baby.

"Give him?" Antonina pointed at the boy.

The small yet unselfish offering elicited a lump in Clare's throat. One she had to swallow past to answer. "Is that all right with you, Helena?"

"Of course," her friend said. "You can give it to him, Antonina."

The girl sat on her knees in front of the boy. After breaking off a part of the orange, Antonina held it out to him. The baby seized it at once and stuffed it into his mouth, then he gave the girl a toothy smile. Clare felt as if she were watching a miracle unfold when Antonina nearly smiled back.

Clare passed out the rest of the orange slices, making sure Antonina got one too. Only then did she eat her portion. The orange skin was dry, but the juice inside tasted marvelous in

Clare's dry mouth. She set about peeling the second orange as Miriam passed around the olives and nuts.

"I thought we could make a sort of mash for him." Clare motioned to the rocks she and Antonina had found.

A tear broke free of Helena's lashes and slid down her dusty cheek. "That would be wonderful. Thank you, Clare and Antonina." At hearing her name, the child glanced up from handing pieces of orange to the baby. "*Grazie*, Antonina," Helena said.

"*Prego*," the girl replied, looking pleased.

Clare piled the last two orange slices, a few olives, and the remaining nuts onto the flat rock. Using the other stone, she slowly ground the food into a pulp. When she finished, she handed her friend the makeshift plate. Helena scooped up the mash and put it in her son's mouth. He wrinkled his nose at first, but he smacked his lips after swallowing as if he wanted more.

Too soon the meager foodstuff was all gone. Clare was thankful for something, however small, inside her stomach—but it wouldn't be enough to stave everyone's hunger for long. An uneasy silence descended over the group as the morning wore on. Some of them, including Antonina and the viscount, fell asleep. Clare couldn't relax though, not when Emmett hadn't yet returned. She noticed Rushford's gaze was also fixed on the road more often than not.

Clare kept herself alert by praying for Emmett and thinking about his request for her to return to England. Hopefully he wouldn't expect her to give him an answer too soon. They still needed to see if the villa in Taormina was standing, and then there was the matter of what to do with Antonina. If the child truly had no one else, then Clare wanted to care for her. Antonina was already attached to Emmett, and Clare herself couldn't help feeling a strong kinship with the girl too.

As time passed, Clare grew more and more thirsty now that her need for some food had been somewhat satisfied. Emmett might have found some way to bring them water. But how long would be it before he returned? Was there a water source beyond the orange grove? Finally she couldn't stand waiting any longer. Even if she didn't find some water, Clare needed a task to keep her mind from imagining all sorts of horrors that might befall her husband in the earthquake-ravaged city.

Clare put her robe back on, then stood and stepped softly toward Rushford. "I'm going to see if I can find a stream or a well. If Antonina wakes, tell her I'm coming back." At his nod, she moved away from the group. When she reached the orange grove, she kept going.

Her feet felt less sore now. They were either going numb or just getting used to no shoes—much like she had in the summers when she'd been a child.

How ironic, Clare thought, shaking her head in mild amusement. She was an heiress and the wife of a future marquess, and yet right now she was making do on next to nothing as her family had so often done during her early childhood. The realization sent renewed purpose pulsing through her, in spite of the resurrection of her queasiness and hunger. Ever present was her thirst too. What she wouldn't give for a bucket full of water.

She didn't think she'd walked far when Clare spied what looked to be a building up ahead. As she came closer, she saw that the house and barn had been demolished by the quake. Only one stone wall remained upright. But there was a well on the far side of the yard. Maybe the owners would be willing to let her take some water back to the field.

"*Ciao*?" Clare called as she approached the ruined cottage. "Is anyone here?"

There was no answer. She started in the direction of the barn when her foot stepped on something soft. Looking down, she saw it was a wrinkled hand attached to a fleshy arm that stuck out of the rubble. Clare screamed in horror and leapt back, her heart racing. A noise from within the wreckage reached her ears.

"Is someone there?" she cried out. "Can anyone hear me?"

An eerie silence greeted her questions. Was someone still alive within the cottage, or was the sound she'd heard only the debris settling? Clare waited a few seconds, then called out again. When there was still no answer, she gave the hand a wide berth and headed toward the well. Since the owners had been killed, they wouldn't care if she drew some water.

A bucket dangled from a rope at the top of the well. Clare twisted the handle to lower the pail. After several cranks, she heard a faint splash as the bucket hit the water. Hopefully the liquid was still drinkable. She turned the crank again to bring the bucket back up, already anticipating the water sliding down her parched throat.

Another rustle came from somewhere behind her, this one noticeably closer. Clare ignored it though. The bucket was nearly to the top of the well, which meant a nice, long drink was just a few more hand cranks away. Besides, she'd already decided the noise had to be the shifting of the house. If there was anyone else here, surely they'd have responded when she called out.

The full bucket finally reached the top of the well. Clare's dry mouth began to water in anticipation of something to drink. She reached out to unlatch the bucket from the rope when she thought she heard footfalls. A shiver of uneasiness ran up her arms, but she focused instead on wrestling the heavy bucket free of the line.

As she set the pail on the well's ledge, she happened to glance down. A dust-covered shoe appeared in her peripheral view. Had there been a shoe in that spot earlier? She didn't think so. But before she could reason out the object's strange appearance, a sharp pain vibrated through her head. Clare let out a moan, then darkness snuffed out everything.

With his arms laden with blankets and the loaf of bread he'd concealed inside, Emmett trudged up the road. It didn't feel as if it had only been a few hours since he'd last walked here. The escape from the hotel felt as if it had happened weeks ago. His arrival in Sicily yesterday felt like another lifetime now. At present, his life, his focus, centered completely on the survival of the group waiting for him in the field.

He rubbed his dirty sleeve over his damp forehead. The temperature wasn't exactly warm, but navigating his way through the still-dangerous city had produced beads of sweat along Emmett's hairline and neck. Risking life and limb among the demolished streets and buildings wasn't the only danger anymore. Now there were thieves roaming Messina, searching among the rubble for anything of value.

After revisiting the rubble that had once been Antonina's home, Emmett had eventually made his way to the harbor. The devastation there was equally as shocking. Broken ships floated in the water, a testament to the tidal wave that had been triggered by the earthquake. Despite the destruction, though, there were still several steamers anchored nearby, whose sailors were doing their best to rescue trapped citizens.

One of them had given Emmett a portion of the bread the man had found in a half-destroyed bakery. The sailor had warned him to keep it hidden though. There was no telling what someone in desperation might do to satisfy the rising need for food and water among the city's newly homeless.

Such total and horrific loss.

Emmett shook his head, weariness adding weight to each step as he forged ahead. The ghastly things he'd seen threatened to overwhelm him, even as he gritted his teeth against the memories. They wouldn't stop tormenting him until he forced his focus to remain on the next stretch of road and what those in his care would need as the chill of evening drew ever nearer.

He finally reached the field. Rushford met him at the edge, his makeshift sling still in place. "I managed to pull some blankets from the rubble at the viscount's villa," Emmett explained, shifting the pile he carried. "There's also some bread."

"Blankets and bread will be welcomed." His valet walked beside him. "Lady Linwood and Antonina found us something to eat too, but that was a while ago."

Clare had procured food? Before Emmett could ask how or where, he saw Antonina jump up and run toward him. Immediately his heart twisted at what he knew was coming. He silently passed his bundle to Rushford, then crouched down so he was eye level with the little girl.

"Where is Angelo?" she asked as she stopped in front of Emmett. "Is he all right? Is he hurt?"

Emmett placed his hand on her shoulder. The words he needed to say felt like they were choking him. "I went back, but Angelo . . ." The image of the boy's broken body among the ruins loomed large in his mind's eye as if he were seeing it all over again. He struggled to drag a full breath into his tight lungs, his pulse thudding. Deep regret at not being able to save the boy seared Emmett's thoughts. He sagged to the side beneath the heavy burden, barely catching himself with his free hand.

He had to fight back, had to push this intense pain away. If not, he'd never be able to help any of them, especially Antonina.

"I'm sorry." Emmett moistened his cracked lips. "Angelo didn't survive the collapse of the building. I don't believe he suffered though."

Antonina's eyes widened and filled with tears. "He is dead then?"

Emmett nodded slowly. "I am so—"

His words, ones that felt wholly inadequate, were cut off as the child threw her arms around his neck. She didn't sob or wail, but he could tell from the trembling of her shoulders that she was crying. After a long minute, he eased her to arm's length. "Do you have any other family or relatives?"

"No." She shook her head. "Only Papa, Mama, and Angelo."

"Then would you like to stay with me and Clare?" He hadn't yet talked to his wife about such an arrangement, but he hoped she would be in agreement. The girl had nothing left here—no family, no home. But he and Clare could provide those things for her.

Antonina appeared to consider his question. "Where do you stay?"

"In Taormina for now," he said, "but our home is actually in England."

"England?" the girl repeated. "That is far away from Sicily."

Emmett rose to his feet. "It is very far away."

"And I get to stay with you in those places?"

"Only if you want to."

Antonina looked past him, back toward Messina. "I think I want to," she said when she peered up at him again.

"*Sì*?" Happiness at her answer reinvigorated his flagging

energy. He'd hoped she would choose to go with them, but he'd wanted it to be her decision.

She offered a solemn nod. "*Sì.*"

Emmett put his arm around Antonina and smiled. He couldn't wait to tell Clare the news. A quick perusal of the rest of the group revealed his wife wasn't among them. A wave of uneasiness threatened to swallow the happy moment. "Where is Clare?"

"She isn't back yet, my lord," Rushford answered.

"Back?" Emmett echoed.

A concerned-looking Miriam joined them. "She went to see if she could find water, but that was some time ago."

His apprehension grew. He didn't like the idea of Clare wandering around the countryside alone. "Do you know which way she went?"

The maid pointed northwest. "Past those trees there."

"I'll see if I can find her." A tug on his hand brought his attention back to Antonina. He could move quicker without her in tow. But he also recognized that he was the closest thing to a father and protector that she had left, and he'd already been gone most of the day. "Do you want to come, Antonina?" he asked in Italian.

She dipped her chin up and down, her mouth set in a tight line of resolve. Clearly she was not going to abide being left behind this time. If he weren't so concerned about Clare, Emmett would have found the wherewithal to chuckle at the little girl's determination. That sort of pluck would surely prove useful to her in the days ahead.

"All right," he conceded. "Rushford? Inside those blankets is a loaf of bread. We can divide it up before Antonina and I go look for Clare."

His valet knelt on the ground and removed the loaf from the blankets. Emmett broke off a piece for Antonina, then, saving a piece for Clare, he passed out the rest of it. The bread was stale, but it still tasted delicious to Emmett. He wished he had a little water to wash it down, though even the small bit of nourishment bolstered his strength.

When the paltry meal was eaten, he and Antonina headed in the direction Miriam had indicated. Neither of them spoke; they simply walked. But her small hand tucked inside his was as comforting to him as he hoped it was to her. After a while, Emmett thought he saw the walls of a building up ahead. Had Clare found assistance there? He picked up his pace while still being mindful of Antonina's short legs.

Once they'd cleared the trees, Emmett stopped. The building he thought he'd seen was just one remaining wall of what had been a house. A nearby barn had also been reduced to rubble by the earthquake. If Clare had come here, would she have moved on in her search for water?

"*Guardare*," Antonina cried. *Look.* She pulled Emmett forward as she pointed to something across the yard.

There, beside the well, lay the prone figure of a woman. Emmett recognized Clare's robe and copper hair. He let go of Antonina and sprinted toward his wife, his heart throbbing painfully with panic. Had he rescued her from the viscount's villa only to lose her now? *Please, Lord, no.*

He knelt in the dirt at Clare's side and touched her shoulder. "Clare? Can you hear me? Where are you hurt?" He was profoundly relieved to see she was still breathing, and that there were no visible signs of blood or broken bones. Yet her eyes were still closed.

A low moan tumbled from her lips. "My head . . ."

He gingerly examined the back of her hair and discovered a large bump. Without opening her eyes, Clare winced. She'd clearly struck her head on something, but Emmett couldn't identify what. There was the well and an overturned bucket, but nothing else. Only then did he notice the shoe prints in the dirt around her. Clare wasn't wearing shoes, though, and the prints weren't Emmett's either. He'd approached his wife from a different direction. Wariness had him glancing around to ascertain if they were alone.

"The baby," Clare whispered. "What if . . . the baby . . ."

Emmett frowned with confusion. Was she talking about Helena's baby? "Little Leo is fine." He placed a hand on her sleeve. "When Antonina and I left, he'd eaten some of the bread I brought back."

Her eyes fluttered open at his words. "Emmett?" Her gaze went wide. At the same instant her cheeks drained of color. "Wh-what are you doing here?"

"I came back to the field, and you were gone. Everyone was concerned that you hadn't returned, so I came to find you." He nodded at Antonina who was kneeling beside him, her expression anxious. "We wanted to see if you were all right."

With his assistance, she slowly sat up. "I don't know what happened . . ." Clare pressed a hand to her forehead and shut her eyes again. "I was getting water from the well when I heard something. I saw what I thought was a shoe on the ground. Then my head started hurting, and I think I fainted."

"I believe you might have been hit on the head by someone."

"Someone?" she repeated as she opened her eyes. "I didn't think there was anyone here." She shuddered and visibly swallowed. "Other than one of the owners, whom I accidentally discovered was . . . dead."

Emmett wished he'd come sooner. Then perhaps he could have spared her from the trauma of being attacked—and discovering a dead body. "My guess is it was a thief. Apparently they've wasted no time in looting the dead and dying."

"But I'm not either."

He shrugged. "A woman by herself would be an easy target."

"I don't have anything of value." Clare gasped as she stared at her hands. "My ring. It's gone."

He looked at her left hand. The wedding ring he'd given her was no longer on her finger. Emmett felt a wince of regret. The ring had been his maternal grandmother's. But the regret faded quickly. The ring was nothing compared to his wife's life. Thankfully the thief had only struck her on the head and left her alone after robbing her.

Rising to his feet, he offered her his hand. "Can you stand?" It was probably best if they didn't linger here, in case the thief came back.

She accepted his help, and leaning heavily into his grip, she got to her feet. But Clare's pained expression became one of total despair when she stuck her hand in the pocket of her robe. "No! My brooch. The one from my father. It's not here either!" She frantically searched both pockets but came up empty-handed. Her lips trembled as she turned toward Emmett, her green eyes full of anguish. "I had it in my pocket, which means whoever took my ring stole my brooch too."

It was the piece of jewelry Emmett had seen her wear most often, save for her wedding ring. She'd once told Emmett that the brooch was a loving reminder of her father and his wisdom, especially now that she lived so far from him and her mother. To lose that reminder, that connection, would be a devastating blow.

"I'm so sorry, Clare."

He hesitated, unsure if any other comfort would be welcome. Antonina had no such qualms. Whether she understood what had happened or not, the little girl rested her head against Clare's arm. The simple yet kind gesture gave Emmett courage. After all, Clare had seemed to appreciate his embrace earlier.

Emmett stepped closer and put his arm around her. As she leaned into him, something inside him clicked softly into place. He felt himself relax as he hadn't in a long time. Quiet settled over the three of them as they stood there together, almost like a family.

He recalled the softening he'd sensed in Clare a few hours earlier, before he'd gone back to Messina. Was it because she still cared? Or was it just her compassionate nature responding to the idea that he'd be in potential danger again? Emmett wasn't any surer of the answer now than he'd been earlier, but her willingness to accept his comfort in this moment gave him hope.

Could caring for Antonina or having a baby bring him and Clare back together? He wanted very much to believe so. Perhaps after today, she would be more willing to consider coming back to England with him—not just for whatever political goals might lie in the future, but to give their marriage and their life together another chance.

Glancing down, Emmett saw Clare wiping tears from her cheeks. The sight of it made his chest constrict with sadness and distress. He hated that she'd lost her treasured brooch after everything else that had happened today. He longed to take away that heartache.

"We might be able to find another brooch in Rome or London. One that looks similar to the one your father gave you."

It was the wrong thing to say. He knew it the instant Clare's shoulders tightened and she slipped out from under his arm. "Maybe. We should probably get back." She wouldn't meet his gaze now. "I don't want to keep worrying everyone else."

"Are you sure you can walk?"

Clare nodded and went to pick up the empty bucket. "Let's get more water first."

"I'll do it," he said, reaching out a hand for the bucket. "You need to be careful after such a violent bump on the head."

Her look was skeptical. "Do you know how to use a well?"

Annoyance colored his response. "I'm confident I can figure it out."

He wasn't completely inept, even as the son of a marquess. While overseeing the repairs, there had been plenty of tasks at their estate that had been new to him, but he'd tried his hand at them anyway. Besides, he'd done far more complicated and difficult things today. Drawing water from a well should be a relatively simple undertaking, and it nettled him that she seemed to doubt his ability.

"Then go ahead." She passed him the bucket, but her eyes were flashing with equal irritation.

Emmett was aware of Antonina watching them. He sent a forced smile her way and tied the bucket to the rope at the well. After a false start or two, he finally managed to get the bucket to go in the direction he wanted—down.

Within a few minutes, he had a full pail of water. Was it drinkable? He scooped a little water into his hand and brought it to his lips. The liquid tasted fine—more than fine, actually. He encouraged Clare and Antonina to have some as well, then he motioned toward the trees. "Shall we head back?"

He let them lead the way. Clare's strides were slow and measured, and not just because she was trying to accommodate the little girl whose hand she held. Emmett imagined her head must be aching with each step. Shame cooled his frustration. How would she know if he could draw water or not? Until today, Emmett hadn't known that Clare could use a well either or forage for food. She'd kept a level head too, without going into hysterics, and continued to respond to Antonina with kindness. And he'd gone and reacted to her simple question about the well.

His conscience would prick at him until he attempted to make things right again. To that end, he walked faster, careful not to slosh the water, and drew alongside his wife. "I was curt just now, and I apologize." He shifted the full pail to his other hand. "Figuring out that well wasn't as easy as I thought it would be."

"You managed it in the end," she reminded him. A moment later, she added, "I appreciate you coming to find me."

"You're welcome." He turned to look at her, hoping to hold her gaze with his. "That was a courageous thing you did, going to look for water."

A brief blush colored her cheeks. "Thank you. It wasn't any more brave than you going back to the city. And you found some bread?"

"A sailor gave it to me. I was also able to salvage some blankets from Vickley's villa."

"That's wonderful."

Perhaps, but Emmett didn't feel brave or wonderful. He felt lacking. Surely his father—or Alder, if his older brother had grown to adulthood and found himself in such a predicament—would have done better. They would have likely found more food or been the ones to find the water source. There likely wouldn't have been any members of their party killed or injured.

But Emmett couldn't admit any of that out loud. It would only add to the stress of their current situation. So he pasted on a smile instead. "We'll get through tonight," he assured her in a light tone, "and hope that tomorrow is better."

Rather than inspire the hopefulness he'd expected, Emmett thought Clare looked even sadder. Was she thinking of her stolen brooch? The possibility pulled the feigned smile from his face. Try as he might, there were still too many things he didn't know how to fix.

Somerset, England, October 1907: Fourteen months earlier

After spending two weeks in Sicily with Emmett for their honeymoon, with few servants and no crowds, Clare was as thrilled as she was overwhelmed by the sight of the large throng gathered on the train platform. Flags and bunting had been festively draped around the station. There was even an arch made of flowers and leaves.

She turned her gaze from the view beyond the train window to her husband seated beside her. "Are all of them actually waiting . . . for us?"

"Not sure about that drowsy-looking chap there or the madam to the left—the one in that horribly garish hat." Emmett chuckled when Clare aimed a feigned glare at him. "Yes, my dear." He kissed the back of her gloved hand, his gaze bright with admiration and a hint of excitement. "Everyone in the village is eager to meet you."

Clare peered out at the crowd again. She could sense their expectant energy through the pane of glass, and it sparked a flicker of enthusiasm inside her as well. Thankfully Miriam had taken extra time on Clare's appearance this morning, though it had been in preparation for seeing Emmett's parents again, not the entire village.

Today she had on a light-gray-and-maroon dress with a

large blue hat atop her carefully styled hair. Around her shoulders, Clare wore the furs Emmett's mother had recommended in a letter to her son as being "proper and fitting" for her daughter-in-law's new role.

Clare checked that her hat and hairpins were still in place. Miriam wasn't here to help, since she and Rushford had gone ahead on an earlier train to ensure everything was ready for them upon their arrival.

"Shall we?" Emmett stood. At her nod, he helped her to her feet.

Tucking her arm in his, Clare followed him from their private train car down the aisle, and to the steps leading down to the platform. She knew the instant they were spotted. A cheer erupted from the waiting assembly. Clare smiled up at her husband, who was grinning himself.

"There's the mayor," he said, nodding at the short man approaching them.

Her husband introduced her to the mayor and the other village dignitaries, and the mayor's daughter handed Clare a pretty bouquet of flowers. Emmett was then asked to make a speech. Clare listened proudly as he spoke of his love for this place and its people. She wasn't the only one moved, either. The villagers watched her husband with respect and pride on their faces.

Would they respond to her in the same way? A worm of panic uncurled inside her. What did she really know about being the wife of a future marquess—the benefactress and leading lady for an entire community? Clare hadn't allowed herself to worry about such things on their honeymoon. She'd basked instead in the Italian sun and the uninterrupted time with her husband. In Sicily, she'd even given in to the nudge to paint. But now that she was back in England, her fears wouldn't stay submerged any longer. They bobbed to the surface of her consciousness, where they seemed to grow larger.

"Lady Linwood?" It took Clare a few seconds to realize the mayor was addressing her. The title still felt foreign to her, like a new article of clothing that didn't yet fit comfortably. "We are most eager to hear from you too."

They wanted her to make a speech? Clare looked in surprise at Emmett. What was she supposed to say? She hadn't expected this. Emmett set his free hand over hers, his smile encouraging.

Taking a deep breath, she compelled her lips to turn upward as well. "Thank you for your warm welcome," she said sincerely and in a voice loud enough to be heard by those in the back. "This is such a beautiful part of England, and all of you have been very hospitable. I can see now why my husband is proud to call this place home." A rumble of approval swept through the crowd. Clare lifted her chin and exchanged a lingering glance with Emmett. "I'm looking forward to making this my home too."

The sound of applause punctuated her words. Her husband leaned down to whisper in her ear, "Brilliantly stated, my dear. They're now as enamored with you as I am."

Clare laughed lightly. "Thank you."

His compliment meant a great deal to her and shored up her confidence. She could do this—she could be a suitable wife to the son of a marquess. After all, she'd come this far with poise, faith, and determination. Surely those qualities, along with God's help, would see her through this new chapter in her life.

No longer needing to manufacture a smile, she walked with Emmett to the waiting carriage. More people lined the streets as they drove through the village. There were even school children waving flags. Clare waved back. After a short distance, the carriage stopped beside a platform.

"More speeches," Emmett explained before helping her exit the vehicle.

They each spoke again, and Clare was given another bouquet to add to the first. There was more clapping and cheering, all of it as enthusiastic as it had been at the station. Then she and Emmett were waved back into the carriage. This time the ride lasted longer, taking them away from the village and into the open countryside. But once again, the carriage came to a stop. A group of smiling men waited for them, though there was no platform in sight. Emmett didn't make any move to climb out either.

"Are we giving another speech?" Clare asked in confusion.

He shook his head. "Not yet. Some of our tenants are going to convey us to Hadwell House."

"Convey us . . ." she repeated, her bewilderment increasing.

"Watch." Emmett motioned to where the horses were being unhitched from the carriage. In their place, the tenants lined up along the shafts. Lifting together, they began walking in tandem, and the carriage rolled forward.

The idea of men pulling their carriage instead of horses wasn't entirely a comfortable one for Clare. But she did her best to relax against the seat. She'd known things would be different here than back at home, though she hadn't expected that would include the ride to the Hadwell estate. The men soon turned onto a gravel drive. Any minute now Clare would get her first glimpse of Hadwell House. This was where she and Emmett would live until spring, when they would purchase their own townhouse in London before the start of the season.

"There's one last speech to make when we reach the house," Emmett said, his tone apologetic. "Do you mind? You're doing splendidly."

She wrapped her arm through his and leaned into his side. "One more speech will definitely put you in my debt, my lord. Especially since you failed to mention I would have to give any."

"I quite agree." His light-blue eyes held amusement. "Name your price."

Clare pretended to think the matter over carefully. "I suppose I could accept payment in, say . . . kisses."

"Ah. Then I look forward to paying off such a debt, my lady."

Her heart sped faster at the low, intimate tone of his voice and the pure happiness emanating from his handsome face. She still couldn't believe she'd found this good man, a man who loved her as much as she loved him.

Before Clare could respond, the carriage swept past the trees, and Hadwell House stood before them. It was much larger than she'd imagined. Two identical square wings flanked the house's main section, which was set back from the drive. The light-colored stone walls boasted numerous multi-paned windows and at least four floors.

Her gaze moved from the house to the people lining the main steps. A bevy of servants waited at attention, along with what appeared to be more of the estate's tenants. Emmett's parents stood closest to the front door.

With Emmett's help, Clare alighted from the carriage for the third time. She kept her arm firmly tucked in his as they approached those assembled on and around the stone steps. When they reached the top of the staircase, Emmett greeted his parents. Then it was Clare's turn.

Her father-in-law gave her a light peck on each cheek before sizing her up. "Welcome to Hadwell House. I believe you will do nicely here."

Clare shot him a strained and somewhat puzzled smile,

unsure of his meaning. Her mother-in-law also kissed her on the cheeks. The gesture held a bit less stiffness and impatience than she'd sensed from the marquess, but Clare still felt little of the enthusiasm from them that she'd experienced from the villagers earlier.

Emmett spoke to those gathered before motioning for Clare to take her turn. She mustered her waning energy to offer her own expression of gratitude for their welcome. The butler then presented them with a wedding gift from the entire household. It was a lovely silver candelabrum. After that, the front door was opened, and Emmett led her and the rest of the entourage inside. Within moments, however, the foyer stood devoid of everyone except the two of them. Even Emmett's parents had disappeared up the grand staircase.

As she took in the marbled foyer, Clare shivered in spite of her furs. Unlike her home in New York, this house echoed with cool silence. Where were the bustle and warmth, the airiness and laughter she'd always known? Her earlier dread returned. She placed her hand against her churning stomach.

"Welcome home, darling," her husband said, clearly unaware of her misgivings.

Clare did her best to meet his expectant look. She didn't want him thinking she was displeased or upset. "Thank you."

"Miriam will take you up to your room." Emmett pressed a warm kiss to Clare's forehead as the maid descended the stairs and approached them. "I need to speak with my father. However, I'll see you at dinner."

She nodded in agreement, though she really wanted to seize his hand and walk right back out the door. And keep walking until they found a place that felt safe and warm. A place that was theirs and theirs alone.

"I'll see you soon," she replied, smiling.

Clare let the smile fall from her lips, though, as she and

Miriam headed to her room. She sensed her confidence at managing her new life slipping away faster than she could hold on to it. In its wake, she was left with little but doubts and a yawning sense of homesickness.

Chapter 6

Something had happened to Emmett, Clare was sure of it. The openness she'd seen in him—and welcomed—before he'd returned to the city had disappeared. His emotions were once again shuttered, especially when they had returned to the field after getting water and she'd quietly asked him about Angelo.

"He didn't make it," Emmett replied in a flat tone. Only the tightening of his jaw hinted at hidden pain.

Clare glanced at Antonina, then back at Emmett, fresh sorrow welling up in her for this orphaned girl who'd lost her entire family. And for her husband, who had tried to save Angelo. "I'm so sorry, Emmett. I can't imagine—"

"We have a little bread for you." He extended the piece toward her, his expression unreadable.

Remorse of a different kind washed through her as she accepted the bread. "Thank you for saving some for me." She wanted so much to shoulder with him the pain and horror he'd experienced today—wanted to believe that if she miscarried again, he would truly shoulder that pain with her too.

Clare hardly tasted the bread for the regret and unshed

tears in her throat. She'd foolishly thought her husband's emotional honesty and empathy would be more than fleeting this time. That after everything that had happened in the past twelve hours or so, Emmett was ready to fully open his heart to her. But it seemed that wasn't going to happen. She tried taking comfort from the reminder that this was one of the main reasons she'd come to Sicily, alone, in the first place, and yet it was little consolation in this moment.

Was her baby all right, even after Clare had been struck on the head? She resisted the urge to touch her stomach, not wanting to do anything that might clue Emmett in to her secret. Her fear had tumbled unconsciously from her lips when her husband had found her lying by the well. She hadn't even realized she'd spoken the word *baby* aloud until Emmett had told her that Helena's baby was fine. She'd been horrified at her blunder, but thankfully her husband had misunderstood her meaning.

Having some food and water had assuaged some of her nausea, but as evening approached, Clare's stomach once again reminded her that she'd had little to eat all day. Prior to that, she'd been doing her best to keep up a conversation with Helena. Emmett had fallen asleep shortly after giving Clare the bread. Rushford too had finally dozed. Antonina had stuck close to Emmett for a while. But eventually the little girl scooted over by Clare. She'd used her fingers to comb through Antonina's long, black tresses, then braided them as she'd done with her own hair.

"Should we find some more oranges?" she asked the child sometime later. It had to be near dinner time, and Little Leo, who had been playing with the rocks they'd found earlier, was fussing again. Probably from hunger.

When Antonina looked confused, Clare pantomimed peeling an orange and eating it. the little girl brightened. "*Sì.* We get . . ."

"Oranges," Clare supplied.

Antonina repeated the word, "Oranges."

"I can help, my lady." Rushford sat up and winced. The poor man needed a doctor to tend to his arm. And though the viscount's head no longer appeared to be bleeding, his gash should be properly examined too.

Clare stood. "You don't have to come, Rushford. Especially if your arm is hurting."

"I need to stretch my legs," the valet said as he rose to his feet.

Miriam also hopped up. "May I come too, my lady?"

"Very well. We'll make a hunting party of it." She smiled at Antonina and held out her hand. "We'll be back soon, Helena. If Emmett wakes before we return, tell him we went to find more oranges." Clare picked up the now-empty water bucket to use to carry whatever foodstuff they found. "Once we come back, someone can go for more water." She would certainly include thanking God for a water source when she prayed tonight.

Helena agreed to share the message, and the four of them headed across the field. Clare's head still hurt, so she kept her steps slow to avoid making the ache any worse. The rest of their party had listened with shocked expressions when she and Emmett had related what had happened to her at the well.

Every time she thought of losing her father's brooch and her wedding ring, she felt anger and anguish all over again. They could find her another ring, but the brooch was irreplaceable, even if they found one similar, as Emmett had suggested. It wouldn't be the one her father had lovingly selected and given to her.

Setting aside her depressing thoughts, Clare turned her concentration on searching for food. They were only able to find a few overly-ripe oranges. But with four people and a better storage container, they collected more olives this time. Everything went into the bucket, which Miriam insisted on carrying. After all, the maid had said, she hadn't been hit on the head or suffered a broken arm.

Emmett met them at the edge of the field when they returned, his face drawn. "You should have woken me." He fell into step beside her. "I would have come too."

"Rushford was with us."

His frown didn't decrease. "It's my responsibility to watch over everyone, Clare."

"Why? Because you aren't injured?"

He looked slightly sheepish before he glanced away. "Well, yes. I only want to help."

"Which we appreciate, Emmett, but the rest of us aren't useless."

"I . . . I didn't mean it like that."

She released her irritation with a sigh, and the reminder that his desire to watch over the rest of them was evidence that he cared. "Who do you think should go for more water?"

"I will."

Clare was grateful he'd volunteered. Right now, she didn't wish to return to the place where she'd been accosted and robbed. "That would be wonderful. We can pass out the food we found first." She shivered and eyed the sky. "Then we might want to gather some wood and make a fire. Even with the blankets, it's going to be cold again tonight."

"We don't have any matches."

She hid a knowing smile as they joined the group. "I think we can figure something out."

The food was handed around, and Clare made more mash for the baby. The group ate the small meal in relative quiet. Afterward, Emmett and Antonina went to collect more water. By then, the evening air had grown chilly. The blankets were distributed, but there weren't enough to go around. Rushford and the viscount insisted the women take them, but Clare knew that without blankets the injured men would need the warmth of a fire to make it through the night.

After asking Miriam and the other three maids to help her, Clare led them on a search for firewood. Bending down to pick up fallen branches renewed her headache, but she did her best to keep going, albeit slowly. Once they each had an armful of kindling, they carried the wood back to the field.

"How will you light the fire, my lady?" one of the maids asked.

"I have a way." If it worked.

It had been more than a decade since her father had taught her how to light a fire using two sticks. Clare wished she had the work gloves her father had worn when he'd shown her the unconventional method, but she'd have to do the best she could with just her hands.

You've blessed us with so much thus far, Lord, she prayed as she and several others cleared away the grass in the center of the group and lined the circular space with rocks. *Please let this work so we can be warm tonight.*

Using the sharp edge of one of the extra rocks, Clare ground the stone into a branch until she had created a small groove in the wood. Next she made a small pile of the torn grass and selected another branch. This was it. If they hoped to have a fire, this was the only way she knew to make it happen. Taking in a long breath, she released it slowly and placed the branch she'd chosen into the groove. Then she began spinning the stick as quickly as she could between her palms.

Again and again she spun the branch, hoping to create enough friction inside the groove to make heat and smoke. Clare's palms began to sting from rubbing against the stick.

No wonder her father had worn gloves. Soon her arms began to tire as well.

She sensed the group watching her. Self-consciousness made her clumsy, and she dropped the branch. Had she given all of them false hope? Clare positioned the stick back into the groove, reminding herself she had to keep trying. She winced at the soreness in her hands as she began turning the stick again. But she pushed away the discomfort and redoubled her focus on her task.

Clare lost track of time as she worked. It wasn't until she heard a soft gasp that she looked down and saw a whiff of smoke. Elated, she spun the stick even faster. The tiny ember grew. She let go of the stick at last and leaned down to blow on the cinder. As it increased in size, Clare fed the tiny flame with bits of grass until it became strong enough to add small pieces of wood. After a few minutes, she had a moderate-sized fire burning.

Someone started clapping, and most of the group joined in. Even Little Leo gave a squeal of delight. "You did it, my lady," Miriam cried with excitement.

"Did what?"

Clare jerked her chin up at the sound of her husband's voice. He stood watching her, a full bucket of water in his hand. Antonina left her place at his side to kneel before the fire. Clare had been so focused on her task she hadn't seen or heard the pair of them return. Guilt had her lowering her gaze to the fire, though she didn't know what she felt guilty for. She'd done nothing wrong. Or maybe it wasn't guilt. Maybe it was concern that Emmett would now realize she hadn't always been an heiress.

"We have a fire," she announced in a falsely cheerful voice, sidestepping his question.

"Which Lady Linwood lit," one of the maids explained.

Clare's cheeks turned warm from more than the growing heat. She felt Emmett's gaze on her as he set down the bucket. But he didn't press her for answers.

The bustle of everyone getting a drink of water shifted the focus away from her. Another of the maids volunteered to be the first to keep the fire going, and Clare willingly relinquished her duties. As she settled on the ground between Antonina and Helena, she could sense the blisters that had formed on her hands.

As darkness fell, the conversations around the fire dwindled to whispered murmurs as the members of the group began to drift off to sleep. Those with blankets curled into them, while the men scooted closer to the fire. Clare drew Antonina's blanket up over her small back. The little girl had fallen asleep with her head on Clare's knee. Clare pulled her own blanket more securely around her shoulders, but she didn't plan to sleep yet. Not after being struck on the head.

Her father had once hit his head when he'd been thrown from a new horse. Clare's mother had insisted that since he probably had a concussion he needed to stay awake as long as possible. If Clare had a concussion too, then she didn't wish to do anything to harm the baby she hopefully still carried. That meant she would try to stay awake as long as possible. She'd offered to take the next shift in tending the fire anyway.

"Can't sleep either?"

Clare had been avoiding looking at Emmett. She'd assumed the quiet from his side of the circle meant he was sleeping. Lifting her gaze from the flames, she peered over at him. He was sitting up too, his elbows resting on his knees.

As she considered how to reply, the first words to come to mind were teasing ones. Even after all the strain and misunderstanding between them, bantering with him still came easily. "Maybe I am asleep," she said in a light tone as she turned back to the fire, "and you are dreaming we're both awake."

His low chuckle sent tickles of feeling up her arms. "If that is the case, then which of us should dream about putting more wood on the fire?"

"I will." Clare reached for a piece of wood, but her blistered hand protested and the stick fell from her grasp. She curled her hand into a fist and winced.

Emmett moved toward her. "That flinch of pain didn't seem dreamlike at all." He unfolded her fingers and studied her hand. "Where did these blisters come from?"

She didn't want to answer, but the feel of his warm hand on hers snarled her thoughts. "It—it's from starting the fire. Which I don't recommend doing without the use of gloves."

He moved to the water bucket and peered inside. Picking up the pail, Emmett returned to her side. He pointed to the robe she still wore beneath her blanket. "May I? I just need the corner."

She nodded, not entirely sure what he meant to do, but too curious to refuse. Emmett took one corner of the robe and dipped it into the bucket, which he tilted forward. Then he placed the damp fabric against her blistered palm. The cold made her jump, causing Antonina to stir in her sleep. But the coolness also felt soothing against Clare's agitated skin.

"Thank you," she whispered.

With a nod, he finished dabbing her hand with the wet cloth before dipping it back into the bucket. "Let me see the other."

Clare didn't have the wherewithal to protest. She was too fascinated by what she was observing. Emmett's expression remained neutral, but his treatment of her hands was methodical and gentle. This glimpse of a side of her husband she'd once seen often and adored filled her with as much gratitude as it did pain. Not sure what to think or how to respond, she held her breath as he worked. Was this small act of kindness an indicator that things in their relationship could improve? Or was this another moment that brought only temporary hope?

"Any better?" he asked, sitting back on his heels.

Clare nodded. "Yes. They sting less now."

"That's good."

To her surprise, he didn't return to his earlier spot after putting more wood on the fire. He took a seat on the other side of Antonina and tucked the blanket around her small feet, his face full of parental concern.

What a wonderful father he would make. The thought, one she'd had many times before, still made Clare want to weep. She hadn't yet been able to give Emmett the children they both wanted, not even the son she was duty-bound to provide. And yet now that she was pregnant again, things were still complicated between them.

"Are you all right," he asked, "with my bringing her along with us?"

Surprised by the question, she looked at him, but his gaze was on Antonina. He'd done a brave and compassionate thing rescuing the little girl, and Clare didn't fault him at all for not wanting to leave her behind.

"Emmett?" She waited until she could see his eyes before she continued. "I'm very glad you brought her along. I wouldn't have been able to walk away and leave her either."

The line of his shoulders relaxed a little. "She has no one left." The hitch in his voice hinted at his deeper, concealed emotions. If only he would share them with her. "I told Antonina she was welcome to stay with us, both here and in England, and she told me she would like that. But after searching for you earlier, I failed to mention it."

Would he take Antonina with him to England even if Clare didn't accompany them? Or would he allow the girl to remain here? Clare had seen the sweet way the child had interacted with Helena's baby. She imagined Antonina would enjoy helping Clare with her baby if she didn't miscarry this time. But would Emmett insist the little girl remain with him? Either way, the decision to return to England had become even more complicated.

"Are you angry with me?" Emmett inquired.

Clare shook her head. "No, not at all. I'm just thinking." She ran her hand down Antonina's braid. "I'm glad she agreed to stay with us. She's a dear little thing, and I'll admit I've already grown fond of her."

"As she has of you." A brief smile touched his mouth as he motioned to the sleeping child, whose head still rested on Clare's leg. "I don't presume to know what her life was like before today or what it might have been if the earthquake hadn't happened. However, I'd like to believe we can offer her more, especially if we raise her as our own. If, of course, that's amenable to you."

"Absolutely," she said without hesitation.

She studied the lovely olive skin of Antonina's face. English society would surely deem it unconventional for her and Emmett to raise as their own a Sicilian child who was not of their same social class. But from the moment Clare had seen the little girl standing with her hand in Emmett's outside the viscount's villa, she'd instinctively known Antonina was now connected to them—in a way that went far beyond providing her with temporary care or room and board. The girl needed love as well as protection and the necessities of life. And Clare wanted to give Antonina all of that.

"What about your family?" She guessed the marquess would not be pleased if Emmett returned to England with a child of Antonina's coloring and stated his intention to provide for her care. As a girl, and one not related by blood, Antonina wouldn't be able to inherit anything either, other than what Emmett and Clare could provide for her.

Emmett shrugged, but the firelight revealed the tightening lines on his brow and around his mouth. "I'm not sure what he'll . . . I mean, they . . . will think." His slip of the tongue indicated he was also thinking most about his father's reaction. "Once we explain, I hope they will see the rightness of such a decision."

"And your political plans? Will raising a Sicilian child affect those?"

His agitation was evident when he ran a hand through his hair. The dark-blond tufts stuck up, though not unattractively. "Honestly, I don't know. I'm simply trying to do what's right by the child and get all of us out of Messina as soon as we're able."

"Fair enough."

Clare's head was beginning to feel fuzzy from the lack of sleep. There would be time enough later on to tackle such complex problems. Right now, as Emmett had said, they simply needed to survive and return to Taormina. Or what was left of it. If the villa was no more, Clare would have a whole new set of troubles to deal with. But she wouldn't leave Sicily, not yet.

Quiet descended between them as Clare added another stick to the flames. A peek at each member of their group revealed everyone was sleeping, even Helena's baby. Gratitude for the warmth of the fire had her offering another prayer of thanks. Her appreciation lasted until Emmett spoke again.

"How did you know how to start the fire without matches, Clare?"

It was the question she'd been dreading all night. Her

eyes darted to his, but she couldn't read the emotion there. Was Emmett angry about her, a high-society lady, acting like a commoner, or merely puzzled that she'd known how to start a fire at all? A muscle in her temple began to throb, along with the increased beating of her pulse. What should she say in answer? If she told him the truth, would it inspire him to be more open too?

She let out a soft sigh and kept her face pointed toward the fire. Seeing her husband's reaction to her story might make it more difficult to tell. "My father taught me how to start a fire using two sticks. You twist the one into a groove you make in the other until it forms an ember. He thought it might be a useful skill to know."

"Whatever for?"

Even his neutral tone couldn't decrease the nervousness growing inside her. Clare fidgeted with the edge of the blanket. There was a thread there she considered pulling. But would it unravel the fabric? The past year she'd felt that way about so many things in her marriage. Jerking too hard on any one thread was liable to undo what was left of the lovely things. Yet some of them had still come undone, and she'd felt powerless to stop them.

"I wasn't always an heiress, Emmett." She left the thread alone and gripped her blanket between her fingers. "I told you once that my family lived in Vermont before we moved to New York City, but I didn't tell you why."

Clare glanced down at the dirtied material of her robe and felt the irony of telling him of her past now, when their wealth and privilege had been temporarily stripped away from them. "My father had apple orchards and a farm, but we were still quite poor most years. I remember as a girl never truly feeling warm from October to May. There were even a handful of times when there was nothing in the larder but a few overly soft apples to eat. Somehow my mother always managed to create something out of nothing, though, so we didn't go completely hungry.

"Being their only child, I learned to work at a very young age, both in the kitchen and around the farm. That's where I learned to ride bareback and how to care for the apples. My father told me I was the best apple picker east of the Mississippi."

She paused, but the only sounds to fill in the silence were the soft snores from those sleeping and the occasional pop of the fire. Emmett didn't speak, but Clare sensed he was watching her. "I was eight years old when my father learned that men's hair pomade is often made with mashed apples. He began experimenting with recipes of his own, certain if he found the right combination it would change things for us. Eventually it did. When his pomade became a hit, he opened a factory in New York and then another. Just as he had around the farm, he insisted on teaching me how a business was run. By the time I debuted into society, my father was already a millionaire several times over, and I was an heiress, but I never forgot the lessons he taught me."

"What did your fellow New Yorkers think of your humble past?"

A blush crept into her cheeks, though she suspected Emmett couldn't see it. "The few who know all of it are loyal employees of my father's. It wasn't our background that caused the scornful reactions when I debuted; it was the fact that my father was a manufacturer and one who still insists on overseeing the factories himself. Many didn't care for his somewhat unpolished manners either, or the fact that his millions aren't old money."

"So you came to England to make a match." He didn't state it as a question, but Clare still nodded. A minute or so passed before he spoke again. This time his tone held frustration and what might be hurt. "Why didn't you tell me any of this before now?"

It was her turn to shrug. "I didn't think it relevant."

"Not relevant? At the very least it would have explained why you detest the cold, Clare. Or how you knew how to start the fire tonight." From the corner of her eye, she saw him gesture at the flames. "I had assumed you'd always led a life similar in many ways to mine." It almost sounded as if he was talking more to himself than to her. "Now I find that's not the case."

Clare swallowed the lump of guilt in her throat. "I'm sorry. I . . . I should have told you before now that I wasn't always an heiress."

She waited for some acknowledgement—of her apology or that it didn't matter that she hadn't begun life as a wealthy heiress—but it didn't come. If disclosing these confessions upset him because she'd hidden her past, how would Emmett react if or when he learned she was pregnant again and had kept it from him?

"I think I'll try to sleep now," she said in a tight voice.

"That's probably wise. I'll tend the fire."

Clare finally looked at him, but she couldn't tell what he was thinking—she hadn't been able to for a long time. "Are you sure? You need sleep too."

"I'll wake Miriam to tend the fire in a few hours if I can't stay awake any longer."

Nodding, she shifted Antonina so both of them could lie on their sides. "I'm sorry again, Emmett. I should have told you all of that sooner."

"Good night, Clare. I hope you're able to get some sleep." His words held no malice, but they were still a dismissal.

Clare bit her lip to keep in the sob that swelled in her

mouth. A few tears escaped, though, sliding into the blanket beneath her cheek. If there was ever any reason for Emmett to depart for England as soon as possible, she'd given him one tonight. And yet instead of relief, a strange sense of disappointment washed over her, making realize just how much she would miss him when he left. her

Somerset, England, December 1907: Twelve months earlier

Seated in the chair closest to the fire, Clare sipped her tea and listened to the conversation swirling about the drawing room. Emmett's dog Bran sat on the rug at her feet, his quiet presence as much a comfort as the heat from the hearth. Lady Hadwell, Lady Melinda, and the other two women who'd been invited to tea spoke to and among themselves, excluding her so completely that it was almost as if they didn't recall Clare was present.

The feeling of being an outsider had become as constant a companion as Bran at her side since she and Emmett had come to live at Hadwell House. Her mother-in-law acted startled whenever she encountered Clare anywhere but in the library or at mealtimes—as if the woman had forgotten she had a daughter-in-law. The marquess rarely spoke to Clare, but when he did, it was always with an air of impatience, even if he was inquiring about her.

She'd attempted to allay her feelings of loneliness and uselessness by learning what she could about managing a household staff. After all, the plan was for her and Emmett to purchase a townhouse shortly before the start of the season, and Clare would be responsible for the hiring and training of the servants. Her formative years had given her far more education on how to manage a household than other American heiresses received. But Clare had quickly discovered there was a vast difference between the familial ties she had enjoyed with her family's staff back home and the stiff formalities that existed between mistress and servant at Hadwell House.

Then there was the seemingly endless array of household rules and regulations she didn't understand. Anytime she questioned Lady Hadwell, in hopes of better understanding why things were done a certain way, her mother-in-law acted confused and irritated at needing to supply an explanation. Clare had eventually stopped asking and instead worked to memorize the perplexing protocols that came with running a large household staff, so she wouldn't prove a disappointment to Emmett.

Time alone with her husband was typically just as elusive. His father kept him busy with estate matters and overseeing the updates to Hadwell House that Clare's money had and would continue to provide. She'd been shocked to discover how many repairs were needed. Signs of age and neglect were everywhere in the centuries-old house—watermarked ceilings, unraveling upholstery, wallpaper peeling back in corners, and a roof in desperate need of repair. There was no electricity either, and the only room that offered a regular fire during the day was the library.

Clare had hoped to turn to painting as a way to fill her largely empty days. But the chilblains she'd developed on her hands from the incessant cold made it difficult for her to hold a paintbrush. Finally, in desperation, she'd asked one of Emmett's sisters during the woman's visit what could be done. Her sister-in-law had instructed her on the right way to bind the blisters on her hands and feet. The chilblains were gone now, but Clare hadn't been able to recreate her desire to put brush to canvas. Until today . . .

She smiled to herself as she brought her tea cup to her lips. She didn't even mind not being included in the conversation.

This morning she'd gone to the village. Clare had given the excuse that the visit was to purchase gifts for Christmas, but her true purpose was to meet with the doctor there. The man had confirmed what Clare herself had suspected for a few weeks—she was going to have a baby.

The same thrill she'd felt at hearing the doctor's words wound through her again. She would be a mother next year, and Emmett a father. It was the start to filling the nursery with all of the children Clare longed to have. She also took satisfaction at being able to give an affirmative answer at last to the incessant questions from Emmett's family and strangers regarding when she was going to produce an heir.

Movement by the door drew her attention. Emmett stood there, looking quite handsome in his riding clothes. His eyes met hers, and he smiled in a way that made everyone else in the room disappear.

"Emmett?" his mother said, her tone one of pleasant surprise. "Did you wish to join us?"

He shook his head as he stepped into the room. "Thank you but not today. I'm going riding and came in search of Bran." He crossed the room to stand before Clare's chair. "I suspected I would find the defector here," he teased. The dog lifted his head and wagged his tail, but he made no move to approach Emmett.

"I'm afraid these days he prefers teatime to accompanying you on a ride, my lord."

"A sure sign you've effectively charmed my dog." He leaned down and kissed her cheek as he added in a murmur, "As you have his master."

The praise spoken in that low voice of his inspired a blush

of pleasure. "If that were true," Clare whispered back, her gaze melding with his, "then I could spirit us both away from here without anyone noticing."

"Shall I cause a commotion in the foyer that would allow you to slip out?"

She feigned a sharp look at him. "Don't tempt me. I'm trying my best to be the consummate wife of a future marquess."

"And I love you for it, my dear." The tender light in his pale-blue eyes spoke as much to his sincerity as the warmth in his voice.

Thankfully he straightened at that moment, or Clare might have taken his face between her hands and kissed him. She adored flirting with him like this, but it was one thing to do so in private and another entirely to banter this way in the company of others.

"I'll see you at dinner," he said, then called for Bran to join him.

The dog looked at Clare as if seeking permission. Biting back a laugh, she nodded for him to go with Emmett. "Go on, Bran." She watched them depart, wishing she could go with them.

As soon as Emmett left the room, Lady Melinda rose from her place on the settee and came to sit in the armchair across from Clare's. The young widow visited regularly with Lady Hadwell and Emmett's sisters whenever they were in residence at Hadwell House. But while she was all smiles and affability to others, Lady Melinda usually treated Clare coolly and with veiled criticism. Clare sensed the widow harbored bitterness towards her and Emmett because he'd chosen to marry someone other than Lady Melinda. This would also account for why the woman seemed eager for Clare to fail in living up to her role as Emmett's wife.

"May I say you're looking well, Lady Linwood?" As usual,

the widow's words sounded pleasant enough, but there was a distinct chill behind them. Lady Melinda took a sip of tea before continuing. "Our English way of life must be appealing to you."

Clare wasn't about to share her real thoughts on the subject. "I can understand why Emmett loves it here."

"This place is in his blood as much as it is for the rest of us."

The excluding way the woman talked grated on Clare, but she wouldn't insult her mother-in-law's guest. "It's important to feel fondly about one's home." Though Clare couldn't imagine ever feeling that way about Hadwell House. It didn't feel like home to her.

"I must say, Lady Linwood," Lady Melinda intoned next, setting her cup in its saucer, "that for a marriage based solely on money, yours does seem to have its moments of happiness."

Clare's eyes widened in surprise, though she wasn't sure which part of the woman's statement she found more shocking—Lady Melinda's knowing, confidential tone that implied she knew the family's secrets or the idea that Emmett would have married for money only.

The widow chortled when Clare remained silent, but her laugh rang false and snide. "Certainly I haven't shared anything you did not already know. I once heard the marquess congratulate his son for doing what he'd been asked to do in finding himself a wealthy wife."

It couldn't be true. Clare hadn't imagined Emmett's love, before or since their wedding. Lady Melinda must have misunderstood what she'd overheard. Or the widow was falsifying her story in another effort to undermine Clare's confidence.

Clare swallowed any nigglings of fear regarding her and

Emmett with her next sip of tea. As a couple, they were happy. And unbeknownst to Lady Melinda, that happiness had and would continue to last for more than brief moments. Especially once Clare told her husband that she was pregnant.

"Your concern is unwarranted," Clare said calmly. "Though Emmett and I do appreciate your desire for our happiness."

The widow's mouth pursed as if she'd tasted something sour. "Of course." She nodded and stood regally before returning to her former seat.

Clare sighed with relief when she realized the conversation had continued to flow without interruption around her. No one else had heard Lady Melinda's allegation. But Clare had.

She lowered her teacup to her lap, no longer able to stomach the drink. If only she'd been able to go with Emmett earlier, then she would have missed the unpleasant conversation with the widow. Because, in spite of her own reassurances, it was still going to take time to completely erase the other woman's accusation and triumphant tone from Clare's memory. Hopefully when she did, the tiny seed of doubt she sensed had sprouted inside her would be expunged too.

Chapter 7

Emmett found the fact that he had slept at all to be remarkable. The hard earth beneath him, the chilly air on his back, and everything his wife had confessed about her past had kept him awake for hours. Eventually he'd started to doze, though, so he had woken Miriam and asked if she would keep the fire going while he tried to get a little sleep.

Sometime later he jerked awake, feeling disoriented. Why was he lying on the ground instead of in his hotel room? Emmett sat up and took in the sight of the fire, the lightening sky, and the other people, all sleeping, save for him and Miriam. Remembering rushed back then, overwhelming his thoughts with all the horror and pain from the day before.

He staggered to his feet as his stomach rumbled with gnawing hunger. "I'm going to get some water," he quietly told the maid, "and see if I can't find more oranges for breakfast. You're welcome to sleep until I return. The fire will be fine until then."

The fire still burned strong, its presence truly a miracle. Without it they might not have survived the cold night. Emmett could admit it was a godsend that Clare had known how to start it.

"Thank you, my lord." Miriam immediately curled up in her blanket and closed her eyes.

Hefting the empty bucket, Emmett set off for the well. The air felt frigid away from the fire's heat. He shivered as he reached the edge of the field. It had already been twenty-four hours since the earthquake, and yet the eleven of them were still homeless and without true relief from their injuries and hunger. Emmett wasn't sure Helena's baby and husband would survive another night out in the open countryside.

Perhaps it was time for all of them to venture back into Messina and see if they could find a reliable means of transport. It seemed the only way to leave the ravished city behind, unless they walked to Taormina. Emmett dismissed that idea at once. Most of their group was in no condition to walk more than thirty miles. Besides, he didn't know how damaged the other city was at present. No matter where they went, he might be leading them into an equally precarious situation. But he didn't want to leave the island altogether without first seeing if his grandfather's villa was still standing. Clare would likely wish to do the same.

Thinking of Clare, he recalled what she'd shared with him last night. Emmett still couldn't believe his heiress wife had once lived as a poor farm child. Some of the shock and anger he'd felt after her confession churned anew inside him as he walked. Why hadn't she told him about her past sooner? Was it because she feared he would judge her? Or had Clare kept her secret because she trusted him so little?

Emmett had asked himself these same questions over and over again as he'd lain awake through most of the night. He didn't judge Clare for her humble beginnings; he simply wished she'd told him, at the very least, before their wedding. What had bothered—and hurt—him most of all, though, was the idea that Clare didn't trust him enough to tell him sooner.

And since she'd withheld this information even during the early days of their marriage, when all had seemed rosy and hopeful between them, he couldn't help wondering if she'd ever truly trusted him at all.

The possibility stung, poking anew at his doubts. Was his wife's humble past further evidence that she had only married him for his title? Going from farm girl to heiress to wife of a future marquess would certainly be a social coup. And yet Clare had never struck him as being socially ambitious.

Even as he'd listened to her story, he hadn't gotten the impression she was soliciting sympathy or exaggerating. She'd shared the details of those difficult years with openness and, as far as Emmett could tell, with only a touch of embarrassment. In addition, she'd never seemed to feel anything but love and admiration for her father, despite his "somewhat unpolished manners," as she'd put it.

Still, if his wife had chosen not to tell him something as poignant as this, what else might she be keeping from him? His mind circled back to the rumors he'd heard. Was Clare too embarrassed to tell him that she had hoped for a titled match, that such a thing had been her reason for coming to England in the first place?

Emmett scraped his fingers through his hair in agitation. His hand came away speckled with dust, in spite of yesterday's rain and sleeping outside. He didn't have the answers. And though not having them was a simmering source of frustration for him, he wasn't sure he wanted answers right now anyway. There were other more critical matters to consider. He needed to get everyone to safety first, then figure out if and when Clare might return to England with him.

Their conversation about Antonina filtered through his thoughts. He'd been relieved to hear Clare also wanted to keep the little girl with them and raise her as a member of their family. There had even been a moment as he'd helped Clare with her blisters when Emmett had sensed her softening toward him again. It had happened when she'd bantered with him about being asleep too.

Over the last twenty-four hours, there had been flickers of returning connection between them, giving Emmett hope that they could return to England as more than a couple living behind a façade of happiness. That they could reconnect beforehand. But then something would happen, like Clare's confession about the past, and the tentative bond would slip away. It made him wonder if they could actually endure having to pretend to be perfectly happy while he campaigned for his seat in Parliament.

For the first time since leaving England a week ago, Emmett was grateful he'd had the wisdom and courage to stand up to his father's idea about having a reporter accompany him to Sicily. There was enough for him to navigate with Clare without someone reporting their every move. But it was only a matter of time before they would have to become accustomed to the constant scrutiny when Emmett began campaigning. And he hated to think what that would do to their already uncertain relationship if they didn't breach the distance between them first.

He couldn't fail to bring Clare back though. If he did, he would fail his father.

His tasks, both before and since the earthquake, pressed heavily against his shoulders. *Thou hast brought us this far, Lord. Please continue to be mindful of us. Help me be the person I must to accomplish what I need to.* He ended his prayer with a heavy sigh as he reached the well.

Emmett drew a full bucket of water. A glance at the ruins behind him gave him an idea, and he set the pail down. Perhaps there was a little food left among the rubble. His search unearthed nothing but some crusts of hardening bread. However, it was still something to eat. He pocketed the bread, picked up the water bucket, and returned to the field.

He came upon Clare, Miriam, and Antonina near the grove of trees. They'd apparently been looking for more oranges. But the only one who carried anything was Antonina.

"We found just the one orange," Clare said as he joined them in their trek back. Antonina lifted the orange for him to see. She looked pleased at her find, but Clare's expression was strained, her face slightly pale.

"There were some bread crusts at the farm." He nearly ended their conversation there, but his conscience wouldn't allow it. Whatever tension and mistrust still brewed between him and Clare, she was his wife, and he cared what happened to her. "How are you feeling this morning?"

She shot him an almost panicked glance, similar to the one yesterday when he'd found her waking up after the robber had knocked her unconscious. Emmett wondered what it meant and if he would ever know the answer. "I'm tired and hungry, same as everyone else."

"And your head?"

Reaching up, she touched the back of her hair. It lay in a long, red-and-gold plait down her back. "My head is still a little sore, but I don't have a headache anymore."

"I'm glad to hear it."

A short distance from the group, Clare stopped and waved for Miriam and Antonina to go ahead. Emmett paused as well, sensing she wished to speak to him in private. Was there more she needed to tell him? Alarm flickered through him at the prospect.

"I want to apologize again, Emmett." The words were full of earnestness, though she didn't meet his eye. "I'm sorry for not telling you about my childhood when we were courting. I don't blame you if you're . . . well, embarrassed . . . by my humble background."

He waited until she finally brought her gaze to his. "You believe I feel embarrassment?"

"I don't know." Frustration threaded her reply. "You didn't say anything last night, so I've been left to guess . . ." He thought he heard her whisper "again."

Emmett set down the bucket. "I was shocked and angry, Clare, not at what you said but at not knowing sooner. However, there is nothing about your childhood that either of us should be ashamed of."

Relief replaced the worry on her face—a face he still found as lovely as ever. He couldn't allow himself to be completely relieved though. Not when their future, today and tomorrow and in the weeks ahead, was still uncertain.

"I'm grateful for your experiences and the benefits they've brought us," he said, hefting the water bucket again. "It was nothing short of a miracle that you were able to light that fire. We would have likely lost some people without it."

A pleased blush drove the paleness from her cheeks. "I'm glad I was able to help. It was nice to feel useful."

As they approached the group, he considered Clare's last words. Did she not usually feel useful? It was another revelation he hadn't expected. Ever since their marriage, she always seemed occupied with something, and yet there had been real satisfaction and a hint of yearning in her voice just now that he didn't think he'd heard before.

The dividing of the bread crusts and the orange drew Emmett's focus elsewhere. Everyone expressed gratitude to him and Antonina for having water to drink and a bit of something in their bellies. The food disappeared quickly, though, along with nearly all of the water. What little remained was used to tend to the viscount's wound and to wash some of the grime from all of their hands and faces. Even the scant washing seemed to lighten everyone's spirits.

However, when Emmett suggested it might be best for them to return to Messina, a cloud of melancholy shrouded the group. Rushford, Clare, and Miriam agreed with his suggestion. But the rest wanted to remain in the field for the time being. Emmett didn't see how he had any other choice but to defer to the wishes of the majority.

The rest of the morning crawled by, with little to break up the monotony save for dozing and light conversation. Occasional tremors still shook the earth now and then, which prompted cries of alarm from some in the group and wide-eyed looks of fear from Antonina. Eventually Emmett could remain inert no longer. He returned to the well for more water, taking Antonina with him as well as two of the maids, who wished to walk around.

He wanted to search the farm ruins for more scraps of food, but the wreckage had already shifted since earlier. Emmett was more likely to end up trapped, or worse, if he disturbed the former cottage anymore. A search of the yard produced nothing else edible. Likewise, the four of them found nothing more to eat on their way back to the field.

A short time later, the piteous cries of Helena's baby and the gnawing in Emmett's own stomach drove him to his feet again. They were in desperate need of bread and a doctor. And they wouldn't find either if they remained where they were.

"We can't stay here," he said, glancing at everyone in turn. "We need more help than this place can provide us."

Helena's face went white as she looked from Emmett to her injured husband. "The city isn't safe either. We could be crushed to death."

Emmett wrestled back yesterday's memories as they threatened to overpower him. "It is a risk to return, but it's also a risk to remain here."

"I don't want to go back to Messina either." Clare rose from where she'd been sitting. "But Emmett is right. We've run out of things to eat and have nothing to help Rushford and Lord Vickley. I think we should return to the city."

Miriam stood as well, her expression resigned but determined. "If you go, my lady, then I go too."

"My place is with you, Lord and Lady Linwood," Rushford said, standing. His slightly haggard face was the only telltale sign, besides his makeshift sling, that his arm still pained him.

Coming to her feet as well, Antonina grasped Emmett's hand firmly in hers. He wasn't sure how much of what they were saying she understood, but he recognized her silent action as a resolution to go where he went, even if it was back into the city she likely feared. Two of the three maids from the viscount's household finally stood too. The remaining young lady peered hesitantly from her friends to her mistress.

"Do you really believe we are in as much danger here as back in Messina?" Helena gave Emmett a searching look.

He paused, wishing he felt more certain that he wasn't leading them into greater trouble. But there were no guarantees of help and safety here or in the city. He—and they—would simply have to keep hoping and praying, whatever they chose to do.

"I don't know what awaits us in Messina," he answered honestly. "We may not find the aid we need, but I do know if we stay here, it will be much longer in coming." His gaze went to her baby and husband. "Too long perhaps."

Helena smoothed back the matted hair of her little boy and breathed out an audible sigh. "He needs milk and bread, and we don't have that here." She climbed to her feet, as did the third maid, and reached out a hand to her husband. "Come, Leo. I don't want to stay here alone."

The viscount rose slowly with his wife's help. Only then did Emmett allow himself to breathe with relief. The group would stay together.

"Very well then." Emmett directed that they tear one of the blankets into strips to tie around the feet of those with no shoes. Once that was completed, he directed Antonina to climb onto his back. "Stay close," he told the rest of them, "and keep a careful watch out for anything dropping from above."

A unified murmur of agreement sounded as they followed him. They left behind the water bucket but brought the remaining blankets. Emmett took the same path back to the city that he had the day before. This time he wasn't alone, though, so he slowed his steps to match those trudging along behind. Clare remained near him. She didn't speak, but he found her presence comforting nonetheless. Her confidence in his decision to return to Messina bolstered his own, bringing with it a renewal of the connection they'd shared.

Still, feeling more confident didn't stop him from praying often that they'd be spared any further harm and find the help they needed.

When they reached the first of the city's outlying streets, their progress slowed to a painful slog. Piles of wreckage had to be carefully scaled, and twice Emmett had them retreat to find a different route when it became clear the way ahead was impassable.

The continued tremors of the earth made both the rubble and the few remaining buildings shutter and shift. More than once their party barely escaped being struck by toppling masonry. At the far edge of one square, the wall of a house had collapsed, leaving the front rooms exposed. The furniture inside was undisturbed, making Emmett feel as if he were viewing a giant dollhouse that awaited its owner's return.

He guessed they were getting closer to the harbor when

Clare put her hand on his arm to stop him. "Do you smell that?"

Emmett sniffed the air. The scent of something baking wafted beneath his nose and sent his gut into fresh spasms of hunger. "It smells like bread."

"That's what I thought. Should we follow it?"

Was it worth changing course to go after something that might end in disappointment? The others gathered around them and began to exclaim over the tantalizing aroma too. It was Antonina, though, who settled the matter when she whispered "*pane*" in the most animated voice Emmett had heard from her yet. That did it—they would go in search of the bread. Besides, he recognized he wasn't likely to convince any of them not to follow the smell now.

"We'll see if we can find where it's coming from." Emmett turned and headed in the opposite direction from where he'd been leading them.

Before long, the smell of bread grew stronger, overcoming every other sense. Emmett moved as fast as he could through the demolished streets, and he wasn't the only one. Even the viscount appeared to have been revived by the heavenly scent and no longer walked half bent over. At last they turned a corner and found themselves at the back of a small crowd. Over the heads of those gathered, Emmett saw some Italian soldiers handing out bread. Behind the soldiers a temporary kitchen had been set up, and this was the source of the wonderful smell.

Would the bread be gone before their group was able to have some? Emmett hoped not. The soldiers' expressions were full of sorrowful kindness. But they were keeping a sharp eye on the crowd too to maintain order.

Finally a warm loaf was placed in Emmett's hands. At once he helped Antonina slide to the ground. He tore the bread in half and gave the girl the larger portion. She ate it hungrily, her dark eyes shining when she peered up at him. Once he'd made certain the rest of the group had their portions, Emmett sank his teeth into his own serving. Nothing had ever tasted sweeter or more filling, and he had to blink back tears of gratitude. Never again would he take a bounteous table for granted.

The wonder and thankfulness he felt was reflected on the face of every other member of their small cluster. Returning to the city hadn't been a fools' errand after all. Another wave of appreciation swept over Emmett as he finished every last crumb.

After everyone had eaten, including Helena's baby boy, Emmett asked one of the soldiers the best way to leave the city. The man told him the rail lines from Messina to Palermo had only just been restored to working order. There were also boats in the harbor providing aid to the homeless and wounded refugees, and others that were conveying evacuees to Sicily's capital city, Palermo, or across the Strait of Messina to other cities in Italy. Emmett asked about the status of Taormina, but the soldier was uncertain how well the other city had fared. He did assure Emmett that Palermo had received no damage, so it was possible Taormina had withstood the devastation too.

Emmett shared what he'd learned with Clare, and she agreed that they ought to try to make their way to Taormina. "What will you do?" he asked the viscount and Helena. "We're going to try our luck at the harbor and hope someone is willing to take us to Taormina."

The viscount exchanged a long look with his wife. The sight of it prompted the tiniest bit of jealousy in Emmett. He missed communicating in that intimate way with Clare.

"We are most appreciative for all of your help, Linwood."

The viscount held out his hand for Emmett to shake. "But since we know Palermo still stands and there are likely doctors there who can patch my forehead, I believe we'll take the train there."

"Will you rebuild your villa?" Clare directed her question to both of them.

Helena shifted her baby from one hip to the other. "Perhaps. Right now I only care about finding some decent clothes and a bed for Little Leo to sleep on."

"Write soon," Clare said as the two women embraced. "Let us know if you stay in Palermo or return to England."

The other woman nodded and reached out to clasp Emmett's hand. "Thank you again, Lord Linwood. None of us would have survived without your help."

Emmett appreciated her thanks, but he hadn't succeeded alone. "All of you were as much a part of our pulling through as I was."

The viscount led his wife, son, and the three maids away from the bread kitchen. When they were no longer in sight, Emmett turned to face the remaining four members of their group. "If the rest of you wish to stay here, I can go to the harbor—"

"We can all come," Clare announced, taking Antonina by the hand. The little girl gave Emmett a decisive nod, which Rushford and Miriam repeated.

He couldn't help but chuckle, and the sensation of it felt as wonderful on his tongue as the bread had earlier. "Very well. We'll *all* go."

They set off for the harbor. It wasn't far, but their trek was constantly hampered by the wreckage and the crowds of other refugees clamoring to leave the ruined city behind. Finally they reached the waterfront. Emmett and Rushford split up to speak with as many sailors as they could, in hopes of finding a captain and vessel willing to convey them to Taormina.

Nearly an hour must have passed before Emmett returned to where Clare, Antonina, and Miriam were still waiting. Their expectant demeanors drooped when he approached and shook his head. "No one is traveling to Taormina today."

"Lord Linwood!" Emmett looked up to see Rushford hurrying toward them through the throng of people. "I found a boat!"

Gratitude swallowed up any disappointment Emmett might have felt at not being the one to secure a ship personally. "Where?"

"Back this way," Rushford said, his breathing coming fast and labored. "They're about to shove off, so we have to hurry."

Emmett swung Antonina onto his back again and moved quickly after the valet. Clare and Miriam kept pace behind them. "You're sure they'll take us to Taormina?"

"I spoke with the captain himself." Rushford winced and gripped his broken arm as another man raced past, jostling him. "That's where they were bound before they heard about the earthquake. He has another passenger to let off at Taormina. And a doctor on board to boot."

"Excellent." His valet would finally get his arm properly cared for.

Emmett glanced back at Antonina and said in Italian, "We're going to take a boat to Taormina." Her small hands gripped him tighter around the neck in an evident show of worry. "It'll be all right. I will be with you and Clare and Miriam and Rushford. You won't be alone." Her grasp relaxed a little. "Hopefully in a few short hours, we'll be sitting down to one of Signora Russo's delicious meals."

When they arrived, out of breath, at the spot Rushford

indicated, a sailor was just preparing to launch the small skiff. Inside sat the captain and two others bound for the waiting steamer. "Climb aboard," the captain said cheerfully, his British accent a welcome reminder of home. "And watch your step."

Once they were all settled, the sailor gave the small boat a shove and hopped inside as the craft slid into the water. The captain introduced himself, and Emmett did the same. As the sailor rowed them away from Messina, the captain exclaimed over the devastating changes to the city. Emmett shared a brief account of their own experiences as they moved toward the steamer.

Clare and Miriam were the first to ascend the ship's ladder, then Emmett helped Antonina. Soon the five of them were aboard the vessel. A small group of people were gathered at the deck railing. Emmett guessed these were the steamer's other passengers.

"We'll have you back to your villa in no time, Lord Linwood," the captain reassured him before striding away.

A gentleman spun away from the railing and stared wide-eyed at Emmett. "Did I hear the captain correctly? You are Lord Linwood?"

"That is correct." The young man with dark-brown hair appeared to be a few years younger than Emmett. "Do I know you?"

With a grin that looked out of place against the backdrop of Messina's destruction, the man pumped Emmett's hand up and down in a hearty handshake. "We've never been formally introduced, but I'm Theo Sharpe. Reporter for the London *Times*. My father and Lord Hadwell are old school chums. In fact, your father is the one who . . ."

Emmett didn't hear another word of Mr. Sharpe's explanation. Not with the ice-cold suspicion chilling him and his thoughts.

His father hadn't backed down after all—he'd simply ignored Emmett's insistence and then bided his time for a day or two before sending someone after him. What was Clare going to think about having a reporter around? Emmett turned toward her and caught her confused expression as she studied Mr. Sharpe. What was Emmett supposed to say? He hadn't expected his father to go behind his back, but he couldn't plead complete innocence of the reporter's presence either.

He hesitated too long. Mr. Sharpe stepped around Emmett and offered his hand to Clare. "You must be Lady Linwood." The young man acted as if they were in a receiving line in a London drawing room rather than standing before him bedraggled and half-starved—and in Clare's case, still shoeless and in her nightgown.

"Yes." She threw Emmett a puzzled look. "What brings you to Messina, Mr. Sharpe?"

The grin was back. "Why, you and your husband, of course. Now that he's going to run for Parliament, Lord Hadwell felt it was important to get both your names in print sooner than later."

Clare's cheeks went white in color. "So you are here to write about . . . us?" Her question was for the reporter, but she peered straight at Emmett. "As a couple?"

"Yes, my lady." Mr. Sharpe rocked back on his heels. "People at home will soon be demanding stories about the illustrious Linwoods, especially now that you've both survived the earthquake."

The young man didn't seem to notice the reddening shade of anger that now spread across Clare's face, but Emmett saw it. "And this was all arranged when?"

"A month or so ago," the reporter replied. "I would've been on the same ship as Lord Linwood, but for some reason,

I was told I wasn't needed right away. I caught the next steamer after his."

In the echo of the man's words, Emmett imagined he heard the loud *snap* of the bond that had temporarily connected him and Clare, like a sail rent into pieces by a fierce wind. How many more times could it endure being patched and mended before it gave out altogether? He considered tossing Mr. Sharpe overboard, and yet that would only bring a temporary reprieve to this newest dilemma. The incorrigible reporter was still likely to turn up in Taormina, eager for a story.

Whether now or later, Emmett would eventually have to respond to the silent demand for answers in Clare's darkening green eyes. Eyes that had looked on him with confidence and appreciation hours ago. That look was gone now, and in its wake, Emmett was left with one sobering reminder. They had escaped with their lives from Messina, but their troubles were far from over. In some ways, he thought as he glanced again at Mr. Sharpe, they were just beginning.

Somerset, England, March 1908: Nine months earlier

Emmett rapped lightly on Clare's door, wondering if she was sleeping. However, when he twisted the handle and stepped into the room, he found his wife sitting before a roaring fire. It had been ten days since her miscarriage, but he still insisted she have a fire in her room during the day. He didn't understand why she was always cold, indoors or out, but a constant source of warmth seemed a small concession after the loss of her pregnancy.

"May I come in?" he asked when she didn't acknowledge him.

At his voice, she turned from staring in the direction of the flames to look over her shoulder. "Oh, Emmett. Yes, do come in."

Her red-rimmed eyes and haunted expression cried at him to reach out to her, to unburden his own sorrow at not being a father this year. But Emmett swallowed the words as he shut the door. He wouldn't add to her grief by sharing his or incite more tears from her.

He took a seat in the chair opposite hers. "How are you feeling?"

"Fine, I suppose." Clare offered him a shrug, then drew

her blanket-like shawl around her shoulders. She had on a dress today, which he hoped was a good sign. "I'm still tired."

Emmett nodded. "The doctor said that was to be expected for some time."

"Yes," she murmured, her gaze once more on the fire.

He breached the space between them and settled his hand over hers where it rested along the chair arm. Her fingers felt cool to the touch, in spite of the warmth of the fire. "We can try again, Clare. The doctor reassured me that there is no reason to believe we won't be parents someday soon."

It wasn't the right thing to say. She slid her hand out from under his and placed it out of reach on her lap. "That may be true, but I don't want to think about that right now. Not after I just lost . . ." Her words faltered as her voice hitched with emotion.

The need to unburden his thoughts, to confide in her, nearly overwhelmed him. But he had to stay strong. Never again would he trouble someone with his mourning as he had all those years ago when his grandfather had died. Instead Emmett had to think of a way to lift Clare's shroud of sorrow and bring back the laughter he missed.

She twisted to look at him. "Is there something you need?"

"I wished to talk about the London house." He bent forward, his arms on his knees, his hands splayed toward the heat. "I know we had to delay our departure . . ." They'd been packed and ready to leave the very morning Clare had begun bleeding. "But I'm afraid we may be hard-pressed to find something if we don't hurry and do so before the season starts next month."

Clare nodded absently. "I suppose you're right."

"Which is why I thought I would pop over to London tomorrow and begin our search. If I find something, I thought

I might solicit the help of one of my sisters in hiring the staff." It was something else he could do to ease things for Clare while she recovered. He glanced her way but couldn't read her features to determine what she was thinking. "I shouldn't be gone more than a fortnight, three weeks at the most. Then I'll return to Hadwell House, and we'll go back to London together."

To his surprise, she suddenly rose to her feet. "I don't want to wait that long."

"For a house?"

Clare shook her head and crossed the room to where her trunk still sat. "For us to go to London. There's no reason I can't go with you now." She slid the trunk away from the wall, but after opening the lid, she sagged against the bedpost.

"Clare, you don't have to come with me." He stood and moved toward her. "You still aren't well, and searching for a house is likely to be tiring."

Her chin rose in defiance, though there were visible tears glittering in her eyes. "I can't stay here. I won't stay."

The firmness of her tone confused him. Did she wish to escape the memories of her miscarriage? Or something else? It was evident she didn't love this place as much as he did, and he'd noticed she hadn't painted anything new in weeks. But Emmett had attributed all of that to adjusting to living in a new country. Not to mention, the winter weather had been especially hard on her. It would be spring soon, and yet in spite of that promise, Clare acted as if she couldn't leave for London soon enough.

"Are you . . . unhappy . . . here?" He hated the bitter way the adjective tasted on his tongue, but he needed to know. Was his wife unhappy living at Hadwell House—or perhaps even unhappy with him?

Several of her tears escaped her lashes and cascaded

down her pale cheeks. "Yes, Emmett. I won't be a mother this summer; I miss my parents something awful; and I feel as if this shawl has become a part of my skin after wearing it so much, and I still can't get warm. So yes, there have been moments and hours and even days of unhappiness. Is that such a crime?"

"No," he answered softly.

Closing the distance between them, he gathered her gently to his chest and let her cry. Each quiet sob squeezed at his lungs and threatened to bring tears to his own eyes.

After a few minutes, her weeping gave way to an occasional shudder. "Do you really wish to come to London with me now?" he asked. If that would bring her smile back, Emmett would spirit her away to the city tonight.

Clare nodded against his now-damp shirt. "I do."

"Very well." He eased back and tilted her face upward. "Is this your way of telling me I'd do a frightful job of hiring a staff on my own?"

Her lips creased slightly at the corners. "You've seen through my ruse, my lord. Besides, I have been preparing for this."

"A fact not to be overlooked." He let the merriment slip from his countenance. "Will you promise not to overexert yourself in our hunt for a house? The season can be exhausting and busy enough as it is." Particularly when his father was dictating the number of events they attended.

Emmett typically enjoyed interacting with friends and acquaintances during the season, but he'd especially been looking forward to being in charge of his own social schedule now that he was married. Unfortunately Lord Hadwell had reminded him the night before of the importance of being seen this season, especially since his wife was no longer pregnant.

Must maintain the image that all is well, his father had intoned.

"I promise I will be careful," Clare said. "May I come, then?"

The earnest look on her lovely features had him whispering "Yes" right before he lowered his mouth to hers in what he imagined would be a brief kiss. Clare would likely draw back quickly as she had for more than a week. However, today she kissed him in return. It wasn't an overly long kiss, but it was no less welcome or delightful.

As he released her, he offered her a smile. "We'll leave first thing tomorrow morning."

"Thank you, Emmett."

For two or three heartbeats, she smiled. The action was nearly as short as her kiss, but it had been there nonetheless. It gave Emmett hope for the first time since finding her crumbled on the floor of her room, in pain. As long as he and Clare could smile and banter together, as long as she wasn't unhappy living with him, then surely they could weather whatever came their way.

Chapter 8

"Would you excuse us for a moment, Mr. Sharpe?" Clare threaded her arm through her husband's and forced a congenial smile for the reporter. Anger still heated her cheeks, but she maintained a calm exterior as she led Emmett to the back of the steamer. She was barely aware of Antonina following behind them.

At the rear of the ship, Clare released her hold and folded her arms tightly against her soiled robe and nightgown. She ought to be embarrassed at her appearance, but she was too grateful for having survived the past two days and too irate with Emmett to care how horribly unkempt she looked right now.

"Why is there a reporter here, Emmett?"

Her husband glanced back down the deck. "He's come to write about us."

"That was *his* explanation. I want *yours*." Clare hadn't missed the subtle panic in her husband's blue eyes when Mr. Sharpe had introduced himself. Emmett had been surprised by the reporter's appearance at this moment but not shocked to learn a reporter had come to find them here. And she wanted to know why.

He ran his hands down his unshaven face. A light beard that she found irritatingly attractive had formed along his jaw. However, the man standing before her in wrinkled, dirty clothes and a worn expression hardly resembled the witty, good-natured Lord Linwood she'd met and married last year.

"My father believes the country could use more reminders that we're happy as a couple. More than you and I simply being seen together in England while I campaign." His tone held little emotion, other than resignation. The steamer was moving by now, and Emmett stared out at the water slipping past them. "He told me before I left for Sicily that he'd hired a reporter to come here with me and write stories about us."

Clare turned to face the railing, hurt mingling dangerously with her anger. To think he'd been upset with her for not sharing sooner about her childhood. "Why didn't you tell me?"

"Because I asked him not to send anyone," Emmett countered. There was no mistaking the frustration leaking into his voice this time, though Clare wasn't sure if it was directed at her, Lord Hadwell, or the both of them. "I committed to coming here to ask you to return to England with me, but I wouldn't abide having someone along to report our every move. However, apparently my wish in that regard was only honored until the day after I boarded the steamer bound for Sicily."

His words inspired the faintest flicker of compassion inside Clare, strong enough that she couldn't ignore it. To have a father who wouldn't honor such a request was awful. "Why do you try so hard to please him?" The question slipped out almost unbidden. She'd wondered it a dozen times or more during their short marriage but hadn't found the courage to ask it outright. Now the query hung taut in the air between them.

"I'm all he has for an heir." Emmett matched her stance at the railing, his hands gripping the metal. "And yet there are many times I wonder if being his flesh and blood is enough." He spoke the last as if he hadn't meant to say it out loud.

Clare shook her head in confusion. "What do you mean?"

"What?"

"An heir is flesh and blood. What more do you need to be?"

Emmett glanced down at Antonina. How much of what they were saying did she understand? "My older brother, Alder, was supposedly everything my father longed for in an heir."

"Y-you had an older brother?" Shock at this news coursed through her.

He nodded impatiently. "Haven't you ever seen his picture hanging in the study?"

"No," Clare said, shaking her head again. She'd never been inside Lord Hadwell's study, nor had she ever wished to. "Why didn't you tell me you had a brother?"

"I . . . don't know." Emmett visibly gripped the railing tighter. "I never knew him. He died as a child before I was born. But he was responsible and serious-minded even as a boy, and my father had high hopes for his future. His death was very difficult on everyone but especially my father."

The confusion inside Clare's head shifted with sudden clarity. "That's why you try so hard to please him, to do everything he asks."

He didn't answer, but his silence was just as affirming. How horrible to constantly live in the shadow of someone he'd never even met. And yet it was still his choice and not entirely the fault of others. Emmett had allowed this stranger of a brother and Lord Hadwell's apparent adoration of Alder to keep himself perpetually grasping at an elusive and continuously changing goal—one of obtaining his father's approval.

"What's the real reason you wish to become an MP, Emmett?" Would he continue to be honest with her, even about this? She still felt angry with him, but Clare couldn't deny also feeling relief and surprise at his willingness to talk openly about his relationship with his father. "Do you truly want to do this for you?"

He threw a pained glance in her direction, then looked away. "I want to help people on a larger scale, yes. However, that isn't the only reason I've chosen to campaign." Emmett pulled in a deep breath as if bracing himself for what he must say next. Or maybe he was steeling himself against her reaction. "My father always wanted to sit in the House of Commons. However, after his father died, he was made Marquess of Hadwell at the age of eighteen."

So that was Emmett's true reason for wanting to be a politician. Clare shut her eyes against the wave of frustration that rolled over her. "That isn't—"

"Look at me, Clare." When she did, he continued. "I know what you think, but this is my chance." He grasped her gently by the shoulders. "Can't you see that? If I fulfill his dream, he'll finally see I'm every bit as worthy of being his heir as Alder was. He'll see that I'm the sort of man and son a father can be proud of."

Never before had Clare seen such vulnerability from him. It pleased and pained her to see it now. Where was such raw honesty in the days and months following both her miscarriages? Or when he'd returned after locating the body of Antonina's brother? Why did Emmett hide away such deep feelings from the world, from her?

Without thinking, she lifted her hand to touch the side of his face. The hairs on his jaw tickled her blistered palm. "This may be a chance to win your father's approval. But if it ends up not being enough, then when it will it end? When will you stop giving into his wishes and whims for your life and start living on your own terms?"

"You don't understand."

He let go of her shoulders and stepped back. She let her arm fall to her side. His rejection of her touch filled her with a far greater ache than his words. Dismissive words she could excuse; especially now that she knew the source of his desperation where his father was concerned. But not wanting her touch, even after all they'd endured the past two days? That she couldn't understand.

It did serve as a stark reminder, though, that her husband's love and support were not guaranteed. Clare was here to care for their unborn child, if she was still pregnant. She couldn't afford to lose focus by risking her heart all over again with Emmett. Doing so would only invite further pain and loneliness into her life.

"What don't I understand?" She held her head up high. "I can see how your father has knowingly or unknowingly preyed upon this comparison of yourself to your brother."

His expression turned thunderous, but he shuttered it a few seconds later. The sight of it annoyed Clare even more. Better to see and hear his anger than for him to attempt to block it out. "You have no siblings for anyone to use as a measuring stick against you."

"You're right." The admission stung a bit, but it was the truth. "That's why I had hoped we would be able to have many children. Not for them to compete and compare, but so they could love and encourage each other in who they are as unique individuals."

He looked instantly contrite. "I'm sorry, Clare. I wasn't suggesting—"

"What do you want to do about the reporter?" she interrupted. She didn't want to keep talking about children. "Does he have to stay with us at the villa?"

Emmett scrubbed a hand through his hair. The lingering dust had turned some of the dark-blond strands white, giving her a glimpse of what he might look like in another twenty years or so. "I imagine he can stay in a hotel." He looked at Antonina, then at Clare again. "That might be for the best anyway."

"He's still going to be intruding at all hours, and we'll be expected to be on our best behavior, won't we?" She didn't bother to disguise the edge behind her rhetorical question. Having a reporter in their midst, even one not staying with them, was going to complicate things even more. "We'll need to appear to be the happy couple whenever he's around."

His mouth formed a grimace. "It isn't what I wanted."

"What is it you want?" she half whispered. Was it still a life with her? Or was it only her money that he wanted?

Emmett attempted a smile, but it fell away quickly. "I want you to consider—and I truly mean consider—returning to England with me and Antonina."

"Me?" the little girl said to Emmett. He nodded and said something to her in Italian.

Clare caught the words *England* and *home*. Was that home to her? She couldn't leave Sicily right now, but she didn't like the idea of being apart from Antonina either. The child had only been in their lives for two days, and yet there was already something special and binding in the little familial unit they'd formed.

"I'll consider returning," she answered calmly, in spite of the way her heart beat rapidly at the implications. "But only after we see how things are at the villa. I'd also like to find some way to help those who lost so much in the earthquake."

That would require a few more weeks, possibly even a month. Plenty of time to determine if she was still pregnant as well as help others in this country Clare had already come to love as much as her own.

Emmett gave a stoic nod, but she could read the gratitude within his suddenly relaxed stance. "That's more than fair. Thank you."

He leaned close and gave her a kiss on the cheek. The affectionate gesture warmed and surprised Clare, especially since he hadn't wished to linger earlier with her hand on his face. Then she saw Mr. Sharpe approaching them. Disappointment riddled the pleasure of Emmett's kiss. He hadn't bestowed it for altruistic reasons; he'd been playing his part for the reporter.

The bread Clare had eaten earlier had greatly helped her hunger and nausea. But the movement of the boat was beginning to wreak havoc on her stomach. "Let's see if the captain has any tea," she announced with a smile.

"Then may I inquire after your experience during the earthquake, Lord and Lady Linwood?" Mr. Sharpe asked.

"Of course." Emmett offered Clare his arm. "Why don't we all sit down to some tea?"

As Clare accepted his grip and held Antonina's hand in her free one, she couldn't help thinking what a balancing act the next few weeks would be—between her and Emmett, between them and Antonina, and finally, between all of them and Mr. Sharpe. She'd learned and inherited plenty of skills from her father. But juggling was one she hadn't mastered yet.

It was still standing! Like the rest of Taormina, his grandfather's villa had weathered the earthquake intact.

Emmett assisted Clare and Antonina out of the cart of the kind farmer who'd offered to drive them from the waterfront to the villa. Mr. Sharpe had thankfully parted company with them after they'd posted telegrams to Emmett's parents, Clare's parents, and the young man's editor at the newspaper, assuring all that they were safe. The reporter had then claimed he was starving, something Emmett felt certain Mr. Sharpe knew nothing about, and headed off to find a restaurant after promising to visit them later at the villa.

Rushing forward up one of the outer staircases, Emmett reached the villa's front door and threw it open wide. "Signora Russo?" he called loudly. The house was all right, but what about their housekeeper and her husband?

The older Sicilian woman had endeared herself to Emmett the first time he'd come here as a boy. Her willingness to teach him Italian and bake him sweets had secured his fondness for life.

"Signora Russo, we're back!"

The door to the servants' stairs opened and crashed against the outer wall as the woman bustled through it. Despite her round girth, she still moved with agility, reaching Emmett's side in only a few strides. She threw her arms around his middle and squeezed. When he was certain he wouldn't be able to breathe again, she released him and promptly burst into tears.

"Oh, *signor, signor*. We were so afraid for you."

She embraced Clare next with no less emotion, then Miriam. Even Rushford received a hug, though Signora Russo was mindful of his patched arm. Antonina had ducked behind Emmett, where she silently watched the boisterous greetings.

Using her apron, Signora Russo dabbed at her wet cheeks as she recounted what had happened in their absence. She and Alessandro were also awakened by the sound and trembling of the earth. They ran outside and saw a mysterious circle of yellow-white light over the bay. The couple made their way to the nearest church, and eventually they joined one of the many religious processions, complete with a carried statue of St. Peter, that were marching through town. When they returned to the villa some time later, Signora Russo continued to petition the saints to protect Lord and Lady Linwood from harm.

"And you were!" she exclaimed with a clap of her hands. "But what is this?" She waved at their disheveled appearance.

Emmett briefly explained how they'd taken refuge in a field outside the city and had spent the night there, with little to eat the past two days. "Is it possible we might eat something now? Before dinner?"

"*Sì, sì.* I grab some fruit, but then . . ." She gave them all a shrewd look. "A bath for all of you before you set one toe in that dining room."

Only then did Signora Russo notice Antonina huddled behind Emmett. "Who is this?"

"This is Antonina." Emmett put his arm around the girl's shoulders. "She lost her family in the quake. Clare and I have invited her to live with us."

The older woman seemed to understand what Emmett hadn't voiced—that the girl wouldn't be a servant but a member of the family. "Little Antonina," she said in Italian as she bent down to view the girl at eye level. "How would you like a nice, hot bath and a new dress? My own daughter is all grown now, but I still have a few of her things."

Antonina looked to Emmett as if asking permission. "It's all right. You can trust Signora Russo." The child bravely lifted her chin and accepted the hand the woman held out to her.

The next hour flew by. Once all of them had eaten some fruit, Emmett headed upstairs. He was more than grateful to scrub away the dust and grime that covered him. When it came time to don a fresh pair of clothes, Rushford struggled to help with his broken arm. Finally Emmett insisted on doing as much as he could on his own. After trying so hard to ensure the survival of others, he felt a bit ridiculous about not dressing himself.

Though only three days had passed since he'd last been here, it felt strange to be inside a house. Emmett found Antonina eating in the dining room, looking somber but not terrified. Her dark hair lay drying down her back, and she wore a simple frock. Perhaps in a few days, once Antonina had settled in at the villa, he and Clare could take her to buy some new clothes.

The girl didn't smile, but her eyes lit up when she saw him. She lifted her plate for him to see what she was eating, prompting a chuckle from Emmett. "Looks and smells *magnifico*," he said as he sat down.

Clare appeared a few minutes later, as well-dressed and poised as ever. The only indicators of the horrors they'd lived through were the white bandages covering the middle of each of her hands. No doubt Signora Russo had expertly tended to Clare's blisters. Her hair was piled once more on top of her head, a fact Emmett noted with a flicker of disappointment. He'd enjoyed seeing her hair in a long braid the past few days.

"Where are Miriam and Rushford?" he asked her.

His wife took a seat beside Antonina. "They're eating in the kitchen. Both of them were able to bathe and change as well."

Emmett slid his napkin onto his lap. "Shall we pray over the food?" he asked Antonina. She blushed as if she'd done something wrong by starting, but he assured her that she was right not to wait.

Bowing his head, Emmett shut his eyes and offered a

prayer in English. He thanked God for His divine mercy in watching over all of them and expressed gratitude for Antonina coming to live with them at the villa. He asked for a blessing on the viscount and his household, then gave thanks for the beautiful meal set before them. When he finished, he noticed there were tears in Clare's eyes. Were they ones of thanksgiving? he wondered as he began to eat.

She hadn't said much to him since his confession on the steamer about his brother and father. When she had spoken, she'd acted pleasant, at least in Mr. Sharpe's company. But Emmett could tell it strained her as much as it did him to pretend things were fine in order to keep up appearances around the reporter. He was relieved to be momentarily rid of the man.

Beneath his relief and gratitude was also a feeling of rawness after sharing his deepest fear with Clare about never gaining his father's approval. Her admonition that Emmett stop trying to live a life according to Lord Hadwell's dictates had stung something fierce.

How could Clare fully grasp what it was like for him? Her parents adored her, exactly as she was. Emmett had seen it the moment the three of them had embraced each other when Mr. Herschel had come to England for the wedding. The contrast between her situation and his own had smarted. However, that didn't excuse his thoughtless remark about his wife not having any siblings. Clare had once confessed how much she'd wanted a brother or sister—it was the reason she anticipated having a whole houseful of children. But was that still what she wanted, with him?

Emmett recalled her earlier question on the boat about what *he* wanted. He'd nearly answered, "To know that you love me for me and not my title." Thankfully he'd swallowed back the words in time. He hadn't been ready in that moment to witness Clare's reaction, especially if she wasn't able or willing to offer the assurance he craved. Instead he'd petitioned her to consider returning to England. That was something else he wanted—needed, really—even if it was far less important to him than his other desire.

He hoped Clare would choose to go back with him, though it wasn't likely to be any easier to fix their marriage there than here. If anything, the strain they'd experienced on the boat, with Mr. Sharpe around, would be exacerbated once Emmett began campaigning.

A knock at the door had all three of them lifting their heads. "That's likely Mr. Sharpe," Emmett said before taking a drink.

Clare frowned and set down her fork as if no longer hungry. "My hope is he'll grow bored of asking us questions after he writes his first story."

Emmett wasn't so sure. His father had likely promised the young man a substantial amount of money for every story about them printed in the paper.

Voices echoed in the foyer, then moved toward the dining room. Belatedly, Emmett considered what Mr. Sharpe would think about Antonina eating with them. But there was nothing he could do about it, nor would he. The girl was a part of their family now.

Signora Russo opened the door. "Signor Sharpe of England to see you, Signor Linwood." The reporter entered the room. "Shall I bring him up a plate?"

"Afraid I've already eaten." Mr. Sharpe eyed the fare on the table. "Though I don't know that I could refuse eating something that smells this delicious."

The older woman beamed with pleasure. "I will get you a plate then."

Without waiting for an invitation, the reporter pulled out

a chair and sat down. His eyes widened when he saw Antonina. "I wasn't aware the child was staying with you."

"She is," Emmett said firmly.

Mr. Sharpe gave a thoughtful nod as he removed a small notebook and pencil from inside his jacket pocket. "Taking in earthquake orphans? That sort of thing makes for a good story."

"Please, don't mention it," Clare interjected. She smoothed Antonina's hair in a gesture that was both motherly and protective. "The child has been through enough already. Let's allow her to recover in peace and anonymity first."

The reporter didn't look particularly pleased with the request, but he put away his writing materials. A minute or so later, Signora Russo appeared with his dinner. Emmett hoped the young man would eat quickly and leave even sooner.

"Where are you staying, signor?" The housekeeper set a heaping plate in front of him.

Mr. Sharpe shrugged. "I hadn't yet settled on a place."

"I'm sure you'll find one of the hotels in town to your liking," Emmett said in a casual tone.

The reporter tossed an expectant glance at him and Clare. "The hotels I walked past did indeed look nice, but I'd hoped to stay close by. That is, if you possibly have any room to spare . . ."

Emmett fought the urge to groan out loud. He couldn't very well insist the man go elsewhere, unless he wanted to incur his father's displeasure. "Of course. You're welcome to stay at the villa. Signora Russo, would you mind preparing a room for our guest?"

"Not at all," she said with a nod before exiting the room.

"Thank you, Lord Linwood." The young man brandished his fork. "This will make reporting about the two of you much easier."

Emmett attempted a smile, but his mouth refused to cooperate. Clare's cheeks were pale, and when she peered at him, her eyes wore a familiar look of panic. One he could relate to. Having Mr. Sharpe stay at the villa might make things easier for the reporter, but he was the only one who benefited from the arrangement. Having the man underfoot day and night was bound to make things exponentially harder for Emmett and Clare.

London, May 1908: Seven months earlier

Seated inside his and Winfield's club, Emmett tried to focus on the conversation with his best friend, but his thoughts kept wandering to Clare and how she was faring. When they'd purchased their townhouse back in March, Clare had selected the household staff. But the hiring and training of the servants as well as furnishing the new home hadn't come without a price—just as Emmett had feared.

Clare had taken ill for an entire week. Even after recovering, though, she'd continued to turn down most of the invitations they received to social events. Emmett couldn't blame her. Attending events with a vast number of people and crowds left her feeling fatigued. So he'd taken to skipping large gatherings as well, though he tried to attend as many private dinners and receptions as he could in order to *be seen* by the right people, as his father had directed.

However, the dearth of high-profile events in their social calendar hadn't gone unnoticed by Lord Hadwell. Emmett had endured more than one unpleasant conversation with his father about the importance of doing more socially. To appease the man, Emmett had suggested hosting dinner parties for two of Clare's friends from New York, Gwen Barton and Syble Rinecroft, who were in London for the season and were American heiresses themselves. Both dinners had gone well, especially the one Winfield had attended for Miss Barton. And Emmett had been cheered by the sight of his wife looking energetic and happy for the first time in weeks. However, that had changed again yesterday.

Clare had gone to visit Helena, who had just arrived in town after giving birth to her first baby three months earlier. Meeting the boy would surely keep Clare's spirits up, or so Emmett had thought. Instead, upon returning to their house, his wife had gone straight up to her room. A short time later Emmett heard her crying.

Confused, he asked her what had happened. Her voice continued to shake with quiet sobs as she told him how holding that beautiful, healthy baby had been a painful reminder of their own loss. He'd tried to offer comfort, but all his assurances that she'd surely hold their own child in her arms someday soon only seemed to push her further into her grief.

This morning she had come down to eat breakfast with him, then excused herself to return to her room. Unsure what else to do, Emmett had gone riding in the park and invited Winfield to join him at the club this afternoon. He wasn't the only one a bit preoccupied either. Every so often his best friend would pause in what he was saying and glance to one side of the room. But Emmett couldn't see anything of interest over there.

"I believe I'll head home," Winfield suddenly announced as he rose to his feet.

Emmett raised his eyebrows. "So early? What's the hurry, Winfield?" As soon as the words were out, he realized his friend was probably bored with Emmett's lackluster attempts at conversation.

"Feeling a bit peaked."

It wasn't the answer Emmett had expected. "You sound

like an old man, chap," he said, laughing. "All you need is a nightcap and pipe to complete the picture."

"Ha. I'm no older than you," Winfield countered. "Besides, I accepted an invitation to the Stouts' dance this evening, and I'd like to rest before I go."

Emmett studied him with growing suspicion. His friend abhorred most occasions that required mingling with society. And yet here he was, planning to go to a dance. Winfield was definitely not acting like himself.

"You're attending another social event? Are you turning into a society man?"

"Hardly." His friend grimaced in a way that made Emmett smile. "But it is my hope that if I put in more of a show this season, my uncle will have less cause for complaint."

Winfield's uncle, the Duke of Moorleigh, wasn't nearly as hounding as Emmett's father when it came to participating in the season, but Emmett also knew the man didn't waste an opportunity to remind his nephew of the importance of being more social. The only society events Winfield didn't try to avoid were evenings at the opera or the theater. For that reason, Emmett had given his best friend full use of his opera box, since he and Clare weren't likely to use it much this season.

"Are you and Lady Linwood attending the dance?" Winfield asked.

A frown pulled at Emmett's mouth. "We were invited, but no, Clare and I won't be attending."

"Is something amiss?"

Emmett attempted a grateful smile. He appreciated his friend's concern, but he didn't wish to discuss his wife's miscarriage and this newest surge of mourning—or his father's annoyance at their lack of social activity. To do so would only be depressing for both of them, and it would mean admitting that he was failing to meet Lord Hadwell's expectations—yet again.

"I'll be all right. You go on, old man."

Winfield's expression was earnest as he said, "If you need anything, Linwood . . ."

Emmett nodded gravely. "I know, Winfield. And I'm grateful for it."

His friend bid him goodbye and headed for the door. Emmett remained where he was for a few more minutes before he decided to leave as well. He didn't necessarily want to return to the cloud of melancholy hanging over his house, so he opted to walk back instead of taking a cab.

He found the hum of activity and the constant flux of people in the streets comforting. And while he missed the wide-open countryside, he liked the energy of London. Clare didn't seem to mind it either, at least in small doses. Would she be more willing to attend some larger events in a few more weeks? Emmett hoped so. The nights when he'd been accompanying her to the theater or the opera during their courtship had been some of his favorite times last season.

I don't know how to help her, Lord.

Emmett stared down at the sidewalk. If only the answers he needed would appear in front of him. All of his efforts seemed to muddy things more, even when he wasn't burdening Clare with his own grief or sorrow. If only there was a way to help her smile return, a way to bring back the banter and teasing and laughter he cherished between them.

Perhaps they simply needed a change of scenery. Emmett lifted his head with renewed optimism. Once the season ended, he wanted to return to the country, but he recognized that Hadwell House wasn't Clare's first choice for a place to live away from London. What if they bought their own estate instead? Some place in Somerset to update and change as they saw fit.

The possibilities brought a smile to his face. Surely having something as wonderful as a house in the country to look forward to and plan for would help cheer his wife.

Confident once more, he quickened his pace, no longer dreading his return home. He'd share his idea with Clare first, then if she agreed, he would write a letter to his father's land agent tonight, inquiring about any estates in the area that were currently for sale. By summer's end, autumn at the latest, he and Clare would hopefully have a place in the country to call their own. A place where they would raise the children he still firmly believed would be theirs.

Chapter 9

Clare sat upright in bed, her heart thrashing at a breakneck pace. The moonlight shining through the thin curtains veiling the balcony showed nothing amiss inside her room. She'd heard a noise, though, loud enough to jerk her from sleep. As she struggled to make sense of the sound, her stomach twisted with familiar queasiness. Should she go downstairs to the kitchen and prepare some tea? What if Mr. Sharpe heard her? She didn't need him asking questions about why she was awake in the middle of the night. It was going to be hard enough trying to sneak away from the villa to see a doctor about her pregnancy without being discovered. For the hundredth time since dinner, she wished the reporter had chosen to stay elsewhere.

A child's cry pierced the air. Antonina! That was the sound that had woken Clare. Would it wake Mr. Sharpe too? She threw off her blankets and grabbed her dressing gown. Pulling it on over her nightdress, she hurried into the hall. She pushed through the door of Antonina's room and found the girl sobbing in bed.

"Antonina?" Clare rushed to her side.

The child didn't appear to be awake, though her cries were real. "Angelo! Angelo!"

"Nina, dear, wake up." She smoothed back the child's hair and touched her damp cheek. "It's all right," Clare soothed. "You're all right. It's only a bad dream."

Antonina's eyelids fluttered open. She murmured something in Italian that Clare didn't understand before she seemed to notice who sat beside her. "Clare?"

"Yes, it's me. Were you dreaming . . . about your brother?"

"*Sì.*" The little girl sat up. In the dim light, her black eyes looked even larger. "He not coming back?"

Clare swallowed the lump that rose into her throat. "No, not here on earth." She gathered Antonina onto her lap and hugged her tight. "But one day, in heaven," she whispered, "you'll see Angelo and your mother and father again."

The child sniffled and pressed her face into Clare's robe. Antonina's shoulders trembled as she wept some more. Clare gently rocked her back and forth as tears filled her own eyes. She didn't doubt that God had put this little girl directly in Emmett's path because He knew they all needed one another.

Kissing the top of Antonina's head, Clare blinked away the salty moisture and murmured words of comfort. She didn't expect the child to understand all of the English words, but they seemed to calm Antonina.

Clare was about to settle the child back in bed when she heard a muffled noise from down the hall. Was someone else awake? Someone who had heard Antonina's crying? Clare hoped it wasn't the reporter. Glancing down, she found Antonina staring up at her. So much for the girl falling back asleep.

"I'll be right back," she reassured her. "I'm going to see what that sound is."

Antonina clung to her, though. Clare couldn't blame her, not after the girl's horrible dream. "All right. We'll go see what it is together."

She kept the girl's hand in her own as they walked quietly into the corridor. But Clare heard nothing more as they moved past her room, then Emmett's, followed by two empty guest rooms, and finally Mr. Sharpe's.

"Hmm," Clare murmured, mostly to herself. "Maybe it was something outside."

They retraced their steps down the hallway, back toward Antonina's bedroom. As they drew alongside Emmett's door the second time, Clare heard the noise again. It sounded like a muffled shout. Would it wake Mr. Sharpe? Clare turned the handle and led Antonina into the room. Emmett shifted restlessly beneath his blankets. Moving closer, Clare thought she detected a sheen of sweat on his face. His eyes were shut, but his lips were moving.

"I can't reach him," he suddenly cried out, making Clare jump and Antonina whimper. Was Emmett dreaming of Angelo too? His next words were her answer. "You'll have to jump, Angelo! I can't reach you."

She needed to wake Emmett—both for himself, to halt his suffering, and to prevent him from rousing anyone else, especially Mr. Sharpe. Taking a seat on the bed, Clare used her free hand to shake Emmett's shoulder. "Emmett! Wake up. You're dreaming. It isn't real, not anymore."

Clare had to shake him twice more before he jerked to a sitting position. "What's wrong? What's happening? Is it another earthquake?"

"No. Everything's fine." Or it would be if Mr. Sharpe kept right on sleeping. "You and Antonina were both having bad dreams." Clare rubbed the child's back.

Emmett scrubbed his hands down his face. "Thank you . . . for waking me."

"Are you all right?"

He nodded slowly, though Clare could tell he was still

shaken. Compassion moved her to reach out and clasp his hand in hers. "Do you want to talk about your dream . . . in a little while?" she asked, glancing pointedly at Antonina. Even if the little girl wouldn't understand the words, it would likely be distressing for her to be in the room when he shared the details.

Emmett didn't answer right away. When he raised his chin to look at Clare, his expression was anguished. But the emotion faded from his features as he said, "No, I'll be fine."

Four little words, innocuous ones, really. And yet they had the power to reopen the chasm between them. Clare bit back a protest as she rose to her feet. "Do you think you can sleep now, Nina?" The child shook her head.

"I'll sit up with her until she's sleepy again." Emmett climbed out of bed and onto his feet.

"Are you sure?"

"Yes, it's only fair after we both woke you."

She considered arguing, but her nausea was getting harder to ignore. Without tea, the best thing to do would be to return to sleep. Clare guided Antonina back to the girl's bedroom, Emmett coming behind them. Inside the room, he opened the balcony door and grabbed one of the armchairs. Rather than positioning it beside the bed, though, he maneuvered the chair so it sat halfway onto the balcony.

"What do you say to sitting outside for a bit?" he said to Antonina, first in English then in Italian. The girl gave a vigorous nod of approval.

Clare stared askance at the two of them. "It's chilly outside." She pulled her robe tighter around her to confirm it.

"I'll be sure she's bundled up nice and warm in some blankets." And he did. Taking two blankets from the bed, Emmett wound them around Antonina, then he scooped her up.

"What if one of you gets sick sitting out there the rest of the night?"

He settled into the chair with Antonina on his knee. "When she falls asleep, I'll put her back in bed and close the door. I promise."

"I don't understand."

His tone was almost pleading. "Being inside tonight is reminding me too much of being in that hotel room. A bit of fresh air, even if it's bracing, is a good reminder that all of us are safe."

Clare could partially relate—tonight she'd struggled to fall asleep at first, trying to convince herself the walls and ceiling were not caving in around her. "I'll bid you both good night then." She bent and kissed Antonina's cheek. "Good night, Nina."

"Good night, Clare."

The child's quiet response wound itself around Clare's heart. "Good night, Emmett," she said next, touching his sleeve.

"Thank you again."

The earnestness in his voice added to the feeling of closeness. Clare returned to her own room, unsure how long it would take her to return to sleep, but praying it would happen soon.

The next thing she became aware of was sunshine spilling in through the window. She'd fallen asleep after all. Hopefully Emmett and Antonina had as well. Miriam arrived a few minutes later with tea. After drinking it all, Clare dressed. She peeked into Antonina's room and was relieved to find the child still slumbering. True to his word, Emmett had set her back in bed, put the chair in place, and shut the balcony door. Had he been able to get any more sleep himself?

She went downstairs to the dining room and stopped

short at the sight of Mr. Sharpe already seated at the table next to Emmett. Clare had momentarily forgotten about the reporter. Both men rose from their chairs when she entered the room.

"Good morning, my dear." Emmett held out a chair for her.

Before she sat, he leaned close and kissed her on the cheek. Clare couldn't help peering at him in surprise. Was his kiss a token of gratitude for her help last night? Or had he felt the same brief closeness she had?

"Quite the caring couple. That'll help win elections, to be sure."

Her attention snapped to Mr. Sharpe, who was watching them like a doting parent. Reality washed over her as Clare dropped into her seat. Neither Emmett's kiss nor his endearment were sincere—nor were they truly meant for her. He was playacting to his audience, and she was required to do the same.

"Good morning, darling." She managed to infuse the greeting with some cheerfulness. "How are you this morning, Mr. Sharpe? Did you sleep well?"

The reporter dabbed his mouth with his napkin. "I slept better than I have in ages, Lady Linwood. Must be the warmer air here."

"I'm sure it must," she murmured as Signora Russo appeared with her plate.

Clare was relieved the man hadn't been awakened by Emmett and Antonina's nightmares, but his presence still complicated things. Though she'd fallen back asleep herself, she was still exhausted from last night. A close look at Emmett revealed lines of fatigue around his mouth and eyes too. But they had to pretend that everything, especially between the two of them, was wonderful.

The thought left her with a growing headache. It was going to be another long day.

By mid-afternoon, Emmett was desperate to escape Mr. Sharpe. He'd already given the young man a tour of the villa and answered questions about his political leanings and even more about his experiences during the earthquake.

Talking about Messina had unfortunately made Emmett recall his nightmare from last night. He'd been climbing the rope outside of the building where Antonina and her brother had lived. However, in his dream, the building began to crumble slowly while he was still hanging from the rope. Emmett shouted at Angelo to jump. But the stones started dropping faster and faster, yanking Angelo away from Emmett's grasp and shaking him to the core. It had taken him a few seconds to realize the shaking was actually Clare trying to wake him.

He'd considered accepting her invitation to tell her about his dream, once Antonina had returned to sleep, especially after Clare had tenderly held his hand. But then he had decided against it. His wife had gone through enough herself during the quake without him burdening her with more shocking details. Besides, sharing something so horrible with anyone still felt too private to him.

Anxious to avoid a repeat of his dream, he'd been more than happy to sit up with Antonina. Emmett had made certain she was sleeping peacefully before he returned to his room. But every time he closed his eyes, he saw Angelo's crushed body. He'd eventually fallen into a restless sleep sometime before dawn.

"I believe I'll go for a walk," he declared as he set aside

the book he'd been trying to read. With the exception of Antonina, who'd asked if she could help Signora Russo, the rest of them had congregated in the drawing room. Clare sat beside him on the settee, hemming another dress that had belonged to Signora Russo's daughter. The size was close enough to Antonina's to be comfortable, but Clare wanted a more exact fit. Mr. Sharpe was writing at the desk in the corner.

The reporter twisted in his chair. "That's a capital idea. I'll join you, Lord Linwood."

Not so capital anymore, Emmett thought grumpily. He was tired of playing his role as his half of a congenial couple, tired of having so little to do after several intense days of survival, and tired of the reporter's constant presence.

"Have you seen any of the cathedrals yet?" he asked, an idea forming. Perhaps there was a way to buy them all a little time away from the young man's questions after all.

Mr. Sharpe shook his head. "No, but I should like to."

"Wonderful." Emmett stood. If he remembered correctly, there was an old priest who was known to give very long, very thorough tours of one of the cathedrals. That was where he'd take Mr. Sharpe first. "Would you like to come with us, dearest?"

Clare's lips pressed together, but he didn't know if it was over a frown or a smile. They'd been trading endearments since this morning. "No, thank you. But Antonina may wish to go."

"I'll see if she wants to come too," he said. "Then I'll meet you in the foyer, Mr. Sharpe."

Emmett made his way downstairs. One voice came from the direction of the kitchen—Signora Russo's—which meant Antonina was still choosing to say little. He was saddened by the thought. As he entered the room, he realized Signora

Russo was speaking both Italian and English in an obvious attempt to teach the child more of the new language.

When Emmett started to ask in Italian if Antonina wanted to go for a walk, his housekeeper wagged her finger at him. "She needs to learn the English."

"You're right, signora." He turned to address Antonina a second time. "Would you like to go for a walk?" Signora Russo nodded in approval, then moved toward the stove. With the housekeeper's back turned, Emmett winked at Antonina and walked his fingers in the air to further demonstrate what he was asking.

One corner of the girl's mouth lifted. It was the nearest thing to a smile Emmett had yet seen from her, and the sight of it warmed him. "Yes, I go walk."

"Yes, I would like to go for a walk," Signora Russo corrected.

After Antonina repeated the words, Emmett applauded her efforts. Signora Russo rummaged up a small coat and had the girl try it on. It was slightly short in the wrists, but it would do. Once ready, he and Antonina went upstairs to meet Mr. Sharpe.

The three of them walked to the nearest cathedral. The reporter looked suitably impressed with the building, even before they went inside. Emmett introduced Mr. Sharpe to the old priest, who was thankfully still around. Before the priest began expounding on the church's vast history, Emmett excused himself and Antonina. "Feel free to return to the villa when you're finished here, Mr. Sharpe."

The young man appeared a bit flummoxed as to what to do, but the priest motioned for him to come along. With a shrug, the reporter complied.

Emmett took in a deep breath that tasted of freedom as he and Antonina headed away from the cathedral. Neither of them spoke as they walked hand in hand down the street, but it was a companionable silence. The contrast between Taormina and Messina made him feel as if he walked on a different planet. Had the viscount seen a doctor yet about the gash to his head? What of the old couple Emmett had assisted from the hotel? Had they escaped?

The farther they walked, the more Emmett realized they weren't alone in taking to the streets today, but they were the only ones empty-handed. Dozens of people passed them, heading in the opposite direction, with bundles in their arms. Curious, Emmett stopped a middle-aged gentleman and inquired where he was going.

"Why, to Giardini," he replied in an American accent.

Emmett studied him in confusion. "It's four miles away. And you're walking all the way there?"

"There's no other way to reach Giaridini now. The earthquake made a real mess of the roads between here and there."

"What is in Giardini?"

It was the older man's turn to look puzzled. "Where have you been, son? There have been refugees and wounded passing through there since yesterday." He hoisted the wrapped bundle in his arms. "They're in desperate need of bread and bandages. Some of them don't even have more than a stitch of clothes on—"

"That's brilliant," Emmett exclaimed. Another idea was formulating in his mind. At the man's severe frown, he quickly shook his head. "Not brilliant that they're in need. It's . . . oh, never mind. Thank you for answering my questions. We must be off now."

He swept Antonina up onto his shoulders and hurried as fast as he could back toward the villa. "Clare?" he called as they entered the house. She was coming down the staircase.

"Oh, you're back already?"

Emmett noticed she had on her hat and coat. "Were you going somewhere?"

"I thought I might step out for a while too," she said, her cheeks turning pink as if with embarrassment. "Did you forget something?"

He set Antonina on her feet. "No. I've just had an idea of how we might help the other earthquake victims. I'll explain once everyone is assembled." Emmett called for the rest of the household to come to the foyer.

Once Miriam, Rushford, and the Russos had joined them, he repeated what the American gentleman had said about the refugees in Giardini. "I'd like to gather up any and all sizes of spare clothing and whatever bread we have in the villa. And material for bandages, if we've got that too." They started to scatter before he recalled something else. "We'll need to wear sturdy shoes to carry everything to Giardini. Apparently the roads are impassable right now for all but foot traffic."

Though it would involve an eight-mile, round-trip walk, everyone wanted to come, including Antonina. The little girl held a sack of bread, while Emmett held another sack of food and a jug of water. He and Clare had both donated clothing for the refugees, which she and Miriam carried. Even Antonina had insisted they give the dress Clare had been hemming to another child in need. The Russos and Rushford had more food, some bandages, and another jug of water between the three of them.

The trek wasn't as arduous as Emmett had believed it would be, though it was still necessary to watch one's step. But friendly conversation and the steady stream of people heading to and from Giardini made the time pass quickly and brought a feeling of camaraderie to the air.

Emmett almost felt badly Mr. Sharpe was missing it. This was a far more interesting story than anything to do with him and Clare. He'd left a note for the reporter on the foyer table, explaining where they had all gone, since the young man was likely to return to the villa before them.

In spite of seeing scores of homeless, wounded, and dying in Messina, Emmett still felt a jolt of shock at the sight that awaited their arrival in Giardini. Many of the people had on little to no clothing, while others were covered in mud. A number of the wounded were without bandages, since they hadn't yet received medical care. On nearly every face, he saw the same dazed expression of shock and hunger that had plagued their own group. Is this how he and the others had looked to their rescuers just yesterday? It felt as though days had passed since they'd left the quake-ravaged city, instead of barely twenty-four hours.

He approached a man about his own age whose leg appeared to be broken. Emmett pulled a loaf of bread from his sack and handed it to the stranger. The other man whispered "*Grazie*," then immediately gave half the loaf to the old man seated beside him. They looked as if they might be son and father.

The stranger's murmur of gratitude was repeated over and over again as Emmett passed around the food and water they'd brought. He never heard a word of complaint. In contrast, everyone seemed thankful and eager to share their portion with those around them.

At first Antonina stuck close to his side. Emmett wasn't sure if she felt shy or alarmed at the obvious suffering. When they came upon a group of children, though, overseen by a nun in a dirty, tattered habit, the girl finally ventured forward to hand some bread to another child. After that, Antonina insisted on helping him pass around the provisions until there was nothing left.

Holding the empty sacks and jug in one hand, Emmett took Antonina's hand in the other and went in search of his wife. He found his valet and the Russos distributing more supplies among the refugees. Miriam was nearby, assisting a group of women who were passing around jugs and cups of water. But where was Clare?

Emmett spied her at last, kneeling beside a middle-aged woman. Using a comb she must have brought along, Clare was untangling the woman's long hair. Even from a distance, Emmett could see the profound effect of the simple act of kindness. The woman had tears spilling down her cheeks, and she appeared to be speaking in low tones to Clare. As he and Antonina drew closer, Emmett could see there were tears in Clare's eyes too.

Not wishing to disrupt the poignant moment and also eager to seize the chance to watch Clare, he stopped before she saw him. The sorrow and empathy in her expression stirred something deep inside him. Here was the woman he'd married—a woman with whom he could laugh and banter but also one whose generosity and kind nature put others immediately at ease.

If only he could unburden his darkest doubts and tragedies to her as this stranger was doing. And yet what if Clare didn't understand, or what if he unintentionally drove her back into the melancholy of her own grief by talking?

Questions burned Emmett's tongue, desperate for release. What was the real reason his wife had come to Sicily without him? Did she want to return with him to England? It had been less than a day of pretending to be a happy couple, but already, it was taking its toll on both of them. Campaigning for a seat in the House of Commons would only intensify the necessity of playacting. Would they ever get past that and go back to when they hadn't needed to pretend? Or was going forward, starting afresh, the only way to heal the rift that seemed to constantly narrow and widen between them?

"Are you finished?"

Emmett glanced up to find Clare standing in front of him. "Uh, yes. We've no more food." He lifted the empty sacks. "Antonina helped me pass it around."

"That's wonderful." Clare gave the little girl a quick embrace around the shoulders. "I only wish there was more we could do for them." Her gaze swept the assembled crowd.

"I do as well."

Their efforts weren't in vain, though. Having been homeless themselves for two days, Emmett recognized the magnitude of what a little bread, water, clothing, and kindness could do. Of course, after two days of privation, he had been able to return to his home and his wealth. He hadn't lost his possessions or his family. There were few people before him who were as fortunate. Nearly all of these people had no homes or livelihoods to return to.

Emmett led Clare and Antonina to where the others were waiting to walk back to Taormina. "We can come again tomorrow and the next day," he reassured Clare, "and for however long they'll have refugees passing through."

"I'd like that."

As they began walking, he threw Clare another glance. "That was a very clever thing you did, bringing a comb along."

"Thank you. It was something I wished we'd had while we were in that field."

"Did that woman tell you her story?"

She nodded, her expression pained. "I didn't understand most of it, but what I did was so sad." Her voice wobbled as Clare continued. "Apparently she lost both her parents, her husband, and three children in the quake. She's the only member of her family who survived."

The tragic tale was a sobering reminder for Emmett. He'd been in no danger of losing his parents and siblings, but Clare might have been killed in the earthquake. That horrid possibility prompted a physical ache inside him—and not just because Clare was someone he'd once cared a great deal about.

She was still his wife, the woman he'd fallen in love with. Surely that was reason enough to try to make things work. If that meant going backward or forward or whatever direction they must to see if they could truly be together again, then that was what Emmett wanted most of all.

Somerset, England, September 1908: Three months earlier

Clare shut her eyes and tilted her face toward the sunshine bursting through the clouds. If only she could store up every drop of warmth and light before she needed to return from her walk. Opening her eyes, she whistled for Bran, who'd gone off exploring. The dog reappeared a few moments later, and Clare commenced her wander down the worn country path.

Maybe instead of returning to the house, she ought to keep walking until she reached the sea. Then she'd commission a boat to take her back home to New York or to Sicily—anywhere but Hadwell House. This estate held so few happy memories for her and so many darker ones now that she had miscarried for the second time.

She'd not been as far along in this pregnancy as she had been the first time. But that didn't take away the physical aches and fatigue or her profound grief at the loss of her dreams to be a mother—again. Tears leaked from her lashes, and Clare made no effort to stop them. It was a relief to let them fall unchecked without being burdened by the disapproving looks of her father-in-law, the expressions of pity from her mother-in-law, or the infuriating optimism of her husband.

There had been one brief moment of shared sadness with

Emmett when the doctor had informed them that Clare's pregnancy had ended. The sorrow and disappointment she'd seen on his handsome face had given her such hope. Hope that this time Emmett would grieve aloud, with her—that they would work through this together. But all too soon, he'd hidden his emotions behind a matter-of-fact expression and words of gratitude for the doctor's assistance.

Unlike last time, Clare hadn't seen another hint of mourning in his eyes in the last month. Any time he spoke with her he seemed determined to maintain his *everything will turn out right in the end* attitude. Still, she'd tried sharing with him her own feelings of grief, hoping it might help them both understand each other better. But whenever she did, Emmett appeared distressed and eager to escape. The last two weeks she'd given up trying altogether. Instead she'd poured out her pain in private, in prayer, in letters to her parents, and occasionally in confessions to Miriam.

This second disappointment of not producing an heir had apparently revived Emmett's efforts to find them a house in the country. When they'd returned last month to Somerset from London, they'd followed up on several possibilities. After Clare had miscarried, though, she'd been too ill to accompany Emmett when he went to scout out properties. Last week, he'd left again on the hunt for a home, and Clare had been almost grateful for his absence.

It wasn't that she wanted to remain at Hadwell House. The trapped feeling she'd experienced living here after her first miscarriage had returned. She'd also found herself thinking often of what Lady Melinda had told her last winter. That Emmett had married Clare first and foremost for her money. Was their increased strain and her husband's single focus to find a house—one that he would use her money to purchase—proof that the widow had been right after all?

"Oh, Bran." Clare paused to rub the dog's fur. "Will things ever be right again?"

Emmett believed so, but it felt like ages to Clare since they'd last teased each other or since he'd given her more than a quick kiss on the cheek at breakfast. She longed for the ease and companionship they'd begun to enjoy once more this summer. Could they be that way again, even after Clare's heart had been shattered repeatedly, not only by the losses but also by the loneliness of suffering through them on her own?

The dog nudged her with his nose, soliciting a small smile from Clare. She was grateful they'd be taking Bran with them wherever they moved. Here, at least, was one member of the family who asked nothing from her that he wasn't also willing to give in return. Bran didn't care if she was an heiress or a milk maid. He didn't look down on her for not being able to stay pregnant either or for not knowing how to get Emmett to talk openly with her.

"Clare!"

She turned at the sound of her husband's voice. Bran did too, then the dog raced toward Emmett, who bent and tussled with him. The happy image they made renewed Clare's tears. Only this time, there was a measure of thankfulness intermingled with the regret. She wouldn't stop feeling her sorrow. If she did, she feared it would fester. But she could welcome and seek out these tiny glints of joy too.

"I thought I might find you walking out this way," Emmett said as he stood.

Clare raised her eyebrows in surprise. He'd noticed where she liked to walk? Were there other things he noticed about her but didn't say? "When did you get back?" She fell into step with him and Bran as they headed toward the house.

"Just now, and I have good news." The grin he sent her way was reminiscent of those he'd offered when they had first met. "I found us a house. It's a few hours' drive from here, and it is called Barksley Hall."

Clare didn't have to manufacture an answering smile. At last they would have a home of their own, one they could fill with laughter, love, and affection—all the things she had envisioned when she'd agreed to marry Emmett.

"That's wonderful," she replied. "How soon can we move in?"

Some of Emmett's excitement faded at her question. "On that, I'm not quite certain. It's a very old house, and as such, it is in need of extensive repairs. The main house, the stables, and the tenant housing all require a great deal of work. However . . ." He turned an expectant gaze on her. "That also means we may do with the place as we please. We can tear down wings or add more—remodel it entirely to our tastes. Anything we like, my dear."

She hadn't heard such warmth behind his endearment in weeks. "When can we begin?"

"We should allow you to completely recover first, Clare." He clasped his hands behind his back. "I don't want you becoming as ill as you did at the start of the season."

Emmett didn't look at her as he said this, but Clare sensed the worry he'd clearly felt back then but hadn't voiced. He did still care about her, even if he refused to share his feelings with her. Was that enough for them to build on going forward?

"I'd first like to take you to see the place in a week or two, if you're up to it. We can stay in the village near the estate while we decide if we want to purchase it." He kicked at a clump of grass with the toe of his shoe. "If we do move forward, then Rushford and I will need to stay nearby, so I can hire the needed help and oversee the project."

Clare knew what he wasn't saying—she would need to remain at Hadwell House during that time. She fought a sigh at the thought of more weeks with only his parents for company. At least Emmett would likely leave Bran with her. "I think that sounds like a good plan. But as soon as there are any livable rooms inside, I'd like to stay there with you."

Emmett turned to face her, his disbelief evident. "You wouldn't rather wait until the place is completely finished?"

"No," Clare said firmly.

He gave a thoughtful nod. "That might work. If we set a few of the rooms to rights, you could stay a week or two while we figure out what changes to make. I want to know how you wish the place to look, Clare. This is to be our home after all."

She'd hoped to stay permanently, not just for a week, but . . . "Our home," she repeated.

On impulse, she slipped her arm through his and tucked close to his side. Emmett again appeared surprised at her response, but after a moment, he rested his hand over hers. The gesture, though simple, felt marvelous. Maybe he'd been right about trying to find them a house of their own. Maybe this project would finally bring the healing and closeness they needed.

Chapter 10

An entire week had passed since the earthquake. And yet Clare still hadn't been able to slip away from the villa, alone, in order to visit the doctor without raising anyone's suspicions, particularly Mr. Sharpe's. Her first attempt the day after their return to Taormina had been complicated by Emmett and Antonina's abrupt return to the villa after going for a walk. Clare's disappointment at not making it to the doctor had quickly faded, though, after Emmett had outlined his idea for bringing aid to the refugees passing through Giardini.

Unfortunately, after missing out on that first trip to the refugees, Mr. Sharpe had doubled his efforts to follow Clare and Emmett around at all times. He was there at every meal and on the long walks they continued to make from Taormina to Giardini and back. The only time the reporter's attention was diverted was during the daily interactions with the refugees. Only then, using Emmett as a translator, did Mr. Sharpe turn his observant eye and questioning tongue on others. He'd already catalogued in his little notebook a great number of stories from the earthquake, which he shared each night at dinner. Some of them were miraculous and others were so heartrending they made Clare weep.

The days were blessedly busy with relief work, leaving little time for Clare to worry over the possible fate of her pregnancy or whether Mr. Sharpe actually believed she and Emmett were happy in their marriage. Nights were different. If she wasn't waking from a bad dream of her own, she was being awakened by Emmett or Antonina and their nightmares.

Anxious to keep their private trauma a secret for as long as possible, Clare would sleep fitfully, afraid she wouldn't hear the other two before Mr. Sharpe did. One night Emmett volunteered to sleep in the chair in Antonina's room to give Clare a reprieve, but his own dreaming had woken the girl. So they'd abandoned that plan. He still wouldn't divulge the details of his nightmare, and Clare had stopped asking. It was evident, though, by the tortured look in his eyes each time she had to wake him that the dream felt much too real.

Her nausea was worse when she was up in the middle of the night. Clare hoped that meant all was proceeding on schedule with her unborn baby. But, after vomiting one night when the other two had gone back to bed, she decided to go belowstairs and make some tea. After that, she prepared it for herself and whoever else couldn't sleep. In spite of all the nocturnal activities, it appeared Mr. Sharpe was still none the wiser, to Clare's immense relief.

The lack of real rest was beginning to take its toll on her, though. No amount of home remedies or cold cream could completely erase the dark smudges forming beneath her eyes.

In contrast, Emmett didn't appear to be affected by little sleep, other than some new lines on his face. If anything, he seemed to have more energy. He worked tirelessly, carrying supplies to the refugees and translating their stories for Mr. Sharpe. Then just yesterday, he'd come up with a long-term plan for assisting the refugees who were currently staying with others in Taormina. He and another British resident of the city would pay a modest wage to any of the male refugees who were willing to repair the roads. The work would begin tomorrow. Emmett had also made arrangements to pay a local cobbler to make shoes for the earthquake victims.

Clare was proud of his efforts. His confidence in himself had grown, even in the short time he'd been away from his father's domineering presence. She was certain now that Emmett would make an excellent MP in his own right. But would she be there to see it? She still hadn't decided if she would return to England with him or not. Maybe once she saw the doctor, she would have a better idea of what to do.

Lowering the comb in her hand, she patted the shoulder of the old woman whose black-gray hair Clare had been brushing. She'd come to be known as the "comb lady." Earlier in the week, she and Miriam and some other women had set up a hair-washing and brushing station for the female refugees. Those who weren't severely injured were able to have the mud, blood, and stones washed from their hair as well as have it combed.

It was a simple thing, but Clare had seen that first day in Giardini how meaningful it could be to have one's hair tended to—the way it made these women feel human again. And just like the woman whose hair Clare had combed that day, these other refugees would share their tales of loss as their hair was washed and brushed.

Clare rose slowly to her feet. Her legs were sore after sitting for so long. She looked to where she'd last seen Antonina, passing out bread with Rushford. The girl had grown more and more morose this week, especially each afternoon when they returned to the villa. But every morning, Antonina insisted on coming along to help the refugees. Clare was worried about her. The child's English vocabulary was increasing each day, but there were still long stretches when Antonina chose not to say much at all.

She spotted Antonina in the crowd and decided to see if the girl wanted to switch tasks. Before Clare could reach her, though, Antonina snapped to attention, her gaze fixed on something or someone up ahead. The child suddenly darted forward, calling out, "Angelo! Angelo!"

Realization slammed into Clare as she hurried after the little girl. Antonina clearly believed her brother might still be alive somehow. Was that why the child had refused to remain behind with someone at the villa while the rest of them visited Giardini? Had she been hoping to find her brother among the refugees? That would explain why, when each day ended in disappointment, Antonina had become more despondent.

"Oh, Nina." Clare knew how the scene before her would play out.

Sure enough, the girl latched onto the shirt of a tall boy. But when he turned around, Antonina froze. It wasn't her brother. Even from a distance, Clare saw the total look of dejection that settled on the child's face before she slumped to her knees with a cry.

Clare rushed toward her. "Antonina!" She gathered the girl onto her lap and rocked her back and forth.

"Not him . . . Clare," Antonina said between sobs. "Not him."

"I know. And I'm so sorry, sweetheart. So very, very sorry."

They had attracted some attention, including that of Mr. Sharpe. The reporter came over. "Who is Angelo?"

"Her brother," Clare responded in a tight voice. She climbed to her feet, then helped Antonina stand as well before putting her arm protectively around the girl's shoulders. "I need to take her back to the villa. Have you seen Lord Linwood?"

For once the young man didn't ask any additional questions. Instead he pointed back toward Taormina. "They're determining where to start work on the roads."

"Thank you."

Mr. Sharpe gave her a nod, as if he understood her gratitude was for more than telling her where to find Emmett. After locating Miriam, Clare explained that she and Antonina were heading back early. The maid took one look at them and volunteered to come too, in the event either of them needed anything. Clare shared their plan a second time with Rushford and the Russos. Then, with Clare holding tight to the child's hand, the three of them began the trek back to Taormina.

They came upon Emmett a short while later. "Heading back already?" he said when he saw them.

Clare nodded. "Antonina isn't . . . feeling well."

"What's wrong?" His expression immediately changed from curiosity to concern.

Clare had Miriam take the child in hand and motioned for Emmett to move a few feet away. "She thought she saw Angelo today," she explained in a quiet voice. "It wasn't him, of course, but she was so upset. I think she's been hoping all week to find him among the refugees."

"I'm not sure I understand." Emmett frowned and glanced back in Antonina's direction. "She knows he isn't still alive."

Clare shrugged. "Knowing something doesn't stop you from hoping it will be different."

His gaze returned to hers. Did Emmett sense that she was talking about more than Antonina and the girl's hopes regarding her brother?

Clare had been given many opportunities to observe her husband the past week, and over and over, she'd seen glimpses of the man she had married. She'd seen him in the way

Emmett interacted with the refugees, in the way he listened to them and reverently repeated their stories to Mr. Sharpe. She'd seen him when he had made Antonina chuckle one afternoon as he told the girl a story. She'd seen him in his request for simple dinners because it meant less work for Signora Russo after baking bread for the refugees.

In those moments, she had seen the man who'd loved her, not her money. The man who would surely weather and feel every difficulty with her. And yet things were still complicated between them. Emmett hadn't grieved with her or wanted her to stay at Barksley Hall. He didn't even really need her to come back to England with him—he needed her money and perhaps her smiling show of support to make him look like a better candidate. But none of that had anything to do with *her*.

"I'm worried," she said, interrupting the yawning silence between them. "She isn't sleeping well, and now this." Looking around, Clare lowered her voice even more. "I think you need to speak with her, Emmett."

He looked genuinely puzzled. "What do you mean?"

"Other than Rushford, you're the only other person who was there with her. With Angelo. If you were to talk to her about that morning—"

Emmett shook his head, his jaw set in a firm line. "I don't see what difference that would make. It would only upset her more."

Why was he so stubborn when it came to talking about hard things? Why couldn't he see that doing so could be healing for both him and Antonina? Clare pressed her lips over the questions. She didn't wish to argue in front of others.

"Is there something else we can do for her?" Emmett asked.

Despite his reticence, Clare knew how much he cared about Antonina. "I'll think about it."

"I will too."

She offered him a brief smile, relieved that at least with Antonina, she wasn't left to manage things entirely on her own. "We'll see you later then." She took a step toward Miriam and Antonina.

Emmett's hand on her elbow stopped her. "Would you like me to walk her back?"

"No," she said, though she was touched by his offer. "You've just begun your project here."

"If you're sure." He lowered his arm, but he continued to peer at her. "Nina is lucky to have someone as kind and attentive as you to be her mother now."

The warmth of his tone and the compliment behind his words poked anew at Clare's buried hopes. She hurried to avert her face as they returned to Antonina's side. She didn't want Emmett seeing the sheen of moisture forming on her lower lashes. But the tears were hard to contain, especially when Emmett crouched down in front of Antonina, murmured reassurances to the girl in Italian, and gave her a hug.

Yes, dear little one, Clare thought as she, Antonina, and Miriam began the long walk back to the villa. *What we know to be true and what we still hope for can be nearly impossible to reconcile.*

It wasn't until they neared Taormina that Clare realized the fortuitous opportunity she'd been given. There was no Mr. Sharpe following them, and even Emmett was occupied for the rest of the afternoon. Maybe now she could finally see the doctor. She'd learned shortly after returning to Sicily that there was an American doctor in town.

Clare peered down at Antonina. The child hadn't spoken

since the incident in Giardini. Would the girl prefer to go straight to the villa with Miriam or remain with Clare? After the emotionally taxing incident, she suspected Antonina would wish to stay with her, wherever she went. Hopefully a visit to the doctor wouldn't take long.

Making up her mind, Clare turned to Miriam. "I'd like to stop by the doctor's before going to the villa." The maid already knew Clare hadn't yet been able to go and had even expressed concern that her mistress not wait much longer.

"I think that's wise, my lady." She looked at Antonina walking silently beside Clare. "Do you want me to take her back to the villa?"

Clare shook her head. "No, I think she'll want me close by. Will you sit with her while I visit with the doctor, though?"

"Of course, my lady."

She smiled in gratitude as they turned the corner onto the next street. Eagerness and a fresh knot of nerves added energy to Clare's footsteps. When the three of them reached the man's office, Dr. Muller informed her there was one patient ahead of her.

Antonina sat on Miriam's lap in one of the chairs set up for waiting. But Clare couldn't sit, preferring to pace the tiny space instead. Finally the person ahead of her exited, and the doctor motioned for her to enter the examining room. She stepped inside and took a seat in the chair he indicated.

"What may I do for you, Lady Linwood?" he asked after Clare had introduced herself.

She blew out her breath slowly. Would he think her negligent for not coming sooner? Regardless, she told herself, she was here now. She shared the history of her previous pregnancies, how far along she believed she was this time, and the doctor's advice she'd received back in England that a warmer climate might increase her chances of avoiding another miscarriage.

"I'm hoping his counsel proves correct," she said, staring down at her hands clasped tightly in her lap. "There's one more thing you need to know." Clare lifted her chin to look directly at the man. "I was in Messina last week, during the earthquake."

Dr. Muller stared with open mouth at her. "I've treated a number of the earthquake victims this week. Very few of them walked away unscathed. But you were not injured at all?"

Clare briefly described the events of those two days. "I would have come sooner when I arrived back in Taormina, but . . . well, it wasn't possible before today. I've still been ill in the morning and at night, and I'm hoping that means everything is still progressing."

"It may."

His noncommittal response left her feeling unnerved once more, but Clare did her best to remain calm. Once the examination was complete and she was again seated in the chair, she waited with thudding heart for the doctor's diagnosis. He took a moment to remove the glasses he'd put on and wipe them with a cloth he pulled from his pocket. His silence was tortuous.

"I believe thanks may be in order, Lady Linwood," he said at last. "To both that preceptive doctor in Britain and the Good Lord in heaven."

It was Clare's turn to gape at him. Did he mean what she hoped? "Are you saying that I'm . . ."

"You are indeed still pregnant." He finally gave her a smile as he put away his glasses.

Too overcome to speak, she pressed her hand to her mouth.

"That being said," the doctor moved toward the door, "you need far more rest, especially after surviving last week's quake."

Clare nodded as she climbed to her feet. "Speaking of rest, my husband and I have taken in a little girl who lost her family in the earthquake. She has nightmares nearly every night."

"Unfortunately, that is all too common after experiencing something traumatic. Has she shown any other signs of distress? Complaints of pain? Lack of appetite?"

Clare tried to remember. Most meals she concentrated so completely on appearing to be friendly with her husband in front of Mr. Sharpe that she was unable to notice much else. But it seemed there'd been a handful of times this week when she'd caught Antonina pushing her food around her plate instead of eating it.

"She hasn't complained of being in any physical pain, though she has shown some lack of appetite. Today has been particularly difficult for her," Clare admitted. "I think she's secretly been hoping her older brother is still alive and that she'll find him among the refugees passing through Giardini. She thought she saw him in the crowd this afternoon."

The doctor's face reflected compassion. "It wasn't him, though, was it?"

Clare shook her head. "She was so distraught."

"I might suggest finding other ways to involve her in the relief work." Dr. Muller opened the door a few inches before turning back to her. "The nightmares and lack of appetite, while difficult to manage, will likely fade with time. Especially if she's given opportunities to express her fears and grief."

If only Emmett could hear the man's advice. "So allowing her to talk about it will help her?"

"When she wants to. Talking, writing, drawing." The doctor waved his hand in the air. "There are many ways to mourn."

She followed him out the door. Seeing her, Antonina

jumped off Miriam's lap and rushed forward to claim Clare's hand again. Clare sent a questioning look in the maid's direction, but Miriam gave a quick shake of her head. Antonina didn't know the reason they were here.

"Is this the child?" Dr. Muller asked.

"Yes, this is Antonina."

He crouched beside the girl and asked something in Italian. Antonina glanced up at Clare, then nodded. After a moment, the doctor straightened. "Though I can't say for certain, she appears to be in good health. And she feels safe with you, which is important after such a frightening ordeal."

"How do you know she feels safe?"

Dr. Muller smiled at them both. "Because that nod of hers was in answer to my question if she liked living with you."

Clare tucked the child against her side as a feeling of love and thankfulness washed through her. Surely this was what it felt like to be a mother. She gave Antonina a smile. "Shall we head to the villa now?"

"Yes." The girl squeezed her hand.

"Thank you for everything, Dr. Muller."

"You are most welcome, Lady Linwood. Remember to get more rest."

"I will." She wasn't sure how, but she would figure out a way to rest more and help Antonina with her grief too.

As they left the doctor's and began the trek toward the villa, Clare felt lighter than she had in a week. She was still pregnant!

Thank You, Father, she silently prayed, *for Thy watchful care and for a chance to finally see the doctor today.*

She expressed gratitude as well for Antonina and for Emmett. While things were still uncertain there, Clare was actually glad he'd come to Sicily. Without him, she and Antonina might not be alive. She also felt grateful for the sweet interactions she'd shared with her husband this past week. Whatever the future held, she would cherish those moments, even when they became distant memories.

Would such moments continue if she went back with Emmett, or were they only possible under these extraordinary circumstances? Another question, this one more sobering, pricked at her elated mood. Would she be able to remain pregnant if she returned to England? Clare didn't know, and the uncertainty settled heavily around her heart. She'd promised to make a decision soon, and she would. But she was beginning to see that whichever choice she made, she could lose something precious to her in the process.

Barksley Hall, December 1908: Four and a half weeks earlier

The house looked marvelous—at least the main bedrooms and the kitchen did. Other areas, such as the dining room, study, and drawing room, were still in various stages of renovation. But Emmett was still pleased with how well the work was coming along. So much so that he was planning to surprise Clare by returning to Hadwell House for the holidays a whole week earlier than he'd originally planned.

He couldn't wait to see her. The estate had taken far more of his time and energy than Emmett had anticipated. He hadn't been able to get away any sooner, which meant it had been nearly a month since he'd last seen his wife.

Hands clasped behind his back, he surveyed the painting that had arrived the day before from London. He'd had the workers hang it in a prominent spot over the hearth in Clare's bedroom. It was another surprise for Clare. She'd painted the beautiful picture of his grandfather's villa in Taormina when they'd honeymooned there last year and had brought the painting to their townhouse in London. However, Emmett thought she might like to keep it here. He hoped that for Clare it would be a memorial, as it was for him, of the first—but not the last—happy period in their marriage. Just like the two weeks Clare had stayed with him at Barksley Hall.

Every day they'd pored over books and sketches together to determine what changes they wanted to make to the house. In the afternoons, they'd gone for walks to view the sea. And every evening, they had dined alone, laughing and bantering as easily and as long into the night as they had in Sicily.

Emmett smiled at the memories as he turned to eye the rest of the room. Clare had known what she was doing when she'd suggested the colors. The walnut-colored wood warmed the cool shades of green and blue that wound their way through the fabrics, the drapes, and the wallpaper. The whole look reminded him very much of Clare.

Did she miss him as much as he did her? Her few letters hadn't said, but Emmett was hopeful. Or he at least tried to be. With Clare at Hadwell House and him at Barksley Hall, there had been moments of doubt. Moments when he'd wondered if the closeness they had shared here would last rather than fade as it had at other times.

He'd been relieved and grateful during their time together to see Clare acting more like herself. Her humor, kindness, and affection during those two weeks had felt like a gift he'd always cherished but hadn't opened in ages.

Could that have been the start of something deeper and long-lasting between them? He wanted to believe so, to believe that the tensions of the past were over and their relationship would now be filled with the warmth and connection he wished for. But the only way to know for certain was to see Clare again.

Emmett exited the room and went to his own. Inside, Rushford was packing his trunk. "A letter came for you, my lord." The valet motioned to the table that stood between the armchairs.

"It's from Clare," Emmett said as he picked up the letter.

Rushford nodded, his eyes lit with a smile. "What do you think her ladyship will say to you returning early for the holidays?"

"My hope is she will find the surprise a delightful one. Perhaps even worthy of a very long kiss." Grinning, Emmett tore open the envelope and removed the single sheet of paper.

His valet paused in his work. "Would you like me to wait to finish packing until you've read your letter?"

"No, I'll take it downstairs." The sooner the packing was complete, the sooner they could commence the drive to Hadwell House.

Emmett waited until he was in the library and seated in one of the newly upholstered chairs before reading his letter. This was the only room in the house he and Clare had left relatively unchanged. Its cheerful fire and shelves of books made for a comfortable place to read or think.

Dear Emmett,

I hope this finds you well. It sounds as if the work on the house is progressing nicely and that you are pleased with this newest round of renovations. I'm glad it's going well. But while we've been apart, I've come to a decision. I'm not sure how to share it. I guess it's probably best that I just state it, even without preamble.

I've decided to spend the holidays somewhere warmer, at the villa actually. I know this is a sudden decision, but I very much believe the warmer temperatures of Sicily will do me good. I leave for Italy in four days. And while I know that's before you are scheduled to arrive back at Hadwell House, I can't delay my leaving.

I wish you the merriest of Christmases. Our time

together at Barksley Hall will remain one of my favorite memories from this year.
Sincerely,
Clare

He lowered the letter to his knee and tried to pull in a full breath through the pressure squeezing his chest. His wife wished to spend the holidays somewhere else, away from him. How could that be true, especially after their time here? Perhaps he'd misunderstood her meaning in his first perusal of the letter.

Gripping the paper tighter at its edge, Emmett read the letter through a second, then a third time. But the words didn't change. Clare was leaving England, without him.

The viselike ache inside him increased, along with his confusion. What had happened between them since Clare had left Barksley Hall last month? She hadn't mentioned being unhappy in her other letters, though Emmett had suspected she felt some loneliness. Did she truly dislike being at his parents' home so much? Or was it *him* she could no longer abide?

Emmett rose to his feet and began to pace the room as anger and hurt coalesced inside him. He welcomed the feelings, as they helped block out the aching near his heart. How could Clare up and leave like this? Without waiting to see him, without waiting to tell him goodbye in person?

A knock on the library door had him lifting his gaze from burning figurative holes in the rug with his glare. "Yes?"

"I'm finished packing, my lord," Rushford answered.

Emmett glanced at the letter he still held, then at the fire. "My plans have changed, I'm afraid. We'll wait to head back to Hadwell House until next week as planned." If Clare had no desire to see him before her departure, then he would grant that wish.

There was a long pause before Rushford said in a puzzled tone, "Shall I unpack then?"

"No, just leave it. Thank you, Rushford." Emmett moved to the hearth and stared down at the flames.

"Is something wrong, my lord? Is Lady Linwood all right?"

Hearing Clare's name threatened to renew his pain. "She's fine. But I've decided there would be too many things left undone if we departed today."

"Very well, my lord."

Emmett listened to the sound of Rushford's fading footsteps as though they were the sound of his dying hopes. All of his fears had been proven right. His and Clare's time together last month had been quite pleasant, but it represented nothing more. Setting his jaw in a firm line, he dropped the letter into the fire and watched the words curdle black in the heat until nothing was left of them except for ashes.

Chapter 11

Two days after Antonina's distressing experience in Giardini, Emmett and Mr. Sharpe returned to a quiet villa. The drawing room, which Clare had cleverly converted into a sewing room to make clothes for the earthquake victims, sat empty.

"Where is everyone?" Mr. Sharpe asked, looking around as he and Emmett hung up their hats and coats.

The reporter had opted to accompany Emmett and the work gang who were repairing the roads rather than stay behind at the villa with the refugee women and children Clare had enlisted the day before to help with the sewing. Emmett had discovered he didn't mind the man's company. In truth, he had grown accustomed to the young man's near-constant presence and had even learned a few things about Mr. Sharpe that softened his view of the reporter.

Mr. Sharpe also struggled with proving himself to his father, who apparently hadn't wanted his son to become a reporter. And when the young man wasn't asking incessant questions or scribbling away in his notebook, he was actually quite funny, with a dry sense of humor Emmett appreciated.

"Clare?" Emmett called out. "Antonina?" Where had

they gone? He led the way down to the kitchen, where Signora Russo was pulling something from the oven.

"Ah, Lord Linwood," she said, looking up. "You and Mr. Sharpe are back."

Emmett nodded. "Do you know where Lady Linwood and Nina have gone?"

"They are in the garden, painting." The housekeeper set the dish on the sideboard.

After thanking her, Emmett and Mr. Sharpe headed outside. "Does your wife paint?" the reporter asked.

"Oh, yes. Quite well."

Emmett thought of the picture of the villa hanging in Clare's bedroom at Barksley Hall and the one she'd painted of him. What was she painting today?

Near the empty fountain, Clare sat before a canvas and easel. Antonina was perched on the fountain's stone bench, a brush in her hand too and an expression of total concentration on her young face. Emmett approached the little girl first. "What are you painting, Nina?"

She hopped off the bench and turned her canvas around. A pile of what appeared to be rocks covered the bottom half of her picture. But were they actually rocks?

"Are those . . . stones?" He crouched in front of her.

A brief smile lifted her lips as she nodded. "It is my house, after earthquake."

Her house after the earthquake? Emmett shot a look of alarm at Clare, but her focus was on her own painting. That meant dealing with this was up to him, but why was Antonina painting a picture of rubble? He struggled for something positive to say. "They do look like stones," he offered as he rose to his feet.

He moved to stand behind his wife so he could view her painting. As with her others, this painting captured a scene with incredible detail. But the subject concerned him. Emmett recognized what had to be a demolished street in Messina. Rain filtered down onto the ruined buildings and masonry. Off in the right-hand corner a small group of people were heading away from the destruction.

"What do you think?" She swiveled to face Emmett, clearly eager to hear his opinion.

To Emmett's relief, Mr. Sharpe answered first. "That is remarkable, Lady Linwood. It looks exactly as you and your husband described it."

"Thank you, Mr. Sharpe," she said as she blushed. Emmett felt a peculiar flicker of jealousy at not having inspired the added color himself.

The reporter leaned forward to point at the tiny people. "Is that your group, fleeing to the countryside?"

"It is." Clare faced her painting again. "I hoped to capture the feel of that morning."

"Why?" The question tumbled from Emmett's mouth before he could stop it.

She frowned and dipped her brush back into the paint. "A wise person recently told me that there are many ways to express grief, even through drawing or painting." Beneath her adept fingers, the paintbrush added depth to the shadows and textures. "So Nina and I are painting pictures to represent the earthquake."

Mr. Sharpe walked to where a few of Clare's other paintings from her time in Sicily sat propped against the nearby stone bench. Before Emmett could go over and view them too, Antonina held up another painting for him to see.

"Look, Emmett."

The face staring back at him—clearly rendered by Clare's skillful brush—looked much like the little girl, but Emmett recognized that it was her brother. It wasn't an exact likeness, and yet it was close enough to set his heart thudding with the memories that filled his nightmares. He pulled in a long breath and pushed it back out.

"How did you . . ." He directed the words to Clare.

His wife shrugged without looking at him. "I sketched something first, using Antonina as a model. When she thought it was close enough to Angelo's likeness, I painted it."

Emmett nearly asked if such a thing was wise given all the child had been through. However, as he watched Antonina lovingly study the painting of her brother, he swallowed back the question. Perhaps Clare was right. He didn't know what they would do with the paintings of rubble, but it was evident how much the portrait of Angelo meant to Antonina. The child didn't have an actual photograph, so the painting would serve as a way to remember him.

"It's an outstanding likeness, Clare," Emmett managed to say with utmost sincerity.

She didn't blush as she had at Mr. Sharpe's compliment, though the tension left her features. "I think it's been good for her to paint her own picture too," she said quietly. "I didn't tell her what to paint, Emmett. The house is what she chose." Clare glanced over her shoulder at him. "I, for one, am glad she did. She needs to let her grief out so she can come to terms with it."

"It was an excellent idea, truly."

Her eyes met his. "You really think so?"

"I—"

Emmett wasn't able to finish, because Mr. Sharpe suddenly announced, "Quite the likeness of you, isn't it, Lord Linwood?" The young man straightened. In his hand, he held the portrait Clare had painted of Emmett.

He stared, uncomprehending, at the picture of himself. How had it come to be here? "You brought it with you?" he finally asked, returning his gaze to Clare.

There was no mistaking who had elicited the blush that reddened her cheeks now. "It's the only other portrait I've completed, so it made sense to bring it along. If I ever choose to do another, with a live model, it'll be nice to see if my skill has improved." Her explanations tumbled over each other. When they stopped, she abruptly stood and began gathering up her supplies. "Antonina, let's clean up and get ready for dinner."

Emmett and Mr. Sharpe helped them, but Clare insisted on carrying her finished paintings herself, including the one of him. She refused to look at him as the four of them went inside. Not that Emmett minded so much. He was too busy thinking.

Clare had brought the portrait—his portrait—to Sicily. It wasn't happenstance that she had either. The picture had been hanging in a frame at Hadwell House, not mixed among her other paintings. That meant she had deliberately removed the portrait to bring it with her. What he couldn't reason out was why.

When they reached her room, she directed them to set her supplies in the hallway. She opened her door as Emmett started down the corridor toward his own room. Something compelled him to look back, though. He found Clare watching him. The look in her eyes was a mixture of awkwardness and regret but also . . . hope. Then she disappeared inside her bedroom.

He'd seen enough, though. Enough to know why she'd brought that particular painting with her—and it changed everything.

Clare still cared for him; she might even still love him. Emmett shook his head in stunned amazement as he entered his room. He didn't know her reasons for leaving England without him, though he was beginning to suspect they had little to do with his title or wanting to live apart. What he did know was that he'd been given a glimpse into the future and the possibility that it might not be too late for them.

Sleep was near impossible for Clare that night. She kept seeing Emmett's look of surprise when he'd discovered she had brought his portrait with her to Taormina. What reason he had assigned to her actions, she didn't know. She wasn't even sure herself what had motivated her to bring the picture along or whether doing so had been a mistake or an excellent idea.

At last she'd finally fallen asleep, only to be awakened some time later by Miriam. The maid had kindly offered to sleep in Antonina's room for a few nights to allow Clare to get more rest. And, to Clare's relief, the little girl had gone two whole nights without a nightmare. Until tonight, when she had apparently startled awake and asked for Clare.

By morning, Clare felt turned inside out and upside down with exhaustion and nausea. She'd been so confident that painting pictures would help Antonina continue to sleep well, but it hadn't. What more could she do to help the girl move through her grief? She hated knowing Antonina was still hurting, especially at night.

Clare didn't bother hiding the lines under her eyes before going down to breakfast. The source of her fatigue included trying to pretend for Mr. Sharpe's benefit that everything was fine. In reality, she wasn't sure from one moment to the next if things were improving or not between her and Emmett. The little girl they'd both come to love was still traumatized by the earthquake, and so was Clare's husband, though Emmett likely wouldn't admit it. Then there was the matter of returning to England and joining the campaign trail, which was likely to be a grueling experience. Clare had yet to decide, too, if she ought to risk returning to someplace cold or remain in Sicily. Her head ached from all the ruminating on what to do in each situation.

Emmett offered a cheery "Good morning" and a perfunctory kiss to her cheek when she entered the dining room. On other days, Clare hadn't minded his now-familiar greeting—there had even been moments when she'd enjoyed it. This morning, however, the playacting grated on her. She let Emmett and Mr. Sharpe do most of the talking as she ate what she needed to in order to assuage her queasiness. Antonina seemed equally out of sorts as Clare. The child mostly picked at her food before asking if she could leave the table.

"Do you want to help with the sewing today?" Clare asked her.

Antonina studied her plate and shook her head.

"Nina?" She waited for the girl to lift her chin. "It's all right. You don't have to help." Maybe being around the other refugee children and their mothers reminded Antonina too much of the family she'd lost. "You can draw or read. Or see if Signora Russo has some dough for you to bake."

The girl appeared to consider the options. "I want to see Signora Russo."

"I think that sounds fun." After offering the child a smile, she watched Antonina exit the dining room. Antonina needed to have fun, to laugh, to be carefree. Hopefully in time she would gain back her spirits, but Clare was still concerned. If only Emmett would talk to the girl.

Clare excused herself a minute or two later. The women would be here soon to start another day of sewing. As she entered the drawing room, she heard footfalls behind her.

"Is everything all right, Clare?" Emmett's voice trailed after her. "You were rather quiet at breakfast."

She started to nod, then thought better of it. "No," she said, turning around. "Everything is not all right." She rubbed at her aching forehead. "Antonina's nightmares, and yours, are making it difficult to get much sleep."

"I should have realized that sooner. I'm sorry."

His sincere tone and troubled expression prompted tears of exhaustion to form in her eyes. Clare blinked them back in order to speak. "I appreciate that."

"Why don't you go lie down?" He stepped back, allowing her a clear path to the door. "Nina is fine, and I can wait to leave until after the sewing gets underway."

A nap, even one this early, sounded wonderful. Still, Clare hesitated. Her getting more sleep this morning would solve only one problem.

"I'm worried about her, Emmett. I really thought painting would help her, but instead she woke up crying after having slept through until morning two nights in a row." Clare glanced toward the door to make sure Mr. Sharpe hadn't followed them. "I'm wondering if there have been too many changes in too short a time—a new house, a new family. Have you noticed she rarely smiles? Every child, regardless of where they live or what they've gone through, needs a reason to smile and an excuse to have fun."

He offered what she guessed was meant to be a reassuring look. "I'm confident she'll come around. It hasn't even been two weeks since the earthquake. We just need to give her more time to adjust."

Instead of inspiring comfort, his optimistic words irritated her. "I don't agree, not entirely. I think she needs more than time. She needs a way to express her grief. If you would only talk with her . . ."

"We discussed that, Clare." Emmett pocketed his hands

and frowned down at the rug. "Talking with her is only going to distress her more, not less."

"Maybe," she countered with barely veiled annoyance. "But I still think it's worth trying." They were talking in circles, and she felt even more fatigued standing here. "I believe I'll take you up on your offer to go lie down." Clare moved toward the door. "I only ask that you not act indifferent toward her sorrow, Emmett."

Her next words, ones she was too weary to hold back, slipped from her lips in a whisper. "As you have with me."

"You think I've felt indifferent toward you?" His hand on her arm halted her retreat.

As she turned to face him, Clare allowed all of the frustration and hurt of the past to flood her answer. "Yes."

"Is that what you believe I feel for you right now?"

She'd never seen such a look on his face before. It was a strange mixture of disappointment and hope, weariness and resolve. Maybe even a little fear. "Yes," she repeated, though it held less bite this time. "By and large, I do think you feel indifferent toward me."

"Then tell me this, Clare." The low timbre of his voice sent a pleasant shiver up her back. "Does this feel like indifference?"

His gaze held hers as he cupped the side of her face, his fingers warm along her jawline and where they brushed the top of her neck. Clare managed to pull in a shaky breath right before he kissed her. Her pulse responded to his touch, though she held the rest of herself still, both eager and afraid of getting lost in his kiss. But when Emmett released her elbow and wrapped his arm around her back, she leaned into him and matched his ardent kiss with her own.

A noise outside the front door startled them apart. Blushing, Clare darted a glance in the direction of the foyer, half-expecting to find Mr. Sharpe standing there, watching. But the foyer stood empty, at least until the group of sewers and their children entered the villa.

Clare turned to Emmett, her heart still beating too fast. Had they really just kissed? What did it mean? She wasn't sure, but there was a tenderness shining in her husband's light-blue eyes that she hadn't seen in a very long time. A question hovered there too.

"You're right," she answered. She took a step away from him and ensured her hair was still in place. "That felt nothing like indifference."

The grin he sent her way made her middle flutter with near-forgotten emotion. "I'm relieved to hear that."

"*Buongiorno*, ladies." Clare nodded to each member of the group as they came into the drawing room. "We'll begin where we ended yesterday."

"I suppose I'd best be off," Emmett said, though he gave her mouth a meaningful glance. Clare blushed again. "Are you going to lie down?"

She shook her head. "I don't feel so tired anymore."

His answering smile erased the last remnants of her exhaustion. "I'll see you this afternoon, my dear." This time, she recognized, his endearment was meant for no one else's benefit but her own.

"Until this afternoon," Clare echoed as he left the room.

Squaring her shoulders, she faced the sewing group with a real smile and renewed energy. And yet the day now seemed to stretch overly long before her. There would be hours to fill before she saw Emmett again and they could finally talk about what had happened between them.

Somerset, England, December 1908: Four weeks earlier

Emmett sipped his drink and studied the holiday decorations tastefully displayed about the drawing room. The bright pine boughs and festoons of ribbon couldn't help but lift one's mood and inspire thoughts of good will. He nearly hadn't come tonight, since people would likely ask why Clare wasn't with him. But his father had baulked at the idea of Emmett staying home. Their family, including Emmett's sisters and their spouses, always attended the neighbors' annual Christmas party. However, it was his mother's suggestion that being around other people might be good for him, which had swayed his decision in favor of attending. And he was glad he had.

When their host and hostess asked after Clare, Emmett had simply replied, "The cold is very difficult for her, so she is in Sicily." The older couple had nodded with sympathy and expressed their delight at his presence. Emmett guessed they were curious as to why he hadn't gone to Italy with his wife but were too polite to ask.

Other than having to repeat the reasons for his wife's absence several more times, he'd enjoyed the conversation at dinner and the superb food. And yet he struggled with frequent bursts of melancholy because he kept thinking of things he wanted to say to Clare—how delicious the current dish was or did she also find it humorous that the gentleman across the table used his napkin so often—only to remember his wife wasn't there.

Emmett hadn't heard from her since receiving her letter that outlined her plans to leave, but he figured she hadn't actually been in Taormina for long. Hopefully a letter would be forthcoming, along with a fuller explanation as to why she'd left.

Setting aside his empty glass, he rose to his feet and crossed the room to examine the painting hanging above the mantel. It was a nice picture of the estate, but it lacked some of the texture and details of Clare's landscapes. Perhaps she would paint Barksley Hall one day, and they could hang her picture in their own drawing room.

"Rather odd, isn't it? For his wife to be gone now," he heard a woman whisper loudly from somewhere behind him.

Emmett winced before reminding himself she might not be talking about Clare. Her companion, whose voice he recognized as Lady Melinda's, responded, "Yes, but most American heiresses are rather odd."

His first guess had been correct—they were discussing his wife after all. Emmett started to turn away, not wanting to hear anymore. But Lady Melinda's next remark bound him in place.

"I do have it on good authority that she only agreed to marry him because it gave her not only a courtesy title but access to an even more prestigious one when he becomes marquess." The widow's tone was cold with judgment and disapproval. It was infuriating, and yet try as he might, Emmett couldn't make himself walk away. "It's also been more than a year since their wedding, but no heir has been forthcoming. I wouldn't be surprised if in the absence of having a child, this trip to Sicily is her preparation for beginning a separate life, away from him. She'll get to keep his title, after all, wherever she lives."

Somehow he found the strength to finally move. Emmett strode to the opposite side of the room, not wishing to hear anymore. What he'd heard already stung badly enough. Could there be any truth to Lady Melinda's words? He didn't want to believe them, but he'd been gone from Hadwell House for weeks now. Weeks in which his wife had likely seen and spoken with the widow. Would Clare have taken the other woman into her confidence?

He tugged at his collar in a vain effort to loosen it. Clare and Lady Melinda hadn't struck him as being friends, especially since the widow appeared to still be bitter over Emmett's choice of a wife. He could even believe that she'd take pleasure from his potential unhappiness with Clare. Melinda had been that way as a girl—it was one of the reasons Emmett had never considered marriage to her. If she couldn't have what she wanted, then she sought to disrupt the happiness of those who did.

Still, her explanations regarding Clare's actions couldn't be devoid of any amount of truth, could they? Surely there was a grain of fact somewhere among the possible embellishments. But which of her statements were truth and which were not?

Had Clare truly only married him for his title? Emmett didn't want to consider it. And yet it was the first thing since Clare's last letter that made any amount of sense. If she'd chosen him solely for a title, then there was little reason for her to stay in England with him, especially when they hadn't yet been able to have a family of their own. Many of his married acquaintances began living separate lives, once the requisite heir and spare were born. Might Clare be doing the same, giving up on the idea of children now that she had his title but couldn't stay pregnant?

The possibilities hurt his head. Worst of all, the likelihood that his wife hadn't married him for love hurt his heart. Too angry and confused to remain at the party, he found his mother and informed her that he was leaving early. Then he made his excuses to the host and hostess.

As he climbed into the carriage for the ride home, Emmett reminded himself that the gnawing ache inside him would eventually fade away. He knew this from experience. And right now, that future event was the only thing for which he felt any degree of confidence.

Chapter 12

Leaning against his shovel, Emmett swiped his forehead with the edge of his dirty sleeve. He'd thought it fairly hard work overseeing the distribution of shoes and clothing to the refugees as well as the delivery of food and water to those working on repairing the roads. But after that, he'd volunteered to help with the actual road work when one of the refugees caught a cold, and he realized that this type of labor made his other duties seem like child's play. Yet no amount of aching muscles or sweaty shirts could dampen his good mood.

"You're grinning again, Lord Linwood. Like a chap pleased with his place in the world." Mr. Sharpe handed Emmett a full ladle of water. The reporter was on drink duty this afternoon. "Or perhaps like a man who received a rather ardent kiss from his wife this morning."

Emmett choked on the cool liquid. When he was done sputtering, he handed back the ladle. "I didn't realize you were watching," he said in slightly hoarse voice.

"Only for a moment." Mr. Sharpe chuckled and dipped the ladle back into the bucket before offering it to Emmett a second time.

His throat was sore from coughing, but he declined a second drink. "Will you write about what you saw?"

"I might." Mr. Sharpe shrugged. "That largely depends on the direction of my story."

"And which direction do you plan to take?"

"Afraid that's undecided at present." The reporter moved on with the water bucket, leaving Emmett to muse over his answer.

So far, the young man had sent only one story to his editor in London, and that one, according to his explanation, had been about Emmett and Clare's experiences during the earthquake in Messina. Why Mr. Sharpe hadn't yet come up with a story about the Linwoods as a happy couple, Emmett didn't know. Perhaps some news stories took longer to write. Besides, the story about the earthquake was very of the moment. A story about the Linwoods as a happy couple could be published at any time.

Emmett found that thoughts about what Mr. Sharpe would write bothered him far less now. Perhaps that was because the kiss the reporter had caught a glimpse of that morning had been real—it had nothing to do with fooling him. It had been about Emmett convincing his wife that he didn't feel indifferent toward her, not in the slightest. And given the way Clare had responded, he felt certain she wasn't indifferent toward him either.

Surely that meant there was hope for them and their marriage. That, even after everything that had happened, they could work things out. He'd talk to Clare about it when he returned to the villa later. And perhaps they would share another memorable kiss too. His earlier grin returned to his face despite the hot, tiring work.

Sometime later a shout from up ahead drew Emmett's attention. He lifted his head to see one of the refugees on the ground, an agonized expression on the man's face. Dropping his shovel, Emmett hurried forward to see what was wrong.

The man had an ugly laceration on his leg from getting too close to one of the workers using a pickaxe. Mr. Sharpe brought over the water, and Emmett used it to wash the wound. Someone handed him a handkerchief, which he tied around the man's leg.

"We need to get you to the doctor," he told him in Italian. The man answered with a grim nod.

Emmett and Mr. Sharpe propped the injured man between them and set off for town. Another worker ran ahead to procure a cart. The walk was slow, and judging by the man's ashen face, very painful. But he managed to stay conscious. By the time they reached the outskirts of Taormina, there was a cart waiting for them. They loaded the injured man into the back, and Emmett scrambled in beside him so he could apply pressure to the wound. The reporter climbed onto the seat next to the driver and told him to take them to the nearest doctor.

To Emmett's surprise, the doctor turned out to be American. Dr. Muller, as he introduced himself, directed the three of them to carry the man inside and set him on the examination table. They were then instructed to sit in the outer room.

Emmett wasn't sure how long they waited before the doctor exited the examining room. "He should be just fine," Dr. Muller announced as he removed his glasses and rubbed them with a cloth. "Once you take him to where he's staying, he'll need to keep off that leg for at least a week."

At Emmett's question about payment, the doctor shook his head. "I'm glad I could help, and that it wasn't more serious."

"*Grazie*, Lord Linwood," the wounded man murmured when Emmett and Mr. Sharpe helped him back out to the cart.

Dr. Muller followed them. "Did I hear him call you Lord Linwood?"

"You did," Emmett replied. He wasn't sure how the doctor recognized his name.

The doctor made no further comment until after they'd assisted the man into the cart and the driver knew where to take him. "I met your wife, Lady Linwood, the other day," Dr. Muller explained.

Why had Clare seen a doctor? Was she ill and hadn't told him? "I see."

"Now, you don't need to worry any more than she has," the doctor said in a kind voice. "Even with her other miscarriages, I'm inclined to believe this baby is going to be all right. If her pregnancy could survive an earthquake, it can surely survive to full term this time."

Clare was pregnant? Emmett felt the shock bleeding into his expression. Aware of Mr. Sharpe's gaze—though, thankfully, the reporter wasn't close enough to hear what was being said—he wiped his hand down his face, hoping to hide his astonishment. How long had his wife known she was expecting?

Dr. Muller's next words provided Emmett with the answer. "The more I've thought on the advice that doctor in England gave her, the more I think it was sound. Maybe a warmer climate has been the answer all along."

That doctor in England . . .

Comprehension pummeled through him, as swift and painful as a hard fist to his stomach. Emmett drew in a ragged breath. Clare had seen a doctor before coming to Sicily, which meant she'd known she was pregnant even then. And yet she hadn't bothered to tell him.

He bid the doctor good day. Hopefully the man didn't hear the anger behind the cordial words. It wasn't the doctor's fault Clare had kept a secret from her husband. *Another secret.*

Bits of memory flickered through Emmett's mind as he set off at a fast walk back toward the work gang. Mr. Sharpe was blessedly silent as he rushed to keep up. No wonder Emmett had suspected Clare of withholding something else after her confession about her childhood. There had also been a number of times when he had asked after her health and she'd appeared startled or panicked by the innocent question. Her response, when he'd found her unconscious by the well, also made sudden sense now. His wife had been afraid that something might have happened to the baby—their baby.

Resentment tightened his jaw, making it ache. He'd been a fool to think one kiss, however amazing, could change things. Clare still didn't trust him, even if she had brought his portrait with her. And without trust, how would things ever be different between them?

Emmett informed the rest of the workers that the other chap would be fine. Then he shouldered his shovel again. There was still work to be done before it was time to return to the villa. But now the thought of seeing Clare no longer held the excitement and appeal it had earlier.

He'd deceived himself into believing there was still hope for them. That this time, this effort, would prove differently. It was a pattern he knew well. After all, Emmett had been chasing his father's approval for more than two decades, and yet it was still out of grasp. It was time to add reconnecting with his wife to his list of continued disappointments.

The members of the sewing group had left, and dinner was ready. But Emmett and Mr. Sharpe still hadn't returned to the villa. Clare set aside the pair of boy's trousers she'd been working on. Antonina lay on the rug at her feet, looking at a book.

What was keeping her husband? Clare hadn't felt this eager to see and talk with him in ages. She stood and went to the drawing-room window, where she parted the curtains. Two figures were striding up the drive. "They're home!" Dropping the curtains into place, she hurried into the foyer.

The front door opened a few seconds later, but it was Mr. Sharpe who entered first. Clare fell back a step. "Lady Linwood." The young man sounded tired, though not unhappy, in spite of his clothes being splattered with dirt.

Emmett came inside next, looking every bit as dirt-covered as Mr. Sharpe. But the sight of his handsome face still made Clare's pulse quicken.

"Did you two did get into a scrape?" she teased.

Instead of chuckling, her husband frowned. "We were short one worker this morning, so I volunteered to help. Mr. Sharpe joined in later, after one of the refugees was injured."

"Is he all right?"

"He will be." Emmett turned his attention to Antonina, who ran up to him and put her hand in his. "How was your day, Nina?"

"It was good."

Clare moved closer to them and tussled the girl's hair. "Antonina helped Signora Russo bake bread, and we finished enough clothing for three families." She placed her hand on Emmett's sleeve. "It's good to have you home, darling."

He fell back a step, out of Clare's reach. "Antonina, will you tell Signora Russo we will be ready for dinner in half an hour?"

The child nodded and headed toward the back stairs. Clare studied Emmett in confusion. Where was the affection and tenderness they'd shared that morning? Did he not realize her eagerness to see him was genuine? She wasn't pretending for Mr. Sharpe's sake.

"Is there something—" she started to ask.

"I need to speak with you in private, Clare." His cool tone belied the heat of anger in his eyes.

She threw a glance at Mr. Sharpe, who looked away. "I'll wash and change for dinner," the young man said before heading up the stairs.

"We can talk in the drawing room." Clare kept her chin up as she led the way, but panic was rapidly turning her insides cold. What did Emmett wish to discuss?

He shut the door behind them, but it was still a long moment before he spoke. "I believe congratulations are in order," he said as he turned to face her. "You're with child again."

"Y-yes. I am." Her dread congealed into a knot of ice. He knew her secret! "How did you find out?"

Emmett moved past her to stand in front of the fireplace, his back to her. "The doctor who treated the injured man recognized my name. Apparently he had met you."

She flinched at his emotionless tone. "I went to see him to make certain I was still pregnant."

"What advice did that doctor in England give you?"

Clare frowned. "What?"

"Dr. Muller said his colleague's advice was sound. What advice was that?"

Clasping her hands together, she directed her answer toward the rug. "He thought a warmer climate would prevent me from miscarrying a third time."

"Is that why you came here?"

The anguish behind his question stabbed her more deeply than his anger. "That was one of the reasons." She took a step forward. This was the same spot where she'd stood this morning when Emmett had kissed her. How cruel that life and relationships could change so drastically in so short a time.

"I couldn't bear to miscarry again." Clare swallowed the emotion crawling up her throat. "If coming here could prevent that, then I felt I had to try."

He turned around, lines of hurt and bewilderment creasing his brow. "You couldn't share that with me? Had I known you needed to be somewhere warmer this time, I would have come with you, Clare."

"I know," she half whispered. "And that's why I didn't say anything."

Emmett reared back as if she'd slapped him. "You didn't want me here?"

"Yes and no." Clare folded her arms protectively over her middle as threads of grief twisted around her heart. "I couldn't bear to endure another loss like that in front of you."

He shook his head. "I don't know what you mean."

"Emmett?" She desperately wanted him to understand, but would he? "I . . . we . . . lost something precious, twice. But I was the only one grieving and feeling and aching." There were tears on her cheeks now. "Aching for these babies I would never hold."

He pinched the bridge of his nose. "That isn't fair. I was as devastated and disappointed as you."

"Then why didn't you show it?" she countered, her frustration adding volume to her voice. "Why didn't you cry with me? Mourn with me?"

Emmett looked away. "I didn't want to upset you anymore than you already were."

It was the same line of thinking he'd used regarding Antonina's grief, but it still made no sense to her. What had happened in her husband's past to convince him it wasn't right to feel sadness or grief? That he was helping people by concealing his emotions from them?

"Your refusal to talk about any of it was far more upsetting than any expression of grief could have been."

"I can't change that now."

The words were hardly more than a murmur, but the ache in them cooled her ire. "Maybe not for me, but you can for Antonina." Before he could protest again, Clare hurried on. "I felt so alone, Emmett. I had no idea if you felt as heartbroken as I did. I longed to be held by you, to cry with you. But you weren't there, not really."

Silence was his only response, and it stung. Still, Clare was grateful she'd finally laid bare the feelings she had harbored for months.

"I should have told you right away that I was pregnant again," she said as she came to stand beside him, "and why I had to come to Sicily. Keeping it from you was wrong, and I'm sorry." Her tears were falling faster than she could brush them away. "It doesn't make it right, but I wasn't sure I could bear your indifference if it all fell apart a third time."

His broad shoulders were no longer rigid with fury but hunched with self-preservation. "Is that what you meant this morning about my feeling indifferent toward you?"

She resisted the urge to offer consolation and instead nodded. If they were ever to be together in every sense of the word, she couldn't hold back portions of her worries and emotions and thoughts from him. She needed to share it all, just as she hoped he would with her.

"Do you really believe Antonina needs someone to . . . mourn . . . with her?"

Was he changing his mind? "Yes, and you are the very best person to do so."

Emmett met her gaze directly. "If I wasn't able to do that with you, how can you be certain I can help Nina?"

"Because you care about her," Clare said with confidence. "And because you already rescued her once. All you need is to find that same courage to do it again."

Dinner was a quiet affair. Emmett tried to contribute to the conversation led by his wife and Mr. Sharpe, but he couldn't stop thinking about Clare's parting words about courage. He hadn't ever looked at grieving with someone as courageous. But the thought of talking to Antonina about her brother and what had happened that day in Messina tightened his collar and made his heart thump harder. So perhaps doing that would be an act of bravery.

He was no longer angry with Clare for not telling him that she was pregnant again. Was he happy with what had happened? No, of course not. However, he'd been unable to cling to his ire after she'd explained her true reason for coming to Sicily without him. How could Emmett remain frustrated when he now saw that the very thing he'd done to avoid upsetting her further had only deepened her sorrow?

Instead of heading into the drawing room with the others after dinner, he wandered upstairs to his room. There he dragged his chair onto the balcony and sat, staring at the garden below.

Had his father been wrong all those years ago when he'd accused Emmett of upsetting his mother and sisters with his continual tears over his grandfather's death? It hadn't occurred to Emmett to question the marquess's conclusions. Surely his father understood such things better than a ten-year-old boy. And yet what about Clare's declaration that she'd needed her husband to grieve with her? If she was right, then Emmett had been holding back from more than her for years now. The thought filled him with deep sadness.

Did he have the courage to test Clare's theory? He didn't want to hurt Antonina any more than she'd already been. On the other hand, his wife believed talking through everything might be the best way to help the child. If he cared about Antonina—which he did, very much—then wasn't it worth trying to speak with her?

As if conjured up by his thoughts, Antonina knocked at his door and entered the room, Clare right behind her. "Good night, Emmett," the little girl said.

She gave him a hug, and the loving gesture squeezed as much at his heart as her little arms did his neck. When she pulled back, he studied her. The smudges under her dark eyes attested to her own fatigue. Seeing them, he made up his mind.

"What do you say to sitting out here with me for a bit, Nina?" he asked. She cast a look over her shoulder at Clare, then shrugged. He interpreted the action to mean she didn't mind. "Why don't you grab a blanket first, so you don't catch cold?"

The little girl disappeared out the door, leaving him and Clare alone. "I'll see that she gets in bed." He ventured a look at his wife. "If that's agreeable with you."

"Of course." She searched his face. "Will you be all right?"

Emmett matched her gaze. "I'll be brave. Beyond that, I'm not sure."

Her eyes widened with understanding. "I have confidence in you."

"Thank you, Clare."

She smiled briefly. "Good night then."

"Good night," he echoed.

Antonina returned as Clare exited the room. After wrapping the blanket around her, he settled her on his knee. "Tell me about Angelo."

The child looked up at him in surprise. "Angelo? He is . . ."

"In Italian," Emmett said. "Tell me in Italian."

She leaned against his chest and began to talk. The garden slowly transformed into shadows as Antonina told him story after story about her brother. Would Emmett have talked the same way about Alder if his brother had lived? He let her talk, only interjecting here and there with a question, a chuckle, or a word of sympathy. He knew where the stories would eventually lead, and that knowledge had his stomach twisting with apprehension long before Antonina's retellings reached the day of the earthquake.

"What happened that morning?" he forced himself to ask.

The little girl recounted waking to the house shaking, the screams of her mother downstairs, the horrible crashing noises, and Angelo crawling into her room on hands and knees. Emmett held her tight when she reached the part about them fleeing onto the balcony.

"He told me God would send us help," Antonina whispered as she gazed up at Emmett. "And then you came."

Emmett dropped his head onto her hair. His eyes stung with the tears he tried to hold back. "I thought I could save him, Nina. I wanted to so badly. But I couldn't reach him in time."

She started to cry. "I want him to come back, Emmett. I miss him so much."

"I know."

He'd once ached the same way for his grandfather, and like this little girl, Emmett hadn't been able to say a proper goodbye either. As thoughts of his grandfather filled his mind, he could no longer suppress the tears. It had been nearly twenty years since he'd last cried. And yet he felt no shame as his shoulders began to shake with sobs. Not when the sound of Antonina's weeping mingled with his own.

Every loss, every disappointment that he'd failed to

mourn seemed to burst forth from some place deep inside him. His grandfather's death, his futile attempts to please his father, his hidden pain over each of Clare's miscarriages. All of it spilled out of him on a purging tide of heartache.

He didn't know how long the two of them sat there grieving. The moon was shining down on the balcony when Emmett realized Antonina had fallen asleep. Only this time, her expression held nothing but peace. Clare had been right—talking about the grief had helped the little girl. It had helped them both.

Emmett hoisted her in his arms and carried her to her room. After settling an extra blanket over her, he watched her for a long moment. Angelo had told his sister that God would send them help. And He had. It hadn't just been help for Antonina, though. God had helped Emmett too. He'd seen the way Emmett was struggling, unsure how to make things right with his wife or if he even had the strength to make another effort. Yet in His infinite mercy, God had guided Emmett—both in coming to Sicily and in finding Antonina—and in doing so had reminded him that the only title God cared about was that of being His child.

"Thank you," Emmett murmured heavenward.

He bent down and kissed Antonina on the forehead. He loved her as much as if she'd been his daughter from the beginning. And he never wanted her to doubt that love, as he'd doubted his father's or as Clare had doubted Emmett's.

Did his wife still doubt? If so, then it was up to him to convince her that he loved her, even now. It no longer seemed relevant or important to him whether she'd married him for his title or not. He would still choose her, every time. Could she possibly feel the same way?

Emmett returned to his room to put away the chair and close the balcony door, his mind awhirl with ideas. Clare hadn't come to Sicily to live apart from him; she'd come because she was hurt and afraid, and because she'd been desperate to protect their child. That alone gave him reason to believe her feelings might still match his own. He would need to find a way, though, to prove that the things that were important to her were important to him too. Somehow he had to show her that he wanted to know and feel and understand her every loss, triumph, fear, and belief.

He'd been given another chance to make things right with her. And this time, Emmett would not take such an opportunity for granted.

A niggling memory slipped into his consciousness as Emmett climbed into bed. It was a long shot, a likely impossibility of a task. But hadn't he once read that with God nothing was impossible? Not even the healing of a marriage. With that thought, he shut his eyes, and for the first time in days, he wasn't afraid to fall asleep.

Chapter 13

Two small hands nudged Clare awake the next morning. She opened one eye, then the other, to find Antonina smiling at her from the side of the bed. "Morning, Clare."

"Good morning," she said as she smiled back. "Did you sleep well?"

The little girl nodded. "I had no bad dream."

"That's wonderful, Nina." Emmett hadn't woken Clare up with his nightmares either. Did that mean his conversation with Antonina had gone well? Now that she was awake, she was eager to ask him.

Miriam appeared beside the bed. "I hope it's all right I let her wake you, my lady. She couldn't wait any longer to see you."

"Of course." Clare slowly sat up. Only then did she notice the sunlight streaming through the curtains at the balcony. "What time is it?"

"After ten," Miriam answered.

No wonder Clare felt so well rested. She hadn't had such a long bout of uninterrupted sleep since before the earthquake. "Has Emmett already had breakfast?"

"He has, my lady. He and Mr. Sharpe both." Miriam

pulled one of Clare's day dresses from the wardrobe. "They left as soon as they finished eating."

Clare looked at the maid in alarm. "Left where?" Had Emmett gone back to England without saying goodbye? Without her and Antonina?

"Rushford said they went to Palermo."

Though she felt a prick of disappointment that Emmett had gone to the capital city without talking to her first, Clare was greatly relieved to hear he hadn't left the country without her. *Like I did to him.* Regret washed through her.

Had her husband been confused, disappointed, and possibly even hurt by her choice to leave England without talking to him face to face? Clare had been afraid to tell him her plans in person, afraid he would try to talk her out of going. But maybe he wouldn't have. Maybe if she'd been truthful with him about the real reason for her leaving, he might have agreed with her plans. Of course, there still would have been the issue of possibly grieving another miscarriage in his presence. And yet yesterday had shown her that Emmett was not opposed to listening to her if she was brave enough to be open and honest about how she felt.

Miriam removed a folded slip of paper from her pocket. "Lord Linwood gave Rushford this note to give to you." She handed it to Clare. "Would you like to dress before your tea, my lady?"

Clare eyed Antonina still standing beside the bed. "I think I'll have my tea first. And what do you say to joining me for breakfast in bed, Nina?" She patted the blanket.

"Yes!" The child scrambled up onto the bed and settled beside her. Today Antonina's black eyes shone with a brightness Clare hadn't seen before. The melancholy had disappeared from her demeanor.

Miriam smiled at them. "I'll bring up a tray, my lady."

"Thank you, Miriam." She unfolded her note from Emmett as Antonina began braiding the ends of Clare's hair. The message wasn't long, but it succeeded in erasing any lingering doubts that Emmett didn't want to see her anymore.

Clare,

I have an errand to attend to in Palermo, but I hope to be back no later than the day after tomorrow. You're still sleeping now, and I don't wish to wake you. Not when I now understand how much you need to rest. Just know that I am thinking of you, my dear.

In truth, I never stopped thinking of you, though I may have fooled myself and you into believing otherwise. I know there is much more we need to discuss and decide. However, in the meantime, I want you to know that I spoke with Antonina last night. And you were right, Clare. It required a great deal of courage, but she wasn't upset. If anything, it was a blessing and a relief that she and I were both able to grieve at last.

I remain yours, now and hopefully always,

Emmett

He'd done it! Emmett had finally allowed himself to mourn. Clare clasped his note to her heart. If Antonina's light countenance was any indication, Emmett must be feeling lighter today too.

In a rush of joy and gratitude, she put her arm around Antonina and snuggled the child to her side. "What do you say to you and I doing something besides sewing today?"

"All right." The girl's voice held a note of excited interest. "What do we do?"

Clare shrugged. "Anything you want."

"Painting."

"Painting?" Clare echoed. "Like the pictures we did the other day?"

The child wrinkled her nose and shook her head. "No. I want to do happy pictures, Clare."

"Me too," she murmured, once she'd swallowed the lump in her throat. "Lots and lots of happy pictures." She twisted to face Antonina. "But first, I think we need some laughter."

Clare tickled the little girl in the side. Antonina's first few giggles were brief and faint. However, the child was soon laughing out loud and attempting to tickle Clare in return. When Miriam entered with their breakfast, they quit their game in favor of eating. But the merry sound of Antonina's laughter seemed to linger in the room for some time, and to Clare, it was the most wonderful thing she'd ever heard.

Emmett exited another shop in Palermo, discouragement dogging his heels. He'd lost count of the number of shops he and Mr. Sharpe had visited between yesterday and today. Any establishment that looked as if it might carry brooches, stolen or not, they'd entered. But so far, the only good thing that had come from this trip was their visit with Helena and the viscount at a nearby hotel.

Clare's friend and her baby were doing well, and the viscount was nearly recovered from his injury. When Helena's husband felt up to it, the family would return to England, with plans to rebuild their villa in the fall. Mr. Sharpe had been interested in getting their story to add to the others he'd collected. This time, as Emmett listened instead of translating, he saw firsthand how the lingering lines of anxiety faded from their faces as they shared their traumatic experiences during the earthquake. If he hadn't already witnessed for himself the importance of talking out one's grief, watching his friends purge their fears and losses aloud would have convinced him that he needed to do the same.

"How many shops are left?" Mr. Sharpe asked as they started across the nearby square.

Emmett shrugged. "Probably more than we can visit before we head back to Taormina tomorrow." He wasn't entirely sure the brooch was even in Palermo. For all he knew, the thief might have left Messina with it right after the earthquake and taken a boat to Naples or Rome or somewhere else in the world.

"You aren't giving up, are you?"

The young man had stopped walking, forcing Emmett to do the same. "Why? Because finding my wife's stolen brooch would make a good story?"

"It would." Mr. Sharpe had the decency to look a bit chagrined at his admission. "But that isn't why I expected you to carry on until the last possible moment."

Emmett regarded him with curiosity. "And why is that?"

"Because you aren't the sort of chap who quits," the reporter countered as if such a thing were obvious. He pocketed his hands and stared at something across the square. "Neither you nor Lady Linwood has stopped trying to make things work between you since I met you on the boat."

Astonishment shot through Emmett. "You mean you . . ."

"Knew that the two of you were just pretending to be a happy couple?" Mr. Sharpe finished in a slightly smug tone.

Emmett nodded mutely. The other man had seen through his and Clare's playacting but hadn't let on, until now.

"I'm a reporter, Lord Linwood. Sniffing out the real details of a story is my job."

Was Emmett supposed to be impressed or alarmed by that answer? He wasn't sure. "Will you share those details with the world?"

"If you mean, will I tell the world about the genuine, enduring, affectionate relationship that exists between Lord and Lady Linwood, then yes."

"But . . ." Emmett shook his head, feeling as relieved as he did bewildered. "You just said you knew we were pretending."

Mr. Sharpe looked directly at him. "Yes, and it became apparent rather quickly that the only ones the two of you were fooling was yourselves. You thought the show wasn't based in any reality, but it's clear how deeply you care for each other."

Emmett couldn't help a surprised chuckle. All this time he and Clare had thought themselves so clever in their interactions around Mr. Sharpe. And yet the reporter was right. Somewhere along the way the playacting hadn't been about acting anymore. He—and hopefully Clare as well—had eventually fallen to the habit of responding to each other from a place of true caring and unending love.

"You are quite astute about a great many things besides journalism, Mr. Sharpe. Your father should be proud of you."

The reporter lifted his shoulders in a shrug. However, Emmett saw how much the compliment meant when Mr. Sharpe straightened to full height, his gaze shining with happiness. "What do you want to do about the brooch then?"

"Can't very well quit after that moving speech, can I?" Emmett said, smiling. "The last store owner suggested trying a shop one street over from here. They don't specialize in jewelry but have been known to carry unique pieces now and then."

Mr. Sharpe waved him forward with a slight bow. "Lead on."

Emmett laughed. He was actually going to miss this intrepid reporter when it came time to part ways. The young man had begun as a threat, then turned into an annoyance, and eventually had become a friend.

The shop they entered held more knickknacks, antiquities, and various odds and ends than Emmett could recall seeing in one place. He squared his shoulders against the seemingly impossible task of finding one brooch among hundreds of items and approached the shop owner. Emmett asked if he had any new pieces of jewelry. The man showed him a bracelet, a locket, and a pair of earrings but no brooch.

Disappointed, Emmett started to turn away as the owner began pulling items out of a tin box on the counter. The objects were all different, some looking more costly than others. "What do you have there?" he asked the man in Italian.

"These all came from refugees of Messina." The man shook his head sadly and remarked on the tragedy of the earthquake. "Some are so desperate for money they've sold off their family heirlooms."

A ripple of hope wound through Emmett. "May I see what you have?"

"Yes, of course," he said, twisting the box around so Emmett could see inside.

Emmett rifled through the items. There were watches, small clocks, hand mirrors, necklaces. At the bottom of the pile, he saw something round and silver. Emmett's heart hammered faster as he lifted the object out of the box. It was a silver brooch in the shape of a flower.

"I found it!" he exclaimed, swiveling to face Mr. Sharpe, who was examining a vase on the other side of the room.

The reporter set the vase down at once and hurried over. "You're certain?"

"Absolutely." Emmett grinned. "This is Clare's brooch."

He turned back to the owner and asked if the man had any wedding rings. Perhaps the thief had sold both pieces to the same shop. But none of the rings were Clare's. Still, Emmett was more than pleased to have found the brooch. Once he'd paid for it, he and Mr. Sharpe exited the shop.

"Now what?" the reporter asked. He looked nearly as elated as Emmett at recovering the lost item.

Emmett rubbed the edges of the brooch, then pocketed it for safekeeping. "You and I are going to head back to Taormina right away." Now that he had what he'd come for, he didn't want to wait any longer to return it to his wife.

By dinner time on the second day of Emmett's trip to Palermo, Clare had uncovered an important truth about herself. She wanted to be with him—not just here in Taormina but in England too.

Two days without Emmett had felt more like two weeks with how much she'd missed him. She missed seeing him at meals, missed his morning kiss, missed talking with him about their daily tasks. All the ways they'd interacted, especially since Mr. Sharpe's sudden arrival, no longer felt forced or difficult. In her husband's absence, Clare realized just how much she'd come to appreciate their interactions—and how much she still loved Emmett. That love had been tried and tested thoroughly over the past year, but it hadn't disappeared as she had once feared. It was still there and had become even stronger now that she'd finally been more open and honest with him about her feelings.

She felt as if a weight had been lifted off her shoulders—and she wasn't the only one. Clare relished seeing the changes in Antonina too. The little girl smiled, laughed, and was full of things to say now. Miriam and Rushford, as well as the Russos, had all commented on the difference in the child's demeanor. Their obvious affection for Antonina and acceptance of her place in the family meant a great deal to Clare.

They were nearly finished with dinner, and Antonina was telling Clare a story, when someone knocked on the front door of the villa. Clare glanced through the open doorway to the foyer. Was it Emmett, eager to surprise them by coming home early?

"Maybe it's Emmett," she said with a smile as she set down her napkin. "Should we go see?"

"Yes!" Antonina tumbled out of her chair in her excitement. She still wore an apron over her dress from helping Signora Russo with the baking earlier.

Standing, Clare followed the girl to the door, her heart beating faster with her own eagerness. Would he be as happy to see her as she was to see him? Would he kiss her again?

"Come, Clare." Antonina latched onto her hand and tugged Clare into the foyer.

She laughed as she allowed the child to drag her forward. Another knock sounded, this one more insistent, before Clare could grab the door handle.

"Emmett," she said as she threw open the door. But it wasn't her husband standing there. Her enthusiasm transformed into instant dread. "Lord and Lady Hadwell?"

"Good evening, Lady Linwood." The marquess stepped past her as though Clare had invited him inside instead of watching him in wide-eyed disbelief. "I see my son has still not employed a butler here."

His wife gave Clare an almost apologetic smile. "It is good to see you again."

"And you . . ." Clare belatedly motioned for Emmett's mother to come in as well. Out on the drive, the couple's valet and lady's maid were unloading luggage from a carriage. "Was Emmett expecting you?"

To Clare's relief, Lord Hadwell shook his head. "He should have been, after his cryptic telegram that shared very little, other than neither of you had been harmed by that earthquake. When I didn't hear from him again, I surmised it was time to see what was impeding his swift return home. Naturally Lady Hadwell wished to see for herself that you were both all right. So here we are."

Irritation crowded out Clare's alarm. Though he hadn't said as much directly, she knew the man was here to find out why Emmett hadn't yet been successful in bringing *her* back to England. "I'm sure Emmett will be pleased to see you." Even if she wasn't.

"Where is he?" The marquess gazed shrewdly around the foyer, almost as if he suspected Clare of hiding his son.

She managed a partial smile. "He had business in Palermo but should be back tomorrow."

Their valet and maid entered with the luggage in tow, and Clare gave them instructions on where to place it upstairs. As she finally shut the door, she pulled in a cleansing breath. It wasn't as if she hadn't been alone with Emmett's parents for weeks at a time already. Though having them in this place that had become a sanctuary for her added another level of difficulty to the hours ahead.

"You there," Lord Hadwell commanded in an arrogant tone. "Help Lady Hadwell's maid with the bags."

None of the other servants were present, so who was the man ordering about? Clare turned and felt something bump into her leg. She glanced down to find Antonina clinging to her skirt, a look of worry and bewilderment on the child's face.

"Did you not hear me, girl?" The marquess frowned at Antonina. "Your help is required."

Clare stiffened in anger and placed a protective arm about the child's shoulders. "This is Antonina. She is not a servant. In this house, she is a member of the family."

"A what?"

Clare might have laughed at the spluttering, red-faced Lord Hadwell if she hadn't been so irate at his condescending attitude and erroneous assumption. "She lost her family in the earthquake, and Emmett and I have taken her into our home." Clare noted the surprised expressions of Lady Hadwell and the two servants before she continued. "I'm sure you're both quite weary from traveling. Why don't you freshen up in your rooms? I'll have Signora Russo set two more places at the table for when you're ready."

Emmett's parents appeared nearly as astonished at her polite dismissal as they did at the news that Antonina was here to stay. But Clare felt invigorated. She'd avoided speaking up around her in-laws for too long, too overawed to assert herself while she was living in their house. But the villa was Emmett's by inheritance, which made Clare the rightful hostess—and as such, she would confidently direct the activities and conversation in her own home. She wouldn't be cowed by the marquess's disapproval.

"Let's finish eating, Nina," she said as the others headed upstairs. The girl still held tightly to Clare's skirt, but her grasp relaxed when they entered the dining room again.

Clare returned to her seat. "Are you all right, sweetheart?"

"Who are they?" Antonina asked.

"Emmett's parents."

The child picked up her fork and frowned. "That man is . . ." She seemed to be searching for the right word. "He is sad."

"Sad?" Clare repeated. She could think of lots of words

for Lord Hadwell, but that one hadn't occurred to her. "What do you mean?"

Antonina's brow scrunched. "His face is angry, but his eyes are sad."

Could that be true? Clare was embarrassed that she'd never noticed the marquess's eyes before. She'd spent more time looking at her lap or her plate or at something across the room when he spoke to her. And yet Antonina had noticed this detail right off.

Memories of what Emmett had told her about his older brother flitted through her mind. Was Lord Hadwell still grieving the death of his oldest son? Clare understood loss—the need to share it and the awful consequences of trying to carry that burden alone. Maybe Emmett had learned from his father to bury his feelings of grief and sorrow. The likelihood engendered compassion in her for both her husband and the marquess.

When she and Antonina were finished with their meal, Clare had the girl come downstairs with her to inform Signora Russo that all of their new guests, servants included, would need dinner. The woman looked as stunned as Clare had been at hearing the marquess was visiting. Apparently the last time Lord and Lady Hadwell had come to the villa together was when Emmett was still a boy.

"Shall we read a book?" Clare asked when she and Antonina returned from downstairs. She didn't wish to subject the child to Lord Hadwell's displeasure by joining the couple at dinner. Instead they would read until Emmett's parents were finished and came into the drawing room.

With a nod, Antonina rushed across the foyer in her eagerness to find the book they'd started last night. At the same time, Lord and Lady Hadwell descended the stairs. The marquess threw a glare at the child's back. Clare fisted her hands in irritation before she attempted to greet them cordially. "Since Nina and I have already eaten, we'll be reading in the drawing room. You're more than welcome to join us after you've finished dinner."

Rather than waiting for their response, she headed into the drawing room. Antonina was already seated on the couch, the chosen book on her lap. Clare sat beside her and picked up the book. The little girl snuggled into her side. A feeling of contentment wrapped itself around Clare as she began to read. The only thing that would have improved the blissful moment was Emmett's presence.

His parents still hadn't yet joined them by the time Antonina had fallen asleep, her head on Clare's shoulder. She gently shook the girl awake and led her into the foyer. Lord and Lady Hadwell were just exiting the dining room.

"I'll put her in bed," Clare said, "then come back down."

Lord Hadwell thankfully stayed silent, but his demeanor conveyed his dissatisfaction. It was a look Clare knew all too well. Ignoring it, she guided Antonina up the stairs. The girl was soon dressed in her nightclothes and in bed.

"Good night, Clare," she murmured sleepily. "I love you."

Tears of joy pricked Clare's eyes. "I love you too, Nina."

She returned downstairs, feeling peaceful until she heard the marquess's raised voice coming from the drawing room. "Did you see her dark complexion? She doesn't belong here. They're better off employing the girl as a maid. Not pretending she's the daughter of the future Marquess of Hadwell."

Clare's earlier ire returned in full force as she marched across the foyer. Still, she slowed her steps as she neared the open doorway. *Please give me courage, Father, to say what I need to without throwing accusations myself.*

"Sorry to keep you waiting." She swept into the room.

Lord Hadwell merely frowned at her from where he sat near the fireplace, but his wife lowered her gaze in evident embarrassment. At least one of them showed enough decency to be ashamed.

Turning back to the door, Clare closed it partway to prevent others from overhearing the marquess in the event his volume rose again. "I hope you enjoyed dinner."

"We did, thank you," Lady Hadwell said with a tight smile.

Clare took a seat on the opposite side of the couch from Emmett's mother. "I heard it has been a long time since you last visited the villa."

"Yes, and apparently it's gone to ruin in that time." The marquess's frown increased to a scowl.

Maintaining an open countenance was difficult, but Clare managed it. "I'm sorry it doesn't meet with your expectations, my lord."

"What I expect is for you to give up your ridiculous scheme of adopting that girl as your child." Lord Hadwell pushed out of his chair and moved to stand before the hearth. His stance reminded Clare of Emmett's the other day. But unlike her husband, she sensed no softening in the marquess.

"My scheme?" she repeated.

Emmett's father nodded curtly. "I doubt my son is behind such foolish notions."

"Actually . . ." Clare folded her hands in her lap. "It was Emmett who first thought of taking Antonina in as our own."

"Regardless, I won't have it," the man countered, whirling to face her. "Emmett needs to build his public image to run for Parliament, not incite curiosity and scrutiny by adopting a Sicilian child of possibly low birth."

Clare dug her fingernails into her palms. "I understand you feel differently about this than Emmett and I do, but it is not your decision."

"Is this your answer to producing an heir? Because she won't inherit anything from me."

Lady Hadwell flinched as much as Clare did. For a moment, angry words met Clare's tongue. Before she could say them, though, she had a thought to look at her father-in-law—truly look. His irritated expression remained unchanged, but his gaze held more than frustration. There was pain and sorrow there too, just as Antonina had said.

"I don't pretend to know what it must be like to lose a child whom you've cared for and loved for years," Clare said, rising to her feet. "I imagine there will always be reminders of that loss. Always moments of wondering what they would have been like at every age. Mourning those milestones and memories that will never be." She'd felt those same things with each miscarriage. "What I do know is that little girl upstairs has brought renewed hope and happiness to me and to Emmett. And she may not inherit anything from you, my lord, but she will from me. I will see she is cared for with my own money, if needs be, and that she is given the same love and affection I would give my flesh and blood."

The marquess eyed her coolly. "She won't be welcome at Hadwell House."

Clare drew herself up straight as she replied, "Then she and I will remain here."

His refusal to listen and understand saddened her, but she wouldn't leave Antonina behind. They would stay in Sicily, even if Clare ached at the thought of living apart from Emmett again. Knowing her husband wouldn't give up Antonina either, she reassured herself that somehow, some way, they would make it work.

"If I don't lose this baby too," Clare said, resting her hand against her stomach. From the corner of her eye, she saw her mother-in-law's gaze widen. "I will raise this child and Antonina here in Sicily."

"You wish to ruin my son's career before it's even started by living apart?"

Clare breathed in and out before responding. "On the contrary, Emmett doesn't need me with him to win an election. He may need my money but only as a way to fund his campaign." Her words grew louder to match her earnestness. "The truth is he doesn't need you either or your management of his life. Emmett will do a marvelous job in Parliament solely based on his own merits. Because that is the type of man he is. He's intelligent and kind and hard-working. And the earthquake has only enhanced those fine qualities.

"Did you know he has played a large role in the relief efforts for the earthquake victims living here in Taormina?" She leveled a look at her father-in-law. "Emmett organized a group of refugees to repair the roads and is giving them wages to help put their lives back together. Their efforts will make travel easier again and restore some sense of normalcy for the people of this town. He also asked a local cobbler to make shoes for those who have none, and he's paying for the shoes. That is the kind of man who will succeed as an MP. The kind of man who doesn't need to be pushed into doing things. You raised an amazing son, my lord. But you won't see that if you never step back and look."

Her fervent speech over, Clare felt suddenly vulnerable. Especially when Lord Hadwell remained silent as he turned toward the fireplace again. Had she said too much? Maybe, but she didn't regret sharing any of it. She only wished she'd been able to help the marquess see things differently.

"I'll bid you both good night, Lord and Lady Hadwell."

Emmett's mother stood and patted Clare's hand, her eyes brimming with tears. "You truly love my son, don't you?"

"I do," Clare said quietly but with conviction.

Lady Hadwell glanced at something over Clare's shoulder and smiled. "It's easy to see how he feels about you."

"What do you mean?"

"It's written all over his face."

Her mother-in-law spun Clare around to face the door. And there, watching her with more adoration than she'd ever seen in his light-blue eyes, was Emmett.

Chapter 14

There was no longer any question in Emmett's mind how his wife felt about him. Not after overhearing her impassioned words to his father and her sweet declaration to his mother just now.

He'd been so eager to see her again, especially after finding her brooch. But the train had been delayed, causing him and Mr. Sharpe to return to Taormina well after dinner. When they'd entered the house, Emmett had heard voices through the partially open door of the drawing room. To his complete astonishment, one of them sounded very much like his father.

Mr. Sharpe had excused himself, leaving Emmett alone outside the drawing room. It was then he overheard his wife mention a decision that wasn't his father's to make. Lord Hadwell had countered with a harsh question about this being Clare's answer to producing an heir.

Realizing they must be talking about Antonina, Emmett nearly burst into the room at that point on a tide of anger, but something whispered at him to pause. Thankfully he'd listened. If he hadn't, he would have missed Clare's kind but firm reply about Antonina's place in their family and about

Emmett's own strengths. Listening to her moving speech about him, he knew he needed no other proof that Clare had married him for love and not his title.

"You're home." Clare hurried toward him, her expression full of relief and happiness. She embraced him tightly, and he relished the feel of her in his arms.

He longed to kiss her thoroughly right then. She had bravely confronted his father, and she'd done it with grace, kindness, and confidence. "I wanted to surprise you," he whispered in her ear. "I have something else for you too, but first there are a few things I need to share with my father." Emmett eased back to rest his forehead against hers. "Wait for me in the garden?"

"I will." She surprised him with a quick kiss to his jaw before she left the room.

Emmett's mother offered him an embrace as well. "I'm so glad you are both all right." She cast a glance over her shoulder to where the marquess stood by the fireplace. "I believe I'll retire and let you two speak alone. Good night, Emmett."

He squeezed her hand. "Good night, Mother." As she left, he squared his shoulders and faced the man across the room. "Hello, Father."

"That wife of yours . . ." Lord Hadwell waved impatiently at the door.

"Is brilliant," Emmett finished, "and articulate and would likely make a better politician than me? I heartily agree with you." He clasped his hands behind his back. "I only wish I'd seen that more fully ages ago."

His father sized him up. "I see you are in one piece."

"I am, but you already knew that from my telegram."

Lord Hadwell shrugged. "Your mother wasn't convinced." Oddly enough, he didn't look at Emmett as he said this, almost as if he was afraid to let his real emotion show through.

Much like I have done, Emmett thought sadly.

He studied his father, who was now intently observing the painting of Taormina that hung on the wall. In that instant, Emmett saw something in Lord Hadwell's eyes he had never seen or noticed before. It was brief, hardly more than a flicker. And yet for just a moment, there was genuine concern in the marquess's gaze.

"You were worried too."

His father sniffed, and the telltale emotion disappeared. "Of course I was. We'd only just mapped out your political career, and I wasn't certain if events here had disrupted that. And I was right to be concerned. Take that Sicilian child, for instance."

"She has a name, Father. It's Antonina."

"As I am well aware. Your wife has already informed me of her intentions to keep the child as her own."

Emmett forced his jaw to relax. "*Our* own. I also want to raise Nina as our daughter, as much as Clare does."

"That wasn't part of our plan," his father barked before stalking to the window.

Running his hand down his face, Emmett pushed out a long breath. What he was about to say would likely seal his father's disapproval forever. Yet he wasn't the same person he'd been back in England. He had greater confidence in himself now and in his own plans for the future. It was time to stop trying to make his father proud, to stop chasing after Alder's shadow.

"I understand that my choice to adopt a child from here was not your plan." Emmett took a step toward him. "It wasn't mine either until the earthquake. However, that event changed a great many things. It changed me, Father."

Lord Hadwell glowered at him. "So what are you saying? You no longer wish to be an MP?"

"On the contrary, I want to be an MP now more than ever. Working with the refugees and helping with the relief efforts has given me a much different perspective. I hope to implement the things I've learned here if I'm elected."

The first semblance of a smile lifted his father's mouth. "Excellent. Then I'm sure we can work out an arrangement for that girl."

Emmett fought back a growl of annoyance at the marquess's dismissive outlook. "I have an arrangement. Antonina is to remain in Taormina with Clare . . . and with me."

"What?" Lord Hadwell wasn't smiling anymore. "You need to begin your campaign, Emmett."

"I need to be here," he countered in an unyielding tone. His place was with Clare and Antonina, whether his father agreed or not. "My wife needs to remain in Sicily, at least until it's warmer back home. A doctor recommended Clare stay somewhere more temperate during this pregnancy. Once we are back in Britain, I can begin campaigning."

The marquess's eyebrows lowered in aggravation. "That may be too late."

"It may, but if I go now, it will be permanently too late for me and Clare. And she matters more to me than any political acclaim." He narrowed the distance between him and his father. "I hope you'll respect my choice in this and as it relates to the daughter we are to adopt. If not, then I'd ask that you not visit us at Barksley Hall or in London when we return. I shall come to you, but I won't have you disparaging any member of my family in our own home."

Rather than throwing an angered remark at him, his father lowered his head. "Alder would have done it differently, I imagine."

The words smarted, but Emmett found they weren't so hard to move past either. "I'm sure he would, and I'm sorry you didn't get the chance to see what he would have done in my place as eldest son and heir."

To Emmett's shock, Lord Hadwell's shoulders drooped, then began to quiver with noiseless sobs. "Father?" He put his hand on the man's back in alarm. "Is something wrong?"

"Your wife was correct," the marquess said in a shuddering voice. "I am reminded of Alder often, and I miss him still." The hand he lifted to swipe at his eyes trembled. "When he died, I pleaded with God to give us another son."

Emmett was too stunned by the emotional display to respond. That, and he sensed his father needed to speak without interruption.

"I nearly gave up believing it would ever happen again, and then you were born." Lord Hadwell's tone softened for a moment. "However, I was unaware of how close we came to losing you too until I read Sharpe's article about the earthquake. Your telegram didn't indicate you and Clare were even in Messina that morning." He leveled a pointed look at Emmett.

Pocketing his hands, Emmett stared out the window. He'd lived through those experiences Mr. Sharpe had described in his article, and yet he still had difficulty believing at times that it wasn't all a dream. To read about them in print must have been equally as shocking for his parents.

"I didn't wish to worry Mother . . . or you, especially since we were blessed to make it out alive and uninjured."

Emmett's candidness seemed to drain what was left of his father's energy. The marquess stumbled to the nearest chair and dropped onto the seat. "If something had happened . . ." He didn't finish but merely shook his head. "That girl, Antonina," he said after a long moment, "she's the child you rescued, the one mentioned in the article?"

"Yes." Emmett sat down as well. "Rushford and I were able to save her but not her brother."

Lord Hadwell dipped his head in a slow nod. "I suppose I can relate to that in a way." Resting his elbow on the chair arm, he massaged his forehead. "I'm not simply here to see what you've been doing, Emmett. Nor to assure myself and your mother that you were indeed safe. I came because I feared losing you, not to death but to your own life."

Emmett frowned. "I'm not sure what you mean."

"Your refusal to have a journalist accompanying you to Sicily angered me. But more than that, it frightened me." He twisted in his seat to look at Emmett. "Why do you think I've always wanted you to follow my plans?"

Did he really wish for an answer? Emmett lifted his shoulders in a shrug. "Because you wanted and expected me to be more like Alder."

"No," the marquess said, his voice full of sadness. "It was because I've always feared that someday I would lose you too. It wasn't only death or illness that I feared. What if you decided you wanted to make your own way in this world without my help? Or chose to live far away? Barksley Hall is already a greater distance from Hadwell House than I would have wished."

Understanding flooded Emmett, along with his own fair share of regret and sorrow. "That's why you wished for me to go into politics now. It was a way to keep me nearby and not solely focused on the work at Barksley Hall."

"You are partly right," his father admitted. "It would also mean being in London together as we've always been. We hardly saw you and Clare this season. However, my motives weren't entirely selfish. I also saw what an asset you would be to Britain and its people."

It was the nearest thing to a compliment Emmett had

heard from him in a very long time. "I appreciate that, Father. But if that is true, why did you send Mr. Sharpe on the next boat after mine, especially when I asked you not to do so?"

"I wanted someone to be my eyes here, to ensure our plans were proceeding as they should." A rare look of chagrin crossed the man's face. "That was wrong of me, and I'm sorry I didn't respect your wishes."

Emmett fought to keep from gaping at his father. He couldn't recall the marquess ever apologizing before.

"When you didn't send word save for that one telegram," his father continued, "I began to believe my fears were being realized. That something had happened while you here to make you change your mind about becoming an MP. Then we arrived and learned from your wife that you had made changes to so many of the plans I had for you."

"And you believe those changes mean you're losing me?"

Lord Hadwell lowered his gaze to his empty hands. "Don't they?"

"Father?" Emmett reached out and grasped his arm. "You are not losing me. Even if I weren't to become an MP, which I very much still hope to do, or if I choose to live farther away than Barksley Hall, I am still your son. That will never change."

The deep lines around the marquess's mouth and eyes eased. "You're right. So what do we do now?"

"You're asking me?" Emmett swallowed back an incredulous laugh. The conversation had brought one astonishment and revelation after another. At his father's nod, he considered the question. "We can't go back and change the past." He'd learned that with Clare. "But we can own our past mistakes—and I have certainly made plenty of my own—and begin again from where we are right now."

Shifting his chair, Lord Hadwell held out his hand. "I would like that."

Emmett poured all of his remorse from the past and his hope for the future into their firm handshake. "I should have been more honest about what I wanted to do with my life and not tried so hard to just be whatever you wanted me to be. And for that, I'm sorry."

The marquess set his other hand over Emmett's. "I suppose I owe an apology to your wife as well," he grumbled before he climbed to his feet. "However, I believe I'll put that off for the morning." His lips twitched with a rare teasing smile. "Something tells me the only person she wishes to speak to tonight is you."

Was Clare still waiting for him? Emmett had taken much longer to speak with his father than he'd expected. He moved with quick strides out of the house and into the garden. The light from indoors shone across the stone terrace. Within its illuminating pool, Clare sat on one of the benches scattered among the paths and foliage. Her red-gold hair had been freed of its pins and glowed like copper in the light as it lay around her shoulders.

She stood when she saw him. "How did it go?"

"Surprisingly well," Emmett answered, hardly able to believe it himself. He motioned for her to sit, then joined her on the bench. Scooping up her hand, he threaded his fingers with hers. At once a feeling of rightness, of contentment, settled inside him. "My father actually voiced an apology, and he plans to do the same with you in the morning."

Clare's green eyes widened. "He was so irate. What happened?"

He shared what his father had confessed about his fears and motives. "It will still take a great deal of time, for both of us, to do and see things differently, but it's a very welcome start."

"I'm so happy for you, Emmett." Looping her other arm through his, she smiled up at him.

There had been a time, not so many weeks ago, when he wasn't sure if he would ever see that beautiful smile directed his way again. "I need to apologize to you too, Clare." He glanced down and squeezed her hand. "You were right, my dear. I did treat you with what must have looked like indifference when you were grieving. It wasn't because I didn't care about you. I never stopped caring. But I recognize now that in my attempt not to hurt or upset you even more, I did exactly that. And I am sorry."

He lifted his gaze to hers and saw tears glittering along her lashes. "If you're willing, I would very much like to hear your feelings, all of them, around this pregnancy and the others."

"I would like that too," she murmured. The gratitude radiating from her told him this was the right step on the path to healing, for both of them.

She began to speak, not holding back anything in her sharing, and Emmett prized her trust in him as much as he did her words. At one point, he released her hand to hold her close. He wasn't silent either. As he'd done with Antonina, he finally gave voice to his own feelings of loss and grief—about Clare's miscarriages, about his grandfather, about how he'd come to believe he was wrong to feel sad.

Clare asked if he was willing to tell her about Angelo and the details of Antonina's rescue, and he did. Relating those events didn't gut him as they had when he'd kept them to himself. Still, there were tears present on both their faces when he'd finished.

"That must have been so awful," Clare said as she

brushed the moisture from her cheeks. "No wonder you were having nightmares."

He rested his cheek against her hair. "I still hate that I wasn't able to save him, but I've made peace with it. Largely because a very intelligent woman told me I needed to talk about it." She gave a light laugh. "I hope this baby will be all right, Clare. But if not, I promise you . . ." He lifted his head to look at her. "You won't suffer this one alone. We will grieve together."

"Thank you."

Slipping his hand into his pocket, Emmett removed the brooch. "I told you that I had something else for you." He twisted her hand, palm up, and placed the piece of jewelry there.

"It's my brooch!" She clasped her fingers around it, her expression one of disbelief and joy. "Where did you find it?"

He smiled as he nestled her against his side once more. "Inside a box in a shop in Palermo. I searched every shop I could find. I know how much it means to you."

Clare kissed his cheek. "I can't believe you found it."

"It was rather a miracle, and in truth, I would have quit trying if it hadn't been for Mr. Sharpe."

"What did he do?" she asked, her surprise evident in her tone.

Emmett fingered the ends of her hair. "He reminded me that I wasn't one to quit. And he told me that we haven't fooled him at all by pretending to be a happy couple."

"Oh no. I'm sorry, Emmett. Maybe if we'd tried harder."

He shook his head. "Mr. Sharpe recognized before I did that we weren't actually pretending anymore."

"You mean . . ."

"Somewhere in all the playacting, it became real for me again."

The fondness in her gaze was as much a confirmation she felt the same way as was her quiet response. "For me too."

He angled his head toward hers, eager to kiss her. But instead of matching his stance, Clare fumbled with his lapel. "Clare? Is something amiss?"

"I owe you an apology too."

"You apologized the other day," he reminded her.

She nodded, but the remorse on her features didn't fade. "There's something else." She pulled in a breath as if to calm herself. Her reluctance had Emmett concerned, though. "For a long time now, I've believed something Lady Melinda told me."

"Lady Melinda?" What other havoc had the widow caused with her gossip?

"During a visit to Hadwell House last year, she mentioned you had only married me for my money."

Emmett sat back. "This was last year and you didn't say anything? Didn't ask me if it was true?"

"I should have." Clare twisted on the bench to face forward. "At first I didn't give any credence to her remarks, knowing she wasn't happy that you'd married me. But then, when I sensed you pulling away, I started to fear she'd been right."

He wanted to feel hurt or frustrated at her for believing Lady Melinda. Yet hadn't he done the same thing? Thanks to the resentful widow, he'd come to believe that Clare had married him solely for his title. But none of the widow's comments had proven to be correct. Instead they'd been weapons of manipulation from an embittered, petulant woman. "I have something to confess as well. After you left for Sicily, I attended a party. Lady Melinda was in attendance too, and I overheard her say that you married me for my title. Unfortunately, I convinced myself that it was also true."

"How tragic," Clare said, peering up at him again. "We both let her resentment-driven gossip feed our fears." Setting her brooch beside her on the bench, she held Emmett's hand between hers. "I didn't marry you for your title, Emmett. I married you because I love you. And I want to be with you, wherever you are." Her voice wavered with emotion as she continued, "So if you are needed in England to campaign, then that's where I'll be too."

She would do that for him? "Even if it means living somewhere cold?"

"Yes." There was no hesitation from her now. "I want to stay with you."

His love for her welled up inside him. "Then you will have to content yourself with remaining in Italy."

"Why?" she asked, the hope in her green eyes growing stronger.

"As I told my father, you need to stay here, which means I need to stay here as well."

"What about your campaign?"

He brushed his finger along her jawline, noting the softness of her skin. "It can wait until all of us return to England. Because while your money is greatly appreciated, Clare, what I need most is you at my side." Emmett placed a kiss against her temple. "I heard what you said to my father about my becoming an MP. However, you only told him half the truth."

"Did I?" Her gaze glinted with awareness.

"The truth is I married an extraordinary woman with talents of her own." He wound his arms around her. "And if I am successful in politics, it will only be to her credit and as a result of her help."

Clare raised her chin, bringing her lips temptingly close to his. "Have I met this extraordinary woman?"

Emmett chuckled. "I believe so. She's beautiful and kind and wise. Best of all, she apparently loves me."

"And do you still love her?" There was teasing but also vulnerability in her question.

"Yes, Clare. I never stopped loving you." He nudged her closer. "And I will keep loving you more openly and more deeply every day."

Nothing, not even another earthquake, could have dissuaded him from kissing his wife right then. Her fervent response matched his own in love and yearning. And in that perfect moment, Emmett felt the joy and healing of being together again at long last.

Epilogue

Barksley Hall, September 1909

Clare studied her canvas. The painting of the estate house was finished, and once it was framed, Emmett had insisted they hang it in a place of prominence over the drawing room fireplace.

The sound of girlish laughter drew her attention away from her paints. Antonina and Emmett were taking turns throwing a ball for Bran, who had bonded as quickly with the girl as he had with Clare. Seated nearby in lawn chairs were Emmett's parents. It had taken time for his family to fully accept Antonina's place with them, but they had come around eventually. The marquess now enjoyed answering Antonina's endless questions and was teaching her how to ride. Lady Hadwell held two-month-old Emmett Jr. in her arms, where the baby had been more often than not since her and her husband's arrival last week.

"Did you finish?" Emmett asked, approaching her.

Clare nodded. "I'm still not sure I can paint people." Standing to one side of the house was a miniature version of herself, holding the baby, alongside Emmett and Antonina.

"It's as incredible as I knew it would be." He settled a kiss just below her jaw on her neck.

A delighted shiver wound through her. "I believe you are biased, my lord."

"True, but that doesn't mean I can't recognize a talented artist." Emmett tugged her from her chair, his fingers touching the new wedding ring he'd given her. "And you, my dear, are a talented artist."

She set down her brush. "If that is so, then how do you plan to pay for such valuable work?"

"I'm hoping," he teased in a low voice, "that this particular artist may be persuaded to accept ardent kisses as currency."

Clare glanced at his parents and blushed. "She may but not here."

"Mother? Father? We're going for a short walk." When his parents waved them on, he lifted his eyebrows at her in silent question.

She couldn't help laughing. "Very discreet."

"That is a talent of mine."

Emmett led her toward their favorite path, the one that wound through the forest and eventually ended at the sea cliffs. Once they were surrounded by trees, he stopped and pulled her toward him. Clare went willingly.

His kiss was thoroughly long and wonderful, and it set her heart racing with happiness. "I love you, Clare."

"I love you too." With her arms around his neck, she gazed up at him. "Are you nervous to start campaigning soon?"

"A little," he admitted. True to his word, her husband had been more open and honest—they both had. "I'm hoping Mr. Sharpe's article will help."

Mr. Sharpe's story about them as a couple had recently

been published in the newspaper in preparation for Emmett's campaign. The reporter had also written a book, which would release in another few months. It was a compilation of the refugees' stories Emmett had translated for him.

Clare smiled up at him. "You mean the article in which he called me as gracious a hostess as I am a wife and mother? And that if women like Lady Linwood were given the right to vote we could very well change the world?"

"Did he also mention how cheeky you can be?"

She laughed. "I loved what he said about you too. That you are a man for our day and one who isn't afraid to use his hands in honest work."

"I hope I'll have the chance to prove his praise accurate." Emmett rested his forehead against hers. "But whether I am elected or not, I'm grateful we'll be side by side for whatever the future holds."

"Now and always," she murmured.

Then she offered him her own thoroughly long and wonderful kiss before they returned to the house, breathless and happy and together.

Author's Note

The Messina, Italy earthquake, which occurred at 5:20 a.m. on December 28, 1908, was one of the worst natural disasters in modern history. It's estimated that between eighty thousand and one hundred thousand people perished. Such massive loss of life has been attributed to the time the earthquake struck, while most people were still sleeping, and the stone construction of the buildings in the affected areas.

The details surrounding the earthquake—including what people experienced when it struck, the escape from a hotel using a mattress, the danger of being crushed to death by toppling masonry, the tidal wave, the happenings in Taormina, thieves stealing valuables, the widespread lack of food and water, and the soldiers from Palermo baking bread—are based on actual accounts. Most of the real-life stories from the earthquake are of loss and heartrending tragedy. There are others, though, of miraculous rescues, including people who were rescued alive after being trapped beneath the rubble eight to twelve days after the earthquake.

The Sicilian capital of Palermo, 125 miles away from Messina, hardly felt the earthquake at all. And while the people in Taormina heard and felt the quake, the town was largely untouched.

The relief given to the refugees passing through the city of Giardini, near Taormina, is also factual. I based the organizing of a work gang to repair the roads, the group to sew clothes for the refugees, and the paying of a cobbler to make shoes on the actual relief work of Katharine Bement Davis, who organized such efforts to aid the refugees in the city of Syracuse, Sicily.

Indispensable to my research about the Messina earthquake were two books: *The Great Earthquake: America*

Comes to Messina's Rescue by Salvatore J. LaGumina and *The Complete Story of the Italian Earthquake Horror* by J. Martin Miller. Both share vivid accounts of the earthquake, its affects, and the relief work.

From the 1870s through the end of the Edwardian Era, more than a hundred American heiresses traveled to England in search of husbands. These "dollar princesses" were searching for the two things they hadn't been able to claim back home—a title and superior social status. Many of the land-rich members of the English peerage were more than happy to accommodate these heiresses and their determined mothers. After all, large country estates took a great deal of money to maintain.

I based Clare's experiences as an American heiress married to a titled Englishman on those described in *To Marry an English Lord* by Gail MacColl and Carol McD. Wallace. This fascinating book gives insight into the often lonely lives these American young ladies found themselves living after the wedding, in old country houses that were always freezing and had fallen into disrepair. There were rules and protocols they didn't understand and the ever-present expectations, too, of producing an heir.

The enthusiastic reception of the young lord and his bride in his home village, the giving of speeches and receiving of bouquets, and the men hauling their carriage to the estate house are also all factual. And while these transatlantic marriages weren't without difficulty and adjustment, there were those who seemed to make it work and appeared to be genuinely happy.

Of interesting note, Winston Churchill's mother was an American heiress as well as Princess Diana's great-grandmother—so was the first woman to sit in the House of Commons. When her MP husband inherited his father's title and had to go to the House of Lords, Nancy Astor won his seat, and in 1918, became the first woman to ever sit in Parliament.

A *USA Today* bestselling author, Stacy Henrie graduated from Brigham Young University with a degree in public relations. Not long after, she switched from writing press releases and newsletters to writing inspirational historical romances. Born and raised in the West, where she currently resides with her family, she enjoys reading, road trips, interior decorating, chocolate, and most of all, laughing with her husband and kids. Her books include *Hope at Dawn*, a 2015 RITA Award finalist for excellence in romance. You can learn more about Stacy and her books by visiting her website, stacyhenrie.com.

45497147R10163

Made in the USA
Middletown, DE
17 May 2019